Candide
and *Other* *Selected Writings*

Voltaire, pseudonym for François-Marie Arouet, was born on 21 November, 1694 in Paris. He is regarded as one of the greatest French writers till date and a key figure in the European philosophical movement known as the Enlightenment. Through critical discourse, satire and wit, his work effectively propagates the idea of progress and commentary against State institutions. Voltaire was precociously talented as a poet. His most-known works included the fictitious *Lettres philosophiques* published in 1734 and the satirical novel *Candide* in 1759. He died on 30 May, 1778 in Paris.

Candide
and *Other Selected Writings*

Voltaire

Published by
Rupa Publications India Pvt. Ltd 2022
7/16, Ansari Road, Daryaganj
New Delhi 110002

Sales Centres:
Allahabad Bengaluru Chennai
Hyderabad Jaipur Kathmandu
Kolkata Mumbai

Edition copyright © Rupa Publications India Pvt. Ltd. 2022

All rights reserved.
No part of this publication may be reproduced, transmitted,
or stored in a retrieval system, in any form or by any means, electronic,
mechanical, photocopying, recording or otherwise, without the prior
permission of the publisher.

P-ISBN: 978-93-5520-848-4
E-ISBN: 978-93-5520-849-1

First impression 2022

10 9 8 7 6 5 4 3 2 1

Printed in India

This book is sold subject to the condition that it shall not, by way of
trade or otherwise, be lent, resold, hired out, or otherwise circulated,
without the publisher's prior consent, in any form of binding or
cover other than that in which it is published.

CONTENTS

Introduction		7
1.	Candide	11
2.	Zadig	109
3.	Nanine	197
4.	André Des Touches in Siam	248
5.	Plato's Dream	255
6.	An Adventure in India	258
7.	Bababec	261

INTRODUCTION

This book is a collection of Voltaire's magnum opus *Candide* and his most-known works *Zadig*, *Nanine*, 'André Des Touches in Siam', 'Plato's Dream', 'An Adventure in India' and 'Bababec'.

Voltaire was primarily a man of language. Through the force of his writing style, opinionated choice of literary genre and the undeniably accomplished manipulation of the book market, he found the means to popularizing the ideas which, until then, had generally been clandestine. The range of his writing is immense, embracing the horizons of every genre. In verse, he wrote in every form—epic poetry, ode, satire and even epistles; his drama, also written in verse, includes both comedies and tragedies. As he became older and more agitated by the growth of atheism, Voltaire's deist beliefs—reiterated throughout his life as well as in his works—started to come out as defensive. The development of a philosophy of action was Voltaire's motivation; his 'common sense' campaign against prejudice and superstition and in favour of religious tolerance was his single greatest contribution to the advancement of the Enlightenment movement.

Candide was first published in 1759 as a French satire. The novella has been translated into a broad variety of languages; the titles for the English translations include *Candide: or, All for the Best* (1759), *Candide: or, The Optimist* (1762) and *Candide: Optimism* (1947). It centers around a young man named Candide who has a secluded existence in an Edenic paradise and is taught Leibnizian optimism by Professor Pangloss, his mentor. The narrative is about the abrupt end of this way of life and Candide's bitter and gradual disillusionment as he observes the overwhelming suffering in the world. In place of Pangloss' Leibnizian maxim that 'everything is for the best' in the 'best of all conceivable worlds', Voltaire ends Candide with the notion that 'we must cultivate our garden'.

Zadig; or, The Book of Fate (1747) is a work of fiction grounded in deeply-reflective philosophical notions. The novella depicts the narrative of Zadig, an ancient Babylonian Zoroastrian philosopher. Voltaire makes no attempt to be historically accurate. Zadig's unusual narrative and unique adventure will be remembered for all of history as the pinnacle of philosophical allusion to 'nothing is either good or bad without comparison'. It is highly reflective in nature, portraying human life as being in the hands of a fate beyond human control. Voltaire's description of the moral revolution taking place in Zadig challenges theological and metaphysical conservatism.

His most celebrated play, a three-act comedy, is called *Nanine, ou le Préjugé Vaincu* (*Nanine*, or *Prejudice Overcome*) originally written in French, produced in 1749, an adaptation of Samuel Richardson's *Pamela, or Virtue Rewarded* (1740) for the French stage. It is written in verses of ten syllables. The absurdity of comedy in rhyme is outrightly prominent in this play. The original begins thus, 'Il faut parler, il faut, Monsieur le Comte, Vous expliquer nettement sur mon Compte.' The reader cannot help but observe what villainous rhymes Comte and Compte are, and perhaps will more readily forgive this comedy being reduced into plain prose.

'André Des Touches in Siam' is a satirical debate between a French musician and a Siamese bureaucrat that depicts a 'utopian' society with an unfair justice system based on old traditions and religious extremism.

'Plato's Dream' (originally in French, *Songe de Platon*) is a short story written in the eighteenth century. It is one of the earliest examples of science fiction written in the modern era, along with his novella *Micromégas* (1752). The narrative, which is presented as a dream and is set in the context of a well-known and religiously accepted figure from history, is a philosophical critique of religious pedagogy. The narrative is based on a dream that Plato, a Greek philosopher, is said to have had in which Demiurgos, a god-like being known as the 'eternal geometer', assigns many 'lesser superbeings' the duty of constructing their own worlds. Demogorgon, the creature that finally builds the planet we know as Earth, is first extremely happy with his creation but soon discovers that the other entities are making fun of his evidently flawed creation.

'An Adventure in India' (originally titled *Aventure indienne*), is another short tale written by Voltaire and published in 1766, depicting Pythagoras' time spent in India. He encounters an oyster, an herb and a group of Hindus determined to burn two men at the stake for allegedly challenging religious tradition. The two men are rescued from the flames by the Greek philosopher. Following that, he is set on fire by a fanatic in his own home. There is an amusing account of Bacchus 'walking across the Red Sea without wetting his feet' and that it is 'faithfully recorded in the Orphic oracles', according to the text. Voltaire suggests a parallel between Bacchus and Moses and adds a further suggestion that the biblical narratives could be just as fantastical as mythical stories. This makes the main plot of the story, and Voltaire at large, enemies of the then existing authorities—whether they be the government or the church. Because of this, it is frequently difficult to grasp the tensions within the Enlightenment movement—to draw a line between deism and atheism, or the Jonathan Israel division between radical and moderate Enlightenments—without also considering style, humour, irony and mockery.

This is classic Voltaire in its portrayal of religious authority as essentially a spectacle. It is expanded upon in the story 'Bababec'. The Brahman's critiques of Bababec appear to be similar to those levelled against religious leaders today. The narrative begins with an assumed Muslim paying a visit to a Brahman friend in the Ganges. The Muslim observes that there are several fakir sects with practices that deviate from the norm. A fakir, for one, feels enraged when he passes a Muslim because of the Muslim's shadow projected onto him. The Gymnosophists were infamous for putting nails into their bodies or carrying chains about with them. The Brahman leads the Muslim to the most well-known of them, Bababec. The Brahman criticises

Bababec, claiming that his life of sitting and suffering with nails in him is no better than the lives of others, particularly those who spend their days giving charity. He persuades Bababec to accompany him on this mission. Bababec, on the other hand, returns to his nails after two weeks since no one was worshipping him.

CANDIDE

OR OPTIMISM

1

HOW CANDIDE WAS BROUGHT UP IN A MAGNIFICENT CASTLE, AND HOW HE WAS EXPELLED THENCE

In a castle of Westphalia, belonging to the Baron of Thunder-ten-Tronckh, lived a youth, whom nature had endowed with the most gentle manners. His countenance was a true picture of his soul. He combined a true judgment with simplicity of spirit, which was the reason, I apprehend, of his being called Candide. The old servants of the family suspected him to have been the son of the Baron's sister, by a good, honest gentleman of the neighborhood, whom that young lady would never marry because he had been able to prove only seventy-one quarterings, the rest of his genealogical tree having been lost through the injuries of time.

The Baron was one of the most powerful lords in Westphalia, for his castle had not only a gate, but windows. His great hall, even, was hung with tapestry. All the dogs of his farmyards formed a pack of hounds at need; his grooms were his huntsmen; and the curate of the village was his grand almoner. They called him "My Lord," and laughed at all his stories.

The Baron's lady weighed about three hundred and fifty pounds, and was therefore a person of great consideration, and she did the honours of the house with a dignity that commanded still greater respect. Her daughter Cunegonde was seventeen years of age, fresh-coloured, comely, plump, and desirable. The Baron's son seemed to be in every respect worthy of his father. The Preceptor Pangloss was the oracle of the family, and little Candide heard his lessons with all the good faith of his age and character.

Pangloss was professor of metaphysico-theologico-cosmolo-nigology. He proved admirably that there is no effect without a cause, and that, in this best of all possible worlds, the Baron's castle was the most magnificent of castles, and his lady the best of all possible Baronesses.

"It is demonstrable," said he, "that things cannot be otherwise than as they are; for all being created for an end, all is necessarily for the best end. Observe, that the nose has been formed to bear spectacles—thus we have spectacles. Legs are visibly designed for stockings—and we have stockings. Stones were made to be hewn, and to construct castles—therefore my lord has a magnificent castle; for the greatest baron in the province ought to be the best lodged. Pigs were made to be eaten—therefore we eat pork all the year round. Consequently they who assert that all is well have said a foolish thing, they should have said all is for the best."

Candide listened attentively and believed innocently; for he thought Miss Cunegonde extremely beautiful, though he never had the courage to tell her so. He concluded that after the happiness of being born of Baron of Thunder-ten-Tronckh, the second degree of happiness was to be Miss Cunegonde, the third that of seeing her every day, and the fourth that of hearing Master Pangloss, the greatest philosopher of the whole province, and consequently of the whole world.

One day Cunegonde, while walking near the castle, in a little wood which they called a park, saw between the bushes, Dr. Pangloss giving a lesson in experimental natural philosophy to her mother's chamber-maid, a little brown wench, very pretty and very docile. As Miss Cunegonde had a great disposition for the sciences, she breathlessly observed the repeated experiments of which she was a witness; she clearly perceived the force of the Doctor's reasons, the effects, and the causes; she turned back greatly flurried, quite pensive, and filled with the desire to be learned; dreaming that she might well be a *sufficient reason* for young Candide, and he for her.

She met Candide on reaching the castle and blushed; Candide

blushed also; she wished him good morrow in a faltering tone, and Candide spoke to her without knowing what he said. The next day after dinner, as they went from table, Cunegonde and Candide found themselves behind a screen; Cunegonde let fall her handkerchief, Candide picked it up, she took him innocently by the hand, the youth as innocently kissed the young lady's hand with particular vivacity, sensibility, and grace; their lips met, their eyes sparkled, their knees trembled, their hands strayed. Baron Thunder-ten-Tronckh passed near the screen and beholding this cause and effect chased Candide from the castle with great kicks on the backside; Cunegonde fainted away; she was boxed on the ears by the Baroness, as soon as she came to herself; and all was consternation in this most magnificent and most agreeable of all possible castles.

2

WHAT BECAME OF CANDIDE AMONG THE BULGARIANS

Candide, driven from terrestrial paradise, walked a long while without knowing where, weeping, raising his eyes to heaven, turning them often towards the most magnificent of castles which imprisoned the purest of noble young ladies. He lay down to sleep without supper, in the middle of a field between two furrows. The snow fell in large flakes. Next day Candide, all benumbed, dragged himself towards the neighbouring town which was called Waldberghofftrarbk-dikdorff, having no money, dying of hunger and fatigue, he stopped sorrowfully at the door of an inn. Two men dressed in blue observed him.

"Comrade," said one, "here is a well-built young fellow, and of proper height."

They went up to Candide and very civilly invited him to dinner.

"Gentlemen," replied Candide, with a most engaging modesty, "you do me great honour, but I have not wherewithal to pay my share."

"Oh, sir," said one of the blues to him, "people of your appearance and of your merit never pay anything: are you not five feet five inches high?"

"Yes, sir, that is my height," answered he, making a low bow.

"Come, sir, seat yourself; not only will we pay your reckoning, but we will never suffer such a man as you to want money; men are only born to assist one another."

"You are right," said Candide; "this is what I was always taught by Mr. Pangloss, and I see plainly that all is for the best."

They begged of him to accept a few crowns. He took them, and wished to give them his note; they refused; they seated themselves at table.

"Love you not deeply?"

"Oh yes," answered he; "I deeply love Miss Cunegonde."

"No," said one of the gentlemen, "we ask you if you do not deeply love the King of the Bulgarians?"

"Not at all," said he; "for I have never seen him."

"What! he is the best of kings, and we must drink his health."

"Oh! very willingly, gentlemen," and he drank.

"That is enough," they tell him. "Now you are the help, the support, the defender, the hero of the Bulgarians. Your fortune is made, and your glory is assured."

Instantly they fettered him, and carried him away to the regiment. There he was made to wheel about to the right, and to the left, to draw his rammer, to return his rammer, to present, to fire, to march, and they gave him thirty blows with a cudgel. The next day he did his exercise a little less badly, and he received but twenty blows. The day following they gave him only ten, and he was regarded by his comrades as a prodigy.

Candide, all stupefied, could not yet very well realise how he was a hero. He resolved one fine day in spring to go for a walk, marching straight before him, believing that it was a privilege of the human as well as of the animal species to make use of their legs as they pleased. He had advanced two leagues when he was overtaken by four others, heroes of six feet, who bound him and carried him to a dungeon. He was asked which he would like the best, to be whipped six-and-thirty times through all the regiment, or to receive at once twelve balls of lead in his brain. He vainly said that human will is free, and that he chose neither the one nor the other. He was forced to make a choice; he determined, in virtue of that gift of God called liberty, to run the gauntlet six-and-thirty times. He bore this twice. The regiment was composed of two thousand men; that composed for him four thousand strokes, which laid bare all his muscles and nerves, from the nape of his neck quite down to his rump. As they were going to proceed to a third whipping, Candide, able to bear no more, begged as a favour that they would be so good as to shoot him. He obtained this favour; they bandaged his eyes, and bade him kneel down. The King of the Bulgarians passed at this moment and ascertained the nature of the crime. As he had great talent, he understood from all that he learnt of Candide that he was a young metaphysician, extremely ignorant of the things of this world, and he accorded him his pardon with a clemency which will bring him praise in all the journals, and throughout all ages.

An able surgeon cured Candide in three weeks by means of emollients taught by Dioscorides. He had already a little skin, and was able to march when the King of the Bulgarians gave battle to the King of the Abares.

3

HOW CANDIDE MADE HIS ESCAPE FROM THE BULGARIANS, AND WHAT AFTERWARDS BECAME OF HIM

There was never anything so gallant, so spruce, so brilliant, and so well disposed as the two armies. Trumpets, fifes, hautboys, drums, and cannon made music such as Hell itself had never heard. The cannons first of all laid flat about six thousand men on each side; the muskets swept away from this best of worlds nine or ten thousand ruffians who infested its surface. The bayonet was also a *sufficient reason* for the death of several thousands. The whole might amount to thirty thousand souls. Candide, who trembled like a philosopher, hid himself as well as he could during this heroic butchery.

At length, while the two kings were causing Te Deum to be sung each in his own camp, Candide resolved to go and reason elsewhere on effects and causes. He passed over heaps of dead and dying, and first reached a neighbouring village; it was in cinders, it was an Abare village which the Bulgarians had burnt according to the laws of war. Here, old men covered with wounds, beheld their wives, hugging their children to their bloody breasts, massacred before their faces; there, their daughters, disembowelled and breathing their last after having satisfied the natural wants of Bulgarian heroes; while others, half burnt in the flames, begged to be despatched. The earth was strewed with brains, arms, and legs.

Candide fled quickly to another village; it belonged to the Bulgarians; and the Abarian heroes had treated it in the same way. Candide, walking always over palpitating limbs or across ruins, arrived at last beyond the seat of war, with a few provisions in his knapsack, and Miss Cunegonde always in his heart. His provisions failed him when he arrived in Holland; but having heard that everybody was rich in that country, and that they were Christians, he did not doubt but he should meet with the same treatment from them as he had met with in the Baron's castle, before Miss Cunegonde's bright eyes were the cause of his expulsion thence.

He asked alms of several grave-looking people, who all answered him, that if he continued to follow this trade they would confine him to the house of correction, where he should be taught to get a living.

The next he addressed was a man who had been haranguing a large assembly for a whole hour on the subject of charity. But the orator, looking askew, said:

"What are you doing here? Are you for the good cause?"

"There can be no effect without a cause," modestly answered Candide; "the whole is necessarily concatenated and arranged for the best. It was necessary for me to have been banished from the presence of Miss Cunegonde, to have afterwards run the gauntlet, and now it is necessary I should beg my bread until I learn to earn it; all this cannot be otherwise."

"My friend," said the orator to him, "do you believe the Pope to be Anti-Christ?"

"I have not heard it," answered Candide; "but whether he be, or whether he be not, I want bread."

"Thou dost not deserve to eat," said the other. "Begone, rogue; begone, wretch; do not come near me again."

The orator's wife, putting her head out of the window, and spying a man that doubted whether the Pope was Anti-Christ, poured over him a full.... Oh, heavens! to what excess does religious zeal carry the ladies.

A man who had never been christened, a good Anabaptist, named James, beheld the cruel and ignominious treatment shown to one of his brethren, an unfeathered biped with a rational soul, he took him home, cleaned him, gave him bread and beer, presented him with two florins, and even wished to teach him the manufacture of Persian stuffs which they make in Holland. Candide, almost prostrating himself before him, cried:

"Master Pangloss has well said that all is for the best in this world, for I am infinitely more touched by your extreme generosity than with the inhumanity of that gentleman in the black coat and his lady."

The next day, as he took a walk, he met a beggar all covered with scabs, his eyes diseased, the end of his nose eaten away, his mouth distorted, his teeth black, choking in his throat, tormented with a violent cough, and spitting out a tooth at each effort.

4

HOW CANDIDE FOUND HIS OLD MASTER PANGLOSS, AND WHAT HAPPENED TO THEM

Candide, yet more moved with compassion than with horror, gave to this shocking beggar the two florins which he had received from the honest Anabaptist James. The spectre looked at him very earnestly, dropped a few tears, and fell upon his neck. Candide recoiled in disgust.

"Alas!" said one wretch to the other, "do you no longer know your dear Pangloss?"

"What do I hear? You, my dear master! you in this terrible plight! What misfortune has happened to you? Why are you no longer in the most magnificent of castles? What has become of Miss Cunegonde, the pearl of girls, and nature's masterpiece?"

"I am so weak that I cannot stand," said Pangloss.

Upon which Candide carried him to the Anabaptist's stable, and gave him a crust of bread. As soon as Pangloss had refreshed himself a little:

"Well," said Candide, "Cunegonde?"

"She is dead," replied the other.

Candide fainted at this word; his friend recalled his senses with a little bad vinegar which he found by chance in the stable. Candide reopened his eyes.

"Cunegonde is dead! Ah, best of worlds, where art thou? But of what illness did she die? Was it not for grief, upon seeing her father kick me out of his magnificent castle?"

"No," said Pangloss, "she was ripped open by the Bulgarian soldiers, after having been violated by many; they broke the Baron's head for attempting to defend her; my lady, her mother, was cut in pieces; my poor pupil was served just in the same manner as his sister; and as for the castle, they have not left one stone upon another, not a barn, nor a sheep, nor a duck, nor a tree; but we have had our revenge, for the Abares have done the very same thing to a neighbouring barony, which belonged to a Bulgarian lord."

At this discourse Candide fainted again; but coming to himself, and having said all that it became him to say, inquired into the cause and effect, as well as into the *sufficient reason* that had reduced Pangloss to so miserable a plight.

"Alas!" said the other, "it was love; love, the comfort of the human species, the preserver of the universe, the soul of all sensible beings, love, tender love."

"Alas!" said Candide, "I know this love, that sovereign of hearts, that soul of our souls; yet it never cost me more than a kiss and twenty kicks on the backside. How could this beautiful cause produce in you an effect so abominable?"

Pangloss made answer in these terms: "Oh, my dear Candide, you remember Paquette, that pretty wench who waited on our noble Baroness; in her arms I tasted the delights of paradise, which produced in me those hell torments with which you see me devoured; she was infected with them, she is perhaps dead of them. This present Paquette received of a learned Grey Friar, who had traced it to its source; he had had it of an old countess, who had received it from a cavalry captain, who owed it to a marchioness, who took it from a page, who had received it from a Jesuit, who when a novice had it in a direct line from one of the companions of Christopher Columbus. For my part I shall give it to nobody, I am dying."

"Oh, Pangloss!" cried Candide, "what a strange genealogy! Is not the Devil the original stock of it?"

"Not at all," replied this great man, "it was a thing unavoidable, a necessary ingredient in the best of worlds; for if Columbus had not in an island of America caught this disease, which contaminates the source of life, frequently even hinders generation, and which is evidently opposed to the great end of nature, we should have neither chocolate nor cochineal. We are also to observe that upon our continent, this distemper is like religious controversy, confined to a particular spot. The Turks, the Indians, the Persians, the Chinese, the Siamese, the Japanese, know nothing of it; but there is a sufficient reason for believing that they will know it in their turn in a few centuries. In the meantime, it has made marvellous progress among us, especially in those great armies composed of honest well-disciplined hirelings, who decide the destiny of states; for we may safely affirm that when an army of thirty thousand men fights another of an equal number, there are about twenty thousand of them p-x-d on each side."

"Well, this is wonderful!" said Candide, "but you must get cured."

"Alas! how can I?" said Pangloss, "I have not a farthing, my friend, and all over the globe there is no letting of blood or taking a glister, without paying, or somebody paying for you."

These last words determined Candide; he went and flung himself at the feet of the charitable Anabaptist James, and gave him so touching a picture of the state to which his friend was reduced, that the good man did not scruple to take Dr. Pangloss into his house, and had him cured at his expense. In the cure Pangloss lost only an eye and an ear. He wrote well, and knew arithmetic perfectly. The Anabaptist James made him his bookkeeper. At the end of two months, being obliged to go to Lisbon about some mercantile affairs, he took the two philosophers with him in his ship. Pangloss explained to him how everything was so constituted that it could not be better. James was not of this opinion.

"It is more likely," said he, "mankind have a little corrupted nature, for they were not born wolves, and they have become wolves; God has given them neither cannon of four-and-twenty pounders, nor bayonets; and yet they have made cannon and bayonets to destroy one another. Into this account I might throw not only bankrupts, but Justice which seizes on the effects of bankrupts to cheat the creditors."

"All this was indispensable," replied the one-eyed doctor, "for private misfortunes make the general good, so that the more private misfortunes there are the greater is the general good."

While he reasoned, the sky darkened, the winds blew from the four quarters, and the ship was assailed by a most terrible tempest within sight of the port of Lisbon.

5

TEMPEST, SHIPWRECK, EARTHQUAKE, AND WHAT BECAME OF DOCTOR PANGLOSS, CANDIDE, AND JAMES THE ANABAPTIST

Half dead of that inconceivable anguish which the rolling of a ship produces, one-half of the passengers were not even sensible of the danger. The other half shrieked and prayed. The sheets were rent, the masts broken, the vessel gaped. Work who would, no one heard, no one commanded. The Anabaptist being upon deck bore a hand; when a brutish sailor struck him roughly and laid him sprawling; but with the violence of the blow he himself tumbled head foremost overboard, and stuck upon a piece of the broken mast. Honest James ran to his assistance, hauled him up, and from the effort he made was precipitated into the sea in sight of the sailor, who left him to perish, without deigning to look at him. Candide drew near and saw his benefactor, who rose above the water one moment and was then swallowed up for ever. He was just going to jump after him, but was prevented by the philosopher Pangloss, who demonstrated to him that the Bay of Lisbon had been made on purpose for the Anabaptist to be drowned. While he was proving this *à priori*, the ship foundered; all perished except Pangloss, Candide, and that brutal sailor who had drowned the good Anabaptist. The villain swam safely to the shore, while Pangloss and Candide were borne thither upon a plank.

As soon as they recovered themselves a little they walked toward Lisbon. They had some money left, with which they hoped to save themselves from starving, after they had escaped drowning. Scarcely had they reached the city, lamenting the death of their benefactor, when they felt the earth tremble under their feet. The sea swelled and foamed in the harbour, and beat to pieces the vessels riding at anchor. Whirlwinds of fire and ashes covered the streets and public places; houses fell, roofs were flung upon the pavements, and the pavements were scattered. Thirty thousand inhabitants of all ages and sexes were crushed under the ruins. The sailor, whistling and swearing, said there was booty to be gained here.

"What can be the *sufficient reason* of this phenomenon?" said Pangloss.

"This is the Last Day!" cried Candide.

The sailor ran among the ruins, facing death to find money; finding it, he took it, got drunk, and having slept himself sober, purchased the favours of the first good-natured wench whom he met on the ruins of the destroyed houses, and in the midst of the dying and the dead. Pangloss pulled him by the sleeve.

"My friend," said he, "this is not right. You sin against the *universal reason*; you choose your time badly."

"S'blood and fury!" answered the other; "I am a sailor and born at Batavia. Four times have I trampled upon the crucifix in four voyages to Japan; a fig for thy universal reason."

Some falling stones had wounded Candide. He lay stretched in the street covered with rubbish.

"Alas!" said he to Pangloss, "get me a little wine and oil; I am dying."

"This concussion of the earth is no new thing," answered Pangloss. "The city of Lima, in America, experienced the same convulsions last year; the same cause, the same effects; there is certainly a train of sulphur under ground from Lima to Lisbon."

"Nothing more probable," said Candide; "but for the love of God a little oil and wine."

"How, probable?" replied the philosopher. "I maintain that the point is capable of being demonstrated."

Candide fainted away, and Pangloss fetched him some water from a neighbouring fountain. The following day they rummaged among the ruins and found provisions, with which they repaired their exhausted strength. After this they joined with others in relieving those inhabitants who had escaped death. Some, whom they had succoured, gave them as good a dinner as they could in such disastrous circumstances; true, the repast was mournful, and the company moistened their bread with tears; but Pangloss consoled them, assuring them that things could not be otherwise.

"For," said he, "all that is is for the best. If there is a volcano at Lisbon it cannot be elsewhere. It is impossible that things should be other than they are; for everything is right."

A little man dressed in black, Familiar of the Inquisition, who sat by him, politely took up his word and said:

"Apparently, then, sir, you do not believe in original sin; for if all is for the best there has then been neither Fall nor punishment."

"I humbly ask your Excellency's pardon," answered Pangloss, still more politely; "for the Fall and curse of man necessarily entered into the system of the best of worlds."

"Sir," said the Familiar, "you do not then believe in liberty?"

"Your Excellency will excuse me," said Pangloss; "liberty is consistent with absolute necessity, for it was necessary we should be free; for, in short, the determinate will——"

Pangloss was in the middle of his sentence, when the Familiar beckoned to his footman, who gave him a glass of wine from Porto or Opporto.

6

HOW THE PORTUGUESE MADE A BEAUTIFUL AUTO-DA-FÉ, TO PREVENT ANY FURTHER EARTHQUAKES; AND HOW CANDIDE WAS PUBLICLY WHIPPED

After the earthquake had destroyed three-fourths of Lisbon, the sages of that country could think of no means more effectual to prevent utter ruin than to give the people a beautiful *auto-da-fé*; for it had been decided by the University of Coimbra, that the burning of a few people alive by a slow fire, and with great ceremony, is an infallible secret to hinder the earth from quaking.

In consequence hereof, they had seized on a Biscayner, convicted of having married his godmother, and on two Portuguese, for rejecting the bacon which larded a chicken they were eating; after dinner, they came and secured Dr. Pangloss, and his disciple Candide, the one for speaking his mind, the other for having listened with an air of approbation. They were conducted to separate apartments, extremely cold, as they were never incommoded by the sun. Eight days after they were dressed in *san-benitos* and their heads ornamented with paper mitres. The mitre and *san-benito* belonging to Candide were painted with reversed flames and with devils that had neither tails nor claws; but Pangloss's devils had claws and tails and the flames were upright. They marched in procession thus habited and heard a very pathetic sermon, followed by fine church music. Candide was whipped in cadence while they were singing; the Biscayner, and the two men who had refused to eat bacon, were burnt; and Pangloss was hanged, though that was not the custom. The same day the earth sustained a most violent concussion.

Candide, terrified, amazed, desperate, all bloody, all palpitating, said to himself:

"If this is the best of possible worlds, what then are the others? Well, if I had been only whipped I could put up with it, for I experienced that among the Bulgarians; but oh, my dear Pangloss! thou greatest of philosophers, that I should have seen you hanged, without knowing for what! Oh, my dear Anabaptist, thou best of men, that thou should'st have been drowned in the very harbour! Oh, Miss Cunegonde, thou pearl of girls! that thou should'st have had thy belly ripped open!"

Thus he was musing, scarce able to stand, preached at, whipped, absolved, and blessed, when an old woman accosted him saying:

"My son, take courage and follow me."

7

HOW THE OLD WOMAN TOOK CARE OF CANDIDE, AND HOW HE FOUND THE OBJECT HE LOVED

Candide did not take courage, but followed the old woman to a decayed house, where she gave him a pot of pomatum to anoint his sores, showed him a very neat little bed, with a suit of clothes hanging up, and left him something to eat and drink.

"Eat, drink, sleep," said she, "and may our lady of Atocha, the great St. Anthony of Padua, and the great St. James of Compostella, receive you under their protection. I shall be back tomorrow."

Candide, amazed at all he had suffered and still more with the charity of the old woman, wished to kiss her hand.

"It is not my hand you must kiss," said the old woman; "I shall be back to-morrow. Anoint yourself with the pomatum, eat and sleep."

Candide, notwithstanding so many disasters, ate and slept. The next morning the old woman brought him his breakfast, looked at his back, and rubbed it herself with another ointment: in like manner she brought him his dinner; and at night she returned with his supper. The day following she went through the very same ceremonies.

"Who are you?" said Candide; "who has inspired you with so much goodness? What return can I make you?"

The good woman made no answer; she returned in the evening, but brought no supper.

"Come with me," she said, "and say nothing."

She took him by the arm, and walked with him about a quarter of a mile into the country; they arrived at a lonely house, surrounded with gardens and canals. The old woman knocked at a little door, it opened, she led Candide up a private staircase into a small apartment richly furnished. She left him on a brocaded sofa, shut the door and went away. Candide thought himself in a dream; indeed, that he had been dreaming unluckily all his life, and that the present moment was the only agreeable part of it all.

The old woman returned very soon, supporting with difficulty a trembling woman of a majestic figure, brilliant with jewels, and covered with a veil.

"Take off that veil," said the old woman to Candide.

The young man approaches, he raises the veil with a timid hand. Oh! what a moment! what surprise! he believes he beholds Miss Cunegonde? he really sees her! it is herself! His strength fails him, he cannot utter a word, but drops at her feet. Cunegonde falls upon the sofa. The old woman supplies a smelling bottle; they come to themselves and recover their speech. As they began with broken accents, with questions and answers interchangeably interrupted with sighs, with tears, and cries. The old woman desired they would make less noise and then she left them to themselves.

"What, is it you?" said Candide, "you live? I find you again in Portugal? then you have not been ravished? then they did not rip open your belly as Doctor Pangloss informed me?"

"Yes, they did," said the beautiful Cunegonde; "but those two accidents are not always mortal."

"But were your father and mother killed?"

"It is but too true," answered Cunegonde, in tears.

"And your brother?"

"My brother also was killed."

"And why are you in Portugal? and how did you know of my being here? and by what strange adventure did you contrive to bring me to this house?"

"I will tell you all that," replied the lady, "but first of all let me know your history, since the innocent kiss you gave me and the kicks which you received."

Candide respectfully obeyed her, and though he was still in a surprise, though his voice was feeble and trembling, though his back still pained him, yet he gave her a most ingenuous account of everything that had befallen him since the moment of their separation. Cunegonde lifted up her eyes to heaven; shed tears upon hearing of the death of the good Anabaptist and of Pangloss; after which she spoke as follows to Candide, who did not lose a word and devoured her with his eyes.

8

THE HISTORY OF CUNEGONDE

"I was in bed and fast asleep when it pleased God to send the Bulgarians to our delightful castle of Thunder-ten-Tronckh; they slew my father and brother, and cut my mother in pieces. A tall Bulgarian, six feet high, perceiving that I had fainted away at this sight, began to ravish me; this made me recover; I regained my senses, I cried, I struggled, I bit, I scratched, I wanted to tear out the tall Bulgarian's eyes—not knowing that what happened at my father's house was the usual practice of war. The brute gave me a cut in the left side with his hanger, and the mark is still upon me."

"Ah! I hope I shall see it," said honest Candide.

"You shall," said Cunegonde, "but let us continue."

"Do so," replied Candide.

Thus she resumed the thread of her story:

"A Bulgarian captain came in, saw me all bleeding, and the soldier not in the least disconcerted. The captain flew into a passion at the disrespectful behaviour of the brute, and slew him on my body. He ordered my wounds to be dressed, and took me to his quarters as a prisoner of war. I washed the few shirts that he had, I did his cooking; he thought me very pretty—he avowed it; on the other hand, I must own he had a good shape, and a soft and white skin; but he had little or no mind or philosophy, and you might see plainly that he had never been instructed by Doctor Pangloss. In three months time, having lost all his money, and being grown tired of my company, he sold me to a Jew, named Don Issachar, who traded to Holland and Portugal, and had a strong passion for women. This Jew was much attached to my person, but could not triumph over it; I resisted him better than the Bulgarian soldier. A modest woman may be ravished once, but her virtue is strengthened by it. In order to render me more tractable, he brought me to this country house. Hitherto I had imagined that nothing could equal the beauty of Thunder-ten-Tronckh Castle; but I found I was mistaken.

"The Grand Inquisitor, seeing me one day at Mass, stared long at me, and sent to tell me that he wished to speak on private matters. I was conducted to his palace, where I acquainted him with the history of my family, and he represented to me how much it was beneath my rank to belong to an Israelite. A proposal was then made to Don Issachar that he should resign me to my lord. Don Issachar, being the court banker, and a man of credit, would hear nothing of it. The Inquisitor threatened him with an *auto-da-fé*. At last my Jew, intimidated, concluded a bargain, by which the house and myself should belong to both in common; the Jew should have for himself Monday, Wednesday, and Saturday, and the Inquisitor should have the rest of the week. It is now six months since this agreement was made. Quarrels have not been wanting, for they could not decide whether the night from Saturday to Sunday belonged to the old law or to the new. For my part, I have so far held out against both, and I verily believe that this is the reason why I am still beloved.

"At length, to avert the scourge of earthquakes, and to intimidate Don Issachar, my Lord Inquisitor was pleased to celebrate an *auto-da-fé*. He did me the honour to invite me to the ceremony. I had a very good seat, and the ladies were served with refreshments between Mass and the execution. I was in truth seized with horror at the burning of those two Jews, and of the honest Biscayner who had married his godmother; but what was my surprise, my fright, my trouble, when I saw in a *san-benito* and mitre a figure which resembled that of Pangloss! I rubbed my eyes, I looked at him attentively, I saw him hung; I fainted. Scarcely had I recovered my senses than I saw you stripped, stark naked, and this was the height of my horror, consternation, grief, and despair. I tell you, truthfully, that your skin is yet whiter and of a more perfect colour than that of my Bulgarian captain. This spectacle redoubled all the feelings which overwhelmed and devoured me. I screamed out, and would have said, 'Stop, barbarians!' but my voice failed me, and my cries would have been useless after you had been severely whipped. How is it possible, said I, that the beloved Candide and the wise Pangloss should both be at Lisbon, the one to receive a hundred lashes, and the other to be hanged by the Grand Inquisitor, of whom I am the well-beloved? Pangloss most cruelly deceived me when he said that everything in the world is for the best.

"Agitated, lost, sometimes beside myself, and sometimes ready to die of weakness, my mind was filled with the massacre of my father, mother, and brother, with the insolence of the ugly Bulgarian soldier, with the stab that he gave me, with my servitude under the Bulgarian captain, with my hideous Don Issachar, with my abominable Inquisitor, with the execution of Doctor Pangloss, with the grand Miserere to which they whipped you, and especially with the kiss I gave you behind the screen the day that I had last seen you. I praised God for bringing you back to me after so many trials, and I charged my old woman to take care of you, and to conduct you hither as soon as possible. She has executed her commission perfectly well; I have tasted the inexpressible pleasure of seeing you again, of hearing you, of speaking with you. But you must be hungry, for myself, I am famished; let us have supper."

They both sat down to table, and, when supper was over, they placed themselves once more on the sofa; where they were when Signor Don Issachar arrived. It was the Jewish Sabbath, and Issachar had come to enjoy his rights, and to explain his tender love.

9

WHAT BECAME OF CUNEGONDE, CANDIDE, THE GRAND INQUISITOR, AND THE JEW

This Issachar was the most choleric Hebrew that had ever been seen in Israel since the Captivity in Babylon.

"What!" said he, "thou bitch of a Galilean, was not the Inquisitor enough for thee? Must this rascal also share with me?"

In saying this he drew a long poniard which he always carried about him; and not imagining that his adversary had any arms he threw himself upon Candide: but our honest Westphalian had received a handsome sword from the old woman along with the suit of clothes. He drew his rapier, despite his gentleness, and laid the Israelite stone dead upon the cushions at Cunegonde's feet.

"Holy Virgin!" cried she, "what will become of us? A man killed in my apartment! If the officers of justice come, we are lost!"

"Had not Pangloss been hanged," said Candide, "he would give us good counsel in this emergency, for he was a profound philosopher. Failing him let us consult the old woman."

She was very prudent and commenced to give her opinion when suddenly another little door opened. It was an hour after midnight, it was the beginning of Sunday. This day belonged to my lord the Inquisitor. He entered, and saw the whipped Candide, sword in hand, a dead man upon the floor, Cunegonde aghast, and the old woman giving counsel.

At this moment, the following is what passed in the soul of Candide, and how he reasoned:

If this holy man call in assistance, he will surely have me burnt; and Cunegonde will perhaps be served in the same manner; he was the cause of my being cruelly whipped; he is my rival; and, as I have now begun to kill, I will kill away, for there is no time to hesitate. This reasoning was clear and instantaneous; so that without giving time to the Inquisitor to recover from his surprise, he pierced him through and through, and cast him beside the Jew.

"Yet again!" said Cunegonde, "now there is no mercy for us, we are excommunicated, our last hour has come. How could you do it? you, naturally so gentle, to slay a Jew and a prelate in two minutes!"

"My beautiful young lady," responded Candide, "when one is a lover, jealous and whipped by the Inquisition, one stops at nothing."

The old woman then put in her word, saying:

"There are three Andalusian horses in the stable with bridles and saddles, let the brave Candide get them ready; madame has money, jewels; let us therefore mount quickly on horseback, though I can sit only on one buttock; let us set out for Cadiz, it is the finest weather in the world, and there is great pleasure in travelling in the cool of the night."

Immediately Candide saddled the three horses, and Cunegonde, the old woman and he, travelled thirty miles at a stretch. While they were journeying, the Holy Brotherhood entered the house; my lord the Inquisitor was interred in a handsome church, and Issachar's body was thrown upon a dunghill.

Candide, Cunegonde, and the old woman, had now reached the little town of Avacena in the midst of the mountains of the Sierra Morena, and were speaking as follows in a public inn.

10

IN WHAT DISTRESS CANDIDE, CUNEGONDE, AND THE OLD WOMAN ARRIVED AT CADIZ; AND OF THEIR EMBARKATION

"Who was it that robbed me of my money and jewels?" said Cunegonde, all bathed in tears. "How shall we live? What shall we do? Where find Inquisitors or Jews who will give me more?"

"Alas!" said the old woman, "I have a shrewd suspicion of a reverend Grey Friar, who stayed last night in the same inn with us at Badajos. God preserve me from judging rashly, but he came into our room twice, and he set out upon his journey long before us."

"Alas!" said Candide, "dear Pangloss has often demonstrated to me that the goods of this world are common to all men, and that each has an equal right to them. But according to these principles the Grey Friar ought to have left us enough to carry us through our journey. Have you nothing at all left, my dear Cunegonde?"

"Not a farthing," said she.

"What then must we do?" said Candide.

"Sell one of the horses," replied the old woman. "I will ride behind Miss Cunegonde, though I can hold myself only on one buttock, and we shall reach Cadiz."

In the same inn there was a Benedictine prior who bought the horse for a cheap price. Candide, Cunegonde, and the old woman, having passed through Lucena, Chillas, and Lebrixa, arrived at length at Cadiz. A fleet was there getting ready, and troops assembling to bring to reason the reverend Jesuit Fathers of Paraguay, accused of having made one of the native tribes in the neighborhood of San Sacrament revolt against the Kings of Spain and Portugal. Candide having been in the Bulgarian service, performed the military exercise before the general of this little army with so graceful an address, with so intrepid an air, and with such agility and expedition, that he was given the command of a company of foot. Now, he was a captain! He set sail with Miss Cunegonde, the old woman, two valets, and the two Andalusian horses, which had belonged to the grand Inquisitor of Portugal.

During their voyage they reasoned a good deal on the philosophy of poor Pangloss.

"We are going into another world," said Candide; "and surely it must be there that all is for the best. For I must confess there is reason to complain a little of what passeth in our world in regard to both natural and moral philosophy."

"I love you with all my heart," said Cunegonde; "but my soul is still full of fright at that which I have seen and experienced."

"All will be well," replied Candide; "the sea of this new world is already better than our European sea; it is calmer, the winds more regular. It is certainly the New World which is the best of all possible worlds."

"God grant it," said Cunegonde; "but I have been so horribly unhappy there that my heart is almost closed to hope."

"You complain," said the old woman; "alas! you have not known such misfortunes as mine."

Cunegonde almost broke out laughing, finding the good woman very amusing, for pretending to have been as unfortunate as she.

"Alas!" said Cunegonde, "my good mother, unless you have been ravished by two Bulgarians, have received two deep wounds in your belly, have had two castles demolished, have had two mothers cut to pieces before your eyes, and two of your lovers whipped at an *auto-da-fé*, I do not conceive how you could be more unfortunate than I. Add that I was born a baroness of seventy-two quarterings—and have been a cook!"

"Miss," replied the old woman, "you do not know my birth; and were I to show you my backside, you would not talk in that manner, but would suspend your judgment."

This speech having raised extreme curiosity in the minds of Cunegonde and Candide, the old woman spoke to them as follows.

11

HISTORY OF THE OLD WOMAN

"I had not always bleared eyes and red eyelids; neither did my nose always touch my chin; nor was I always a servant. I am the daughter of Pope Urban X, and of the Princess of Palestrina. Until the age of fourteen I was brought up in a palace, to which all the castles of your German barons would scarcely have served for stables; and one of my robes was worth more than all the magnificence of Westphalia. As I grew up I improved in beauty, wit, and every graceful accomplishment, in the midst of pleasures, hopes, and respectful homage. Already I inspired love. My throat was formed, and such a throat! white, firm, and shaped like that of the Venus of Medici; and what eyes! what eyelids! what black eyebrows! such flames darted from my dark pupils that they eclipsed the scintillation of the stars—as I was told by the poets in our part of the world. My waiting women, when dressing and undressing me, used to fall into an ecstasy, whether they viewed me before or behind; how glad would the gentlemen have been to perform that office for them!

"I was affianced to the most excellent Prince of Massa Carara. Such a prince! as handsome as myself, sweet-tempered, agreeable, brilliantly witty, and sparkling with love. I loved him as one loves for the first time—with idolatry, with transport. The nuptials were prepared. There was surprising pomp and magnificence; there were *fêtes*, carousals, continual *opera bouffe*; and all Italy composed sonnets in my praise, though not one of them was passable. I was just upon the point of reaching the summit of bliss, when an old marchioness who had been mistress to the Prince, my husband, invited him to drink chocolate with her. He died in less than two hours of most terrible convulsions. But this is only a bagatelle. My mother, in despair, and scarcely less afflicted than myself, determined to absent herself for some time from so fatal a place. She had a very fine estate in the neighbourhood of Gaeta. We embarked on board a galley of the country which was gilded like the great altar of St. Peter's at Rome. A Sallee corsair swooped down and boarded us. Our men defended themselves like the Pope's soldiers; they flung themselves upon their knees, and threw down their arms, begging of the corsair an absolution *in articulo mortis*.

"Instantly they were stripped as bare as monkeys; my mother, our maids of honour, and myself were all served in the same manner. It is amazing with what expedition those gentry undress people. But what surprised me most was, that they thrust their fingers into the part of our bodies which the generality of women suffer no other instrument but—pipes to enter. It appeared to me a very strange kind of ceremony; but thus one judges of things when one has not seen the world. I afterwards learnt that it was to try whether we had concealed any diamonds. This is the practice established from time immemorial, among civilised nations that scour the seas. I was informed that the very religious Knights of Malta never fail to make this search when they take any Turkish prisoners of either sex. It is a law of nations from which they never deviate.

"I need not tell *you* how great a hardship it was for a young princess and her mother to be made slaves and carried to Morocco. You may easily imagine all we had to suffer on board the pirate vessel. My mother was still very handsome; our maids of honour, and even our waiting women, had more charms than are to be found in all Africa. As for myself, I was ravishing, was exquisite, grace itself, and I was a virgin! I did not remain so long; this flower, which had been reserved for the handsome Prince of Massa Carara, was plucked by the corsair captain. He was an abominable negro, and yet believed that he did me a great deal of honour. Certainly the Princess of Palestrina and myself must have been very strong to go through all that we experienced until our arrival at Morocco. But let us pass on; these are such common things as not to be worth mentioning.

"Morocco swam in blood when we arrived. Fifty sons of the Emperor Muley-Ismael had each their adherents; this produced fifty civil wars, of blacks against blacks, and blacks against tawnies, and tawnies against tawnies, and mulattoes against mulattoes. In short it was a continual carnage throughout the empire.

"No sooner were we landed, than the blacks of a contrary faction to that of my captain attempted to rob him of his booty. Next to jewels and gold we were the most valuable things he had. I was witness to such a battle as you have never seen in your European climates. The northern nations have not that heat in their blood, nor that raging lust for women, so common in Africa. It seems that you Europeans have only milk in your veins; but it is vitriol, it is fire which runs in those of the inhabitants of Mount Atlas and the neighbouring countries. They fought with the fury of the lions, tigers, and serpents of the country, to see who should have us. A Moor seized my mother by the right arm, while my captain's lieutenant held her by the left; a Moorish soldier had hold of her by one leg, and one of our corsairs held her by the other. Thus almost all our women were drawn in quarters by four men. My captain concealed me behind him; and with his drawn scimitar cut and slashed every one that opposed his fury. At length I saw all our Italian women, and my mother herself, torn, mangled, massacred, by the monsters who disputed over them. The slaves, my companions, those who had taken them, soldiers, sailors, blacks, whites, mulattoes, and at last my captain, all were killed, and I remained dying on a heap of dead. Such scenes as this were transacted through an extent of three hundred leagues—and yet they never missed the five prayers a day ordained by Mahomet.

"With difficulty I disengaged myself from such a heap of slaughtered bodies, and crawled to a large orange tree on the bank of a neighbouring rivulet, where I fell, oppressed with fright, fatigue, horror, despair, and hunger. Immediately after, my senses, overpowered, gave themselves up to sleep, which was yet more swooning than repose. I was in this state of weakness and insensibility, between life and death, when I felt myself pressed by something that moved upon my body. I opened my eyes, and saw a white man, of good countenance, who sighed, and who said between his teeth: '*O che sciagura d'essere senza coglioni!*'"

12

THE ADVENTURES OF THE OLD WOMAN CONTINUED

"Astonished and delighted to hear my native language, and no less surprised at what this man said, I made answer that there were much greater misfortunes than that of which he complained. I told him in a few words of the horrors which I had endured, and fainted a second time. He carried me to a neighbouring house, put me to bed, gave me food, waited upon me, consoled me, flattered me; he told me that he had never seen any one so beautiful as I, and that he never so much regretted the loss of what it was impossible to recover.

"'I was born at Naples,' said he, 'there they geld two or three thousand children every year; some die of the operation, others acquire a voice more beautiful than that of women, and others are raised to offices of state. This operation was performed on me with great success and I was chapel musician to madam, the Princess of Palestrina.'

"'To my mother!' cried I.

"'Your mother!' cried he, weeping. 'What! Can you be that young princess whom I brought up until the age of six years, and who promised so early to be as beautiful as you?'

"'It is I, indeed; but my mother lies four hundred yards hence, torn in quarters, under a heap of dead bodies.'

"I told him all my adventures, and he made me acquainted with his; telling me that he had been sent to the Emperor of Morocco by a Christian power, to conclude a treaty with that prince, in consequence of which he was to be furnished with military stores and ships to help to demolish the commerce of other Christian Governments.

"'My mission is done,' said this honest eunuch; 'I go to embark for Ceuta, and will take you to Italy. *Ma che sciagura d'essere senza coglioni!*'

"I thanked him with tears of commiseration; and instead of taking me to Italy he conducted me to Algiers, where he sold me to the Dey. Scarcely was I sold, than the plague which had made the tour of Africa, Asia, and Europe, broke out with great malignancy in Algiers. You have seen earthquakes; but pray, miss, have you ever had the plague?"

"Never," answered Cunegonde.

"If you had," said the old woman, "you would acknowledge that it is far more terrible than an earthquake. It is common in Africa, and I caught it. Imagine to yourself the distressed situation of the daughter of a Pope, only fifteen years old, who, in less than three months, had felt the miseries of poverty and slavery, had been ravished almost every day, had beheld her mother drawn in quarters, had experienced famine and war, and was dying of the plague in Algiers. I did not die, however, but my eunuch, and the Dey, and almost the whole seraglio of Algiers perished.

"As soon as the first fury of this terrible pestilence was over, a sale was made of the Dey's slaves; I was purchased by a merchant, and carried to Tunis; this man sold me to another merchant, who sold me again to another at Tripoli; from Tripoli I was sold to Alexandria, from Alexandria to Smyrna, and from Smyrna to Constantinople. At length I became the property of an Aga of the Janissaries, who was soon ordered away to the defence of Azof, then besieged by the Russians.

"The Aga, who was a very gallant man, took his whole seraglio with him, and lodged us in a small fort on the Palus Méotides, guarded by two black eunuchs and twenty soldiers. The Turks killed prodigious numbers of the Russians, but the latter had their revenge. Azof was destroyed by fire, the inhabitants put to the sword, neither sex nor age was spared; until there remained only our little fort, and the enemy wanted to starve us out. The twenty Janissaries had sworn they would never surrender. The extremities of famine to which they were reduced, obliged them to eat our two eunuchs, for fear of violating their oath. And at the end of a few days they resolved also to devour the women.

"We had a very pious and humane Iman, who preached an excellent sermon, exhorting them not to kill us all at once.

"'Only cut off a buttock of each of those ladies,' said he, 'and you'll fare extremely well; if you must go to it again, there will be the same entertainment a few days hence; heaven will accept of so charitable an action, and send you relief.'

"He had great eloquence; he persuaded them; we underwent this terrible operation. The Iman applied the same balsam to us, as he does to children after circumcision; and we all nearly died.

"Scarcely had the Janissaries finished the repast with which we had furnished them, than the Russians came in flat-bottomed boats; not a Janissary escaped. The Russians paid no attention to the condition we were in. There are French surgeons in all parts of the world; one of them who was very clever took us under his care—he cured us; and as long as I live I shall remember that as soon as my wounds were healed he made proposals to me. He bid us all be of good cheer, telling us that the like had happened in many sieges, and that it was according to the laws of war.

"As soon as my companions could walk, they were obliged to set out for Moscow. I fell to the share of a Boyard who made me his gardener, and gave me twenty lashes a day. But this nobleman having in two years' time been broke upon the wheel along with thirty more Boyards for some broils at court, I profited by that event; I fled. I traversed all Russia; I was a long time an inn-holder's servant at Riga, the same at Rostock, at Vismar, at Leipzig, at Cassel, at Utrecht, at Leyden, at the Hague, at Rotterdam. I waxed old in misery and disgrace, having only one-half of my posteriors, and always remembering I was a Pope's daughter. A hundred times I was upon the point of killing myself; but still I loved life. This ridiculous foible is perhaps one of our most fatal characteristics; for is there anything more absurd than to wish to carry continually a burden which one can always throw down? to detest existence and yet to cling to one's existence? in brief, to caress the serpent which devours us, till he has eaten our very heart?

"In the different countries which it has been my lot to traverse, and the numerous inns where I have been servant, I have taken notice of a vast number of people who held their own existence in abhorrence, and yet I never knew of more than eight who voluntarily put an end to their misery; three negroes, four Englishmen, and a German professor named Robek. I ended by being servant to the

Jew, Don Issachar, who placed me near your presence, my fair lady. I am determined to share your fate, and have been much more affected with your misfortunes than with my own. I would never even have spoken to you of my misfortunes, had you not piqued me a little, and if it were not customary to tell stories on board a ship in order to pass away the time. In short, Miss Cunegonde, I have had experience, I know the world; therefore I advise you to divert yourself, and prevail upon each passenger to tell his story; and if there be one of them all, that has not cursed his life many a time, that has not frequently looked upon himself as the unhappiest of mortals, I give you leave to throw me headforemost into the sea."

13

HOW CANDIDE WAS FORCED AWAY FROM HIS FAIR CUNEGONDE AND THE OLD WOMAN

The beautiful Cunegonde having heard the old woman's history, paid her all the civilities due to a person of her rank and merit. She likewise accepted her proposal, and engaged all the passengers, one after the other, to relate their adventures; and then both she and Candide allowed that the old woman was in the right.

"It is a great pity," said Candide, "that the sage Pangloss was hanged contrary to custom at an *auto-da-fé*; he would tell us most amazing things in regard to the physical and moral evils that overspread earth and sea, and I should be able, with due respect, to make a few objections."

While each passenger was recounting his story, the ship made her way. They landed at Buenos Ayres. Cunegonde, Captain Candide, and the old woman, waited on the Governor, Don Fernando d'Ibaraa, y Figueora, y Mascarenes, y Lampourdos, y Souza. This nobleman had a stateliness becoming a person who bore so many names. He spoke to men with so noble a disdain, carried his nose so loftily, raised his voice so unmercifully, assumed so imperious an air, and stalked with such intolerable pride, that those who saluted him were strongly inclined to give him a good drubbing. Cunegonde appeared to him the most beautiful he had ever met. The first thing he did was to ask whether she was not the captain's wife. The manner in which he asked the question alarmed Candide; he durst not say she was his wife, because indeed she was not; neither durst he say she was his sister, because it was not so; and although this obliging lie had been formerly much in favour among the ancients, and although it could be useful to the moderns, his soul was too pure to betray the truth.

"Miss Cunegonde," said he, "is to do me the honour to marry me, and we beseech your excellency to deign to sanction our marriage."

Don Fernando d'Ibaraa, y Figueora, y Mascarenes, y Lampourdos, y Souza, turning up his moustachios, smiled mockingly, and ordered Captain Candide to go and review his company. Candide obeyed, and the Governor remained alone with Miss Cunegonde. He declared his passion, protesting he would marry her the next day in the face of the church, or otherwise, just as should be agreeable to herself. Cunegonde asked a quarter of an hour to consider of it, to consult the old woman, and to take her resolution.

The old woman spoke thus to Cunegonde:

"Miss, you have seventy-two quarterings, and not a farthing; it is now in your power to be wife to the greatest lord in South America, who has very beautiful moustachios. Is it for you to pique yourself upon inviolable fidelity? You have been ravished by Bulgarians; a Jew and an Inquisitor have enjoyed your favours. Misfortune gives sufficient excuse. I own, that if I were in your place, I should have no scruple in marrying the Governor and in making the fortune of Captain Candide."

While the old woman spoke with all the prudence which age and experience gave, a small ship entered the port on board of which were an Alcalde and his alguazils, and this was what had happened.

As the old woman had shrewdly guessed, it was a Grey Friar who stole Cunegonde's money and jewels in the town of Badajos, when she and Candide were escaping. The Friar wanted to sell some of the diamonds to a jeweller; the jeweller knew them to be the Grand Inquisitor's. The Friar before he was hanged confessed he had stolen them. He described the persons, and the route they had taken. The flight of Cunegonde and Candide was already known. They were traced to Cadiz. A vessel was immediately sent in pursuit of them. The vessel was already in the port of Buenos Ayres. The report spread that the Alcalde was going to land, and that he was in pursuit of the murderers of my lord the Grand Inquisitor. The prudent old woman saw at once what was to be done.

"You cannot run away," said she to Cunegonde, "and you have nothing to fear, for it was not you that killed my lord; besides the Governor who loves you will not suffer you to be ill-treated; therefore stay."

She then ran immediately to Candide.

"Fly," said she, "or in an hour you will be burnt."

There was not a moment to lose; but how could he part from Cunegonde, and where could he flee for shelter?

14

HOW CANDIDE AND CACAMBO WERE RECEIVED BY THE JESUITS OF PARAGUAY

Candide had brought such a valet with him from Cadiz, as one often meets with on the coasts of Spain and in the American colonies. He was a quarter Spaniard, born of a mongrel in Tucuman; he had been singing-boy, sacristan, sailor, monk, pedlar, soldier, and lackey. His name was Cacambo, and he loved his master, because his master was a very good man. He quickly saddled the two Andalusian horses.

"Come, master, let us follow the old woman's advice; let us start, and run without looking behind us."

Candide shed tears.

"Oh! my dear Cunegonde! must I leave you just at a time when the Governor was going to sanction our nuptials? Cunegonde, brought to such a distance what will become of you?"

"She will do as well as she can," said Cacambo; "the women are never at a loss, God provides for them, let us run."

"Whither art thou carrying me? Where shall we go? What shall we do without Cunegonde?" said Candide.

"By St. James of Compostella," said Cacambo, "you were going to fight against the Jesuits; let us go to fight for them; I know the road well, I'll conduct you to their kingdom, where they will be charmed to have a captain that understands the Bulgarian exercise. You'll make a prodigious fortune; if we cannot find our account in one world we shall in another. It is a great pleasure to see and do new things."

"You have before been in Paraguay, then?" said Candide.

"Ay, sure," answered Cacambo, "I was servant in the College of the Assumption, and am acquainted with the government of the good Fathers as well as I am with the streets of Cadiz. It is an admirable government. The kingdom is upwards of three hundred leagues in diameter, and divided into thirty provinces; there the Fathers possess all, and the people nothing; it is a masterpiece of reason and justice. For my part I see nothing so divine as the Fathers who here make war upon the kings of Spain and Portugal, and in Europe confess those kings; who here kill Spaniards, and in Madrid send them to heaven; this delights me, let us push forward. You are going to be the happiest of mortals. What pleasure will it be to those Fathers to hear that a captain who knows the Bulgarian exercise has come to them!"

As soon as they reached the first barrier, Cacambo told the advanced guard that a captain wanted to speak with my lord the Commandant. Notice was given to the main guard, and immediately a Paraguayan officer ran and laid himself at the feet of the

Commandant, to impart this news to him. Candide and Cacambo were disarmed, and their two Andalusian horses seized. The strangers were introduced between two files of musketeers; the Commandant was at the further end, with the three-cornered cap on his head, his gown tucked up, a sword by his side, and a spontoon in his hand. He beckoned, and straightway the new-comers were encompassed by four-and-twenty soldiers. A sergeant told them they must wait, that the Commandant could not speak to them, and that the reverend Father Provincial does not suffer any Spaniard to open his mouth but in his presence, or to stay above three hours in the province.

"And where is the reverend Father Provincial?" said Cacambo.

"He is upon the parade just after celebrating mass," answered the sergeant, "and you cannot kiss his spurs till three hours hence."

"However," said Cacambo, "the captain is not a Spaniard, but a German, he is ready to perish with hunger as well as myself; cannot we have something for breakfast, while we wait for his reverence?"

The sergeant went immediately to acquaint the Commandant with what he had heard.

"God be praised!" said the reverend Commandant, "since he is a German, I may speak to him; take him to my arbour."

Candide was at once conducted to a beautiful summer-house, ornamented with a very pretty colonnade of green and gold marble, and with trellises, enclosing parraquets, humming-birds, fly-birds, guinea-hens, and all other rare birds. An excellent breakfast was provided in vessels of gold; and while the Paraguayans were eating maize out of wooden dishes, in the open fields and exposed to the heat of the sun, the reverend Father Commandant retired to his arbour.

He was a very handsome young man, with a full face, white skin but high in colour; he had an arched eyebrow, a lively eye, red ears, vermilion lips, a bold air, but such a boldness as neither belonged to a Spaniard nor a Jesuit. They returned their arms to Candide and Cacambo, and also the two Andalusian horses; to whom Cacambo gave some oats to eat just by the arbour, having an eye upon them all the while for fear of a surprise.

Candide first kissed the hem of the Commandant's robe, then they sat down to table.

"You are, then, a German?" said the Jesuit to him in that language.

"Yes, reverend Father," answered Candide.

As they pronounced these words they looked at each other with great amazement, and with such an emotion as they could not conceal.

"And from what part of Germany do you come?" said the Jesuit.

"I am from the dirty province of Westphalia," answered Candide; "I was born in the Castle of Thunder-ten-Tronckh."

"Oh! Heavens! is it possible?" cried the Commandant.

"What a miracle!" cried Candide.

"Is it really you?" said the Commandant.

"It is not possible!" said Candide.

They drew back; they embraced; they shed rivulets of tears.

"What, is it you, reverend Father? You, the brother of the fair Cunegonde! You, that was slain by the Bulgarians! You, the Baron's son! You, a Jesuit in Paraguay! I must confess this is a strange world that we live in. Oh, Pangloss! Pangloss! how glad you would be if you had not been hanged!"

The Commandant sent away the negro slaves and the Paraguayans, who served them with liquors in goblets of rock-crystal. He thanked God and St. Ignatius a thousand times; he clasped Candide in his arms; and their faces were all bathed with tears.

"You will be more surprised, more affected, and transported," said Candide, "when I tell you that Cunegonde, your sister, whom you believe to have been ripped open, is in perfect health."

"Where?"

"In your neighbourhood, with the Governor of Buenos Ayres; and I was going to fight against you."

Every word which they uttered in this long conversation but added wonder to wonder. Their souls fluttered on their tongues, listened in their ears, and sparkled in their eyes. As they were Germans, they sat a good while at table, waiting for the reverend Father Provincial, and the Commandant spoke to his dear Candide as follows.

15

HOW CANDIDE KILLED THE BROTHER OF HIS DEAR CUNEGONDE

"I shall have ever present to my memory the dreadful day, on which I saw my father and mother killed, and my sister ravished. When the Bulgarians retired, my dear sister could not be found; but my mother, my father, and myself, with two maid-servants and three little boys all of whom had been slain, were put in a hearse, to be conveyed for interment to a chapel belonging to the Jesuits, within two leagues of our family seat. A Jesuit sprinkled us with some holy water; it was horribly salt; a few drops of it fell into my eyes; the father perceived that my eyelids stirred a little; he put his hand upon my heart and felt it beat. I received assistance, and at the end of three weeks I recovered. You know, my dear Candide, I was very pretty; but I grew much prettier, and the reverend Father Didrie, Superior of that House, conceived the tenderest friendship for me; he gave me the habit of the order, some years after I was sent to Rome. The Father-General needed new levies of young German-Jesuits. The sovereigns of Paraguay admit as few Spanish Jesuits as possible; they prefer those of other nations as being more subordinate to their commands. I was judged fit by the reverend Father-General to go and work in this vineyard. We set out—a Pole, a Tyrolese, and myself. Upon my arrival I was honoured with a sub-deaconship and a lieutenancy. I am to-day colonel and priest. We shall give a warm reception to the King of Spain's troops; I will answer for it that they shall be excommunicated and well beaten. Providence sends you here to assist us. But is it, indeed, true that my dear sister Cunegonde is in the neighbourhood, with the Governor of Buenos Ayres?"

Candide assured him on oath that nothing was more true, and their tears began afresh.

The Baron could not refrain from embracing Candide; he called him his brother, his saviour.

"Ah! perhaps," said he, "we shall together, my dear Candide, enter the town as conquerors, and recover my sister Cunegonde."

"That is all I want," said Candide, "for I intended to marry her, and I still hope to do so."

"You insolent!" replied the Baron, "would you have the impudence to marry my sister who has seventy-two quarterings! I find thou hast the most consummate effrontery to dare to mention so presumptuous a design!"

Candide, petrified at this speech, made answer:

"Reverend Father, all the quarterings in the world signify nothing; I rescued your sister from the arms of a Jew and of an Inquisitor; she has great obligations to me, she wishes to marry me; Master Pangloss always told me that all men are equal, and certainly I will marry her."

"We shall see that, thou scoundrel!" said the Jesuit Baron de Thunder-ten-Tronckh, and that instant struck him across the face with the flat of his sword. Candide in an instant drew his rapier, and plunged it up to the hilt in the Jesuit's belly; but in pulling it out reeking hot, he burst into tears.

"Good God!" said he, "I have killed my old master, my friend, my brother-in-law! I am the best-natured creature in the world, and yet I have already killed three men, and of these three two were priests."

Cacambo, who stood sentry by the door of the arbour, ran to him.

"We have nothing more for it than to sell our lives as dearly as we can," said his master to him, "without doubt some one will soon enter the arbour, and we must die sword in hand."

Cacambo, who had been in a great many scrapes in his lifetime, did not lose his head; he took the Baron's Jesuit habit, put it on Candide, gave him the square cap, and made him mount on horseback. All this was done in the twinkling of an eye.

"Let us gallop fast, master, everybody will take you for a Jesuit, going to give directions to your men, and we shall have passed the frontiers before they will be able to overtake us."

He flew as he spoke these words, crying out aloud in Spanish: "Make way, make way, for the reverend Father Colonel."

16

ADVENTURES OF THE TWO TRAVELLERS, WITH TWO GIRLS, TWO MONKEYS, AND THE SAVAGES CALLED OREILLONS

Candide and his valet had got beyond the barrier, before it was known in the camp that the German Jesuit was dead. The wary Cacambo had taken care to fill his wallet with bread, chocolate, bacon, fruit, and a few bottles of wine. With their Andalusian horses they penetrated into an unknown country, where they perceived no beaten track. At length they came to a beautiful meadow intersected with purling rills. Here our two adventurers fed their horses. Cacambo proposed to his master to take some food, and he set him an example.

"How can you ask me to eat ham," said Candide, "after killing the Baron's son, and being doomed never more to see the beautiful Cunegonde? What will it avail me to spin out my wretched days and drag them far from her in remorse and despair? And what will the *Journal of Trevoux* say?"

While he was thus lamenting his fate, he went on eating. The sun went down. The two wanderers heard some little cries which seemed to be uttered by women. They did not know whether they were cries of pain or joy; but they started up precipitately with that inquietude and alarm which every little thing inspires in an unknown country. The noise was made by two naked girls, who tripped along the mead, while two monkeys were pursuing them and biting their buttocks. Candide was moved with pity; he had learned to fire a gun in the Bulgarian service, and he was so clever at it, that he could hit a filbert in a hedge without touching a leaf of the tree. He took up his double-barrelled Spanish fusil, let it off, and killed the two monkeys.

"God be praised! My dear Cacambo, I have rescued those two poor creatures from a most perilous situation. If I have committed a sin in killing an Inquisitor and a Jesuit, I have made ample amends by saving the lives of these girls. Perhaps they are young ladies of family; and this adventure may procure us great advantages in this country."

He was continuing, but stopped short when he saw the two girls tenderly embracing the monkeys, bathing their bodies in tears, and rending the air with the most dismal lamentations.

"Little did I expect to see such good-nature," said he at length to Cacambo; who made answer:

"Master, you have done a fine thing now; you have slain the sweethearts of those two young ladies."

"The sweethearts! Is it possible? You are jesting, Cacambo, I can never believe it!"

"Dear master," replied Cacambo; "you are surprised at everything. Why should you think it so strange that in some countries there are monkeys which insinuate themselves into the good graces of the ladies; they are a fourth part human, as I am a fourth part Spaniard."

"Alas!" replied Candide, "I remember to have heard Master Pangloss say, that formerly such accidents used to happen; that these mixtures were productive of Centaurs, Fauns, and Satyrs; and that many of the ancients had seen such monsters, but I looked upon the whole as fabulous."

"You ought now to be convinced," said Cacambo, "that it is the truth, and you see what use is made of those creatures, by persons that have not had a proper education; all I fear is that those ladies will play us some ugly trick."

These sound reflections induced Candide to leave the meadow and to plunge into a wood. He supped there with Cacambo; and after cursing the Portuguese inquisitor, the Governor of Buenos Ayres, and the Baron, they fell asleep on moss. On awaking they felt that they could not move; for during the night the Oreillons, who inhabited that country, and to whom the ladies had denounced them, had bound them with cords made of the bark of trees. They were encompassed by fifty naked Oreillons, armed with bows and arrows, with clubs and flint hatchets. Some were making a large cauldron boil, others were preparing spits, and all cried:

"A Jesuit! a Jesuit! we shall be revenged, we shall have excellent cheer, let us eat the Jesuit, let us eat him up!"

"I told you, my dear master," cried Cacambo sadly, "that those two girls would play us some ugly trick."

Candide seeing the cauldron and the spits, cried:

"We are certainly going to be either roasted or boiled. Ah! what would Master Pangloss say, were he to see how pure nature is formed? Everything is right, may be, but I declare it is very hard to have lost Miss Cunegonde and to be put upon a spit by Oreillons."

Cacambo never lost his head.

"Do not despair," said he to the disconsolate Candide, "I understand a little of the jargon of these people, I will speak to them."

"Be sure," said Candide, "to represent to them how frightfully inhuman it is to cook men, and how very un-Christian."

"Gentlemen," said Cacambo, "you reckon you are to-day going to feast upon a Jesuit. It is all very well, nothing is more unjust than thus to treat your enemies. Indeed, the law of nature teaches us to kill our neighbour, and such is the practice all over the world. If we do not accustom ourselves to eating them, it is because we have better fare. But you have not the same resources as we; certainly it is much better to devour your enemies than to resign to the crows and rooks the fruits of your victory. But, gentlemen, surely you would not choose to eat your friends. You believe that you are going to spit a Jesuit, and he is your defender. It is the enemy of your enemies that you are going to roast. As for myself, I was born in your country; this gentleman is my master, and, far from being a Jesuit, he has just killed one, whose spoils he wears; and thence comes your mistake. To convince you of the truth of what I say, take his habit and carry it to the first barrier of the Jesuit kingdom, and inform yourselves whether my master did not kill a Jesuit officer. It will not take you long, and you can always eat us if you find that I have lied to you. But I have told you the truth. You are too well acquainted with the principles of public law, humanity, and justice not to pardon us."

The Oreillons found this speech very reasonable. They deputed two of their principal people with all expedition to inquire into the truth of the matter; these executed their commission like men of sense, and soon returned with good news. The Oreillons untied their prisoners, showed them all sorts of civilities, offered them girls, gave them refreshment, and reconducted them to the confines of their territories, proclaiming with great joy:

"He is no Jesuit! He is no Jesuit!"

Candide could not help being surprised at the cause of his deliverance.

"What people!" said he; "what men! what manners! If I had not been so lucky as to run Miss Cunegonde's brother through the body, I should have been devoured without redemption. But, after all, pure nature is good, since these people, instead of feasting upon my flesh, have shown me a thousand civilities, when then I was not a Jesuit."

17

ARRIVAL OF CANDIDE AND HIS VALET AT EL DORADO, AND WHAT THEY SAW THERE

"You see," said Cacambo to Candide, as soon as they had reached the frontiers of the Oreillons, "that this hemisphere is not better than the others, take my word for it; let us go back to Europe by the shortest way."

"How go back?" said Candide, "and where shall we go? to my own country? The Bulgarians and the Abares are slaying all; to Portugal? there I shall be burnt; and if we abide here we are every moment in danger of being spitted. But how can I resolve to quit a part of the world where my dear Cunegonde resides?"

"Let us turn towards Cayenne," said Cacambo, "there we shall find Frenchmen, who wander all over the world; they may assist us; God will perhaps have pity on us."

It was not easy to get to Cayenne; they knew vaguely in which direction to go, but rivers, precipices, robbers, savages, obstructed them all the way. Their horses died of fatigue. Their provisions were consumed; they fed a whole month upon wild fruits, and found themselves at last near a little river bordered with cocoa trees, which sustained their lives and their hopes.

Cacambo, who was as good a counsellor as the old woman, said to Candide:

"We are able to hold out no longer; we have walked enough. I see an empty canoe near the river-side; let us fill it with cocoanuts, throw ourselves into it, and go with the current; a river always leads to some inhabited spot. If we do not find pleasant things we shall at least find new things."

"With all my heart," said Candide, "let us recommend ourselves to Providence."

They rowed a few leagues, between banks, in some places flowery, in others barren; in some parts smooth, in others rugged.

The stream ever widened, and at length lost itself under an arch of frightful rocks which reached to the sky. The two travellers had the courage to commit themselves to the current. The river, suddenly contracting at this place, whirled them along with a dreadful noise and rapidity. At the end of four-and-twenty hours they saw daylight again, but their canoe was dashed to pieces against the rocks. For a league they had to creep from rock to rock, until at length they discovered an extensive plain, bounded by inaccessible mountains. The country was cultivated as much for pleasure as for necessity. On all sides the useful was also the beautiful. The roads were covered, or rather adorned, with carriages of a glittering form and substance, in which were men and women of surprising beauty, drawn by large red sheep which surpassed in fleetness the finest coursers of Andalusia, Tetuan, and Mequinez.

"Here, however, is a country," said Candide, "which is better than Westphalia."

He stepped out with Cacambo towards the first village which he saw. Some children dressed in tattered brocades played at quoits on the outskirts. Our travellers from the other world amused themselves by looking on. The quoits were large round pieces, yellow, red, and green, which cast a singular lustre! The travellers picked a few of them off the ground; this was of gold, that of emeralds, the other of rubies—the least of them would have been the greatest ornament on the Mogul's throne.

"Without doubt," said Cacambo, "these children must be the king's sons that are playing at quoits!"

The village schoolmaster appeared at this moment and called them to school.

"There," said Candide, "is the preceptor of the royal family."

The little truants immediately quitted their game, leaving the quoits on the ground with all their other playthings. Candide gathered them up, ran to the master, and presented them to him in a most humble manner, giving him to understand by signs that their royal highnesses had forgotten their gold and jewels. The schoolmaster, smiling, flung them upon the ground; then, looking at Candide with a good deal of surprise, went about his business.

The travellers, however, took care to gather up the gold, the rubies, and the emeralds.

"Where are we?" cried Candide. "The king's children in this country must be well brought up, since they are taught to despise gold and precious stones."

Cacambo was as much surprised as Candide. At length they drew near the first house in the village. It was built like an European palace. A crowd of people pressed about the door, and there were still more in the house. They heard most agreeable music, and were aware of a delicious odour of cooking. Cacambo went up to the door and heard they were talking Peruvian; it was his mother tongue, for it is well known that Cacambo was born in Tucuman, in a village where no other language was spoken.

"I will be your interpreter here," said he to Candide; "let us go in, it is a public-house."

Immediately two waiters and two girls, dressed in cloth of gold, and their hair tied up with ribbons, invited them to sit down to table with the landlord. They served four dishes of soup, each garnished with two young parrots; a boiled condor which weighed two hundred pounds; two roasted monkeys, of excellent flavour; three hundred humming-birds in one dish, and six hundred fly-birds in another; exquisite ragouts; delicious pastries; the whole served up in dishes of a kind of rock-crystal. The waiters and girls poured out several liqueurs drawn from the sugar-cane.

Most of the company were chapmen and waggoners, all extremely polite; they asked Cacambo a few questions with the greatest circumspection, and answered his in the most obliging manner.

As soon as dinner was over, Cacambo believed as well as Candide that they might well pay their reckoning by laying down two of those large gold pieces which they had picked up. The landlord and landlady shouted with laughter and held their sides. When the fit was over:

"Gentlemen," said the landlord, "it is plain you are strangers, and such guests we are not accustomed to see; pardon us therefore for laughing when you offered us the pebbles from our highroads in payment of your reckoning. You doubtless have not the money of the country; but it is not necessary to have any money at all to dine in this house. All hostelries established for the convenience of commerce are paid by the government. You have fared but very indifferently because this is a poor village; but everywhere else, you will be received as you deserve."

Cacambo explained this whole discourse with great astonishment to Candide, who was as greatly astonished to hear it.

"What sort of a country then is this," said they to one another; "a country unknown to all the rest of the world, and where nature is of a kind so different from ours? It is probably the country where all is well; for there absolutely must be one such place. And, whatever Master Pangloss might say, I often found that things went very ill in Westphalia."

18

WHAT THEY SAW IN THE COUNTRY OF EL DORADO

Cacambo expressed his curiosity to the landlord, who made answer:

"I am very ignorant, but not the worse on that account. However, we have in this neighbourhood an old man retired from Court who is the most learned and most communicative person in the kingdom."

At once he took Cacambo to the old man. Candide acted now only a second character, and accompanied his valet. They entered a very plain house, for the door was only of silver, and the ceilings were only of gold, but wrought in so elegant a taste as to vie with the richest. The antechamber, indeed, was only encrusted with rubies and emeralds, but the order in which everything was arranged made amends for this great simplicity.

The old man received the strangers on his sofa, which was stuffed with humming-birds' feathers, and ordered his servants to present them with liqueurs in diamond goblets; after which he satisfied their curiosity in the following terms:

"I am now one hundred and seventy-two years old, and I learnt of my late father, Master of the Horse to the King, the amazing revolutions of Peru, of which he had been an eyewitness. The kingdom we now inhabit is the ancient country of the Incas, who quitted it very imprudently to conquer another part of the world, and were at length destroyed by the Spaniards.

"More wise by far were the princes of their family, who remained in their native country; and they ordained, with the consent of the whole nation, that none of the inhabitants should ever be permitted to quit this little kingdom; and this has preserved our innocence and happiness. The Spaniards have had a confused notion of this country, and have called it *El Dorado*; and an Englishman, whose name was Sir Walter Raleigh, came very near it about a hundred years ago; but being surrounded by inaccessible rocks and precipices, we have hitherto been sheltered from the rapaciousness of European nations, who have an inconceivable passion for the pebbles and dirt of our land, for the sake of which they would murder us to the last man."

The conversation was long: it turned chiefly on their form of government, their manners, their women, their public entertainments, and the arts. At length Candide, having always had a taste for metaphysics, made Cacambo ask whether there was any religion in that country.

The old man reddened a little.

"How then," said he, "can you doubt it? Do you take us for ungrateful wretches?"

Cacambo humbly asked, "What was the religion in El Dorado?"

The old man reddened again.

"Can there be two religions?" said he. "We have, I believe, the religion of all the world: we worship God night and morning."

"Do you worship but one God?" said Cacambo, who still acted as interpreter in representing Candide's doubts.

"Surely," said the old man, "there are not two, nor three, nor four. I must confess the people from your side of the world ask very extraordinary questions."

Candide was not yet tired of interrogating the good old man; he wanted to know in what manner they prayed to God in El Dorado.

"We do not pray to Him," said the worthy sage; "we have nothing to ask of Him; He has given us all we need, and we return Him thanks without ceasing."

Candide having a curiosity to see the priests asked where they were. The good old man smiled.

"My friend," said he, "we are all priests. The King and all the heads of families sing solemn canticles of thanksgiving every morning, accompanied by five or six thousand musicians."

"What! have you no monks who teach, who dispute, who govern, who cabal, and who burn people that are not of their opinion?"

"We must be mad, indeed, if that were the case," said the old man; "here we are all of one opinion, and we know not what you mean by monks."

During this whole discourse Candide was in raptures, and he said to himself:

"This is vastly different from Westphalia and the Baron's castle. Had our friend Pangloss seen El Dorado he would no longer have said that the castle of Thunder-ten-Tronckh was the finest upon earth. It is evident that one must travel."

After this long conversation the old man ordered a coach and six sheep to be got ready, and twelve of his domestics to conduct the travellers to Court.

"Excuse me," said he, "if my age deprives me of the honour of accompanying you. The King will receive you in a manner that cannot displease you; and no doubt you will make an allowance for the customs of the country, if some things should not be to your liking."

Candide and Cacambo got into the coach, the six sheep flew,

and in less than four hours they reached the King's palace situated at the extremity of the capital. The portal was two hundred and twenty feet high, and one hundred wide; but words are wanting to express the materials of which it was built. It is plain such materials must have prodigious superiority over those pebbles and sand which we call gold and precious stones.

Twenty beautiful damsels of the King's guard received Candide and Cacambo as they alighted from the coach, conducted them to the bath, and dressed them in robes woven of the down of humming-birds; after which the great crown officers, of both sexes, led them to the King's apartment, between two files of musicians, a thousand on each side. When they drew near to the audience chamber Cacambo asked one of the great officers in what way he should pay his obeisance to his Majesty; whether they should throw themselves upon their knees or on their stomachs; whether they should put their hands upon their heads or behind their backs; whether they should lick the dust off the floor; in a word, what was the ceremony?

"The custom," said the great officer, "is to embrace the King, and to kiss him on each cheek."

Candide and Cacambo threw themselves round his Majesty's neck. He received them with all the goodness imaginable, and politely invited them to supper.

While waiting they were shown the city, and saw the public edifices raised as high as the clouds, the market places ornamented with a thousand columns, the fountains of spring water, those of rose water, those of liqueurs drawn from sugar-cane, incessantly flowing into the great squares, which were paved with a kind of precious stone, which gave off a delicious fragrancy like that of cloves and cinnamon. Candide asked to see the court of justice, the parliament. They told him they had none, and that they were strangers to lawsuits. He asked if they had any prisons, and they answered no. But what surprised him most and gave him the greatest pleasure was the palace of sciences, where he saw a gallery two thousand feet long, and filled with instruments employed in mathematics and physics.

After rambling about the city the whole afternoon, and seeing but a thousandth part of it, they were reconducted to the royal palace, where Candide sat down to table with his Majesty, his valet Cacambo, and several ladies. Never was there a better entertainment, and never was more wit shown at a table than that which fell from his Majesty. Cacambo explained the King's *bon-mots* to Candide, and notwithstanding they were translated they still appeared to be *bon-mots*. Of all the things that surprised Candide this was not the least.

They spent a month in this hospitable place. Candide frequently said to Cacambo:

"I own, my friend, once more that the castle where I was born is nothing in comparison with this; but, after all, Miss Cunegonde is not here, and you have, without doubt, some mistress in Europe. If we abide here we shall only be upon a footing with the rest, whereas, if we return to our old world, only with twelve sheep laden with the pebbles of El Dorado, we shall be richer than all the kings in Europe. We shall have no more Inquisitors to fear, and we may easily recover Miss Cunegonde."

This speech was agreeable to Cacambo; mankind are so fond of roving, of making a figure in their own country, and of boasting of what they have seen in their travels, that the two happy ones resolved to be no longer so, but to ask his Majesty's leave to quit the country.

"You are foolish," said the King. "I am sensible that my kingdom is but a small place, but when a person is comfortably settled in any part he should abide there. I have not the right to detain strangers. It is a tyranny which neither our manners nor our laws permit. All men are free. Go when you wish, but the going will be very difficult. It is impossible to ascend that rapid river on which you came as by a miracle, and which runs under vaulted rocks. The mountains which surround my kingdom are ten thousand feet high, and as steep as walls; they are each over ten leagues in breadth, and there is no other way to descend them than by precipices. However, since you absolutely wish to depart, I shall give orders to my engineers to construct a machine that will convey you very safely. When we have conducted you over the mountains no one can accompany you further, for my subjects have made a vow never to quit the kingdom, and they are too wise to break it. Ask me besides anything that you please."

"We desire nothing of your Majesty," says Candide, "but a few sheep laden with provisions, pebbles, and the earth of this country."

The King laughed.

"I cannot conceive," said he, "what pleasure you Europeans find in our yellow clay, but take as much as you like, and great good may it do you."

At once he gave directions that his engineers should construct a machine to hoist up these two extraordinary men out of the kingdom. Three thousand good mathematicians went to work; it was ready in fifteen days, and did not cost more than twenty million sterling in the specie of that country. They placed Candide and Cacambo on the machine. There were two great red sheep saddled and bridled to ride upon as soon as they were beyond the mountains, twenty pack-sheep laden with provisions, thirty with presents of the curiosities of the country, and fifty with gold, diamonds, and precious stones. The King embraced the two wanderers very tenderly.

Their departure, with the ingenious manner in which they and their sheep were hoisted over the mountains, was a splendid spectacle. The mathematicians took their leave after conveying them to a place of safety, and Candide had no other desire, no other aim, than to present his sheep to Miss Cunegonde.

"Now," said he, "we are able to pay the Governor of Buenos Ayres if Miss Cunegonde can be ransomed. Let us journey towards Cayenne. Let us embark, and we will afterwards see what kingdom we shall be able to purchase."

19

WHAT HAPPENED TO THEM AT SURINAM AND HOW CANDIDE GOT ACQUAINTED WITH MARTIN

Our travellers spent the first day very agreeably. They were delighted with possessing more treasure than all Asia, Europe, and Africa could scrape together. Candide, in his raptures, cut Cunegonde's name on the trees. The second day two of their sheep plunged into a morass, where they and their burdens were lost; two more died of fatigue a few days after; seven or eight perished with hunger in a desert; and others subsequently fell down precipices. At length, after travelling a hundred days, only two sheep remained. Said Candide to Cacambo:

"My friend, you see how perishable are the riches of this world; there is nothing solid but virtue, and the happiness of seeing Cunegonde once more."

"I grant all you say," said Cacambo, "but we have still two sheep remaining, with more treasure than the King of Spain will ever have; and I see a town which I take to be Surinam, belonging to the Dutch. We are at the end of all our troubles, and at the beginning of happiness."

As they drew near the town, they saw a negro stretched upon the ground, with only one moiety of his clothes, that is, of his blue linen drawers; the poor man had lost his left leg and his right hand.

"Good God!" said Candide in Dutch, "what art thou doing there, friend, in that shocking condition?"

"I am waiting for my master, Mynheer Vanderdendur, the famous merchant," answered the negro.

"Was it Mynheer Vanderdendur," said Candide, "that treated thee thus?"

"Yes, sir," said the negro, "it is the custom. They give us a pair of linen drawers for our whole garment twice a year. When we work at the sugar-canes, and the mill snatches hold of a finger, they cut off the hand; and when we attempt to run away, they cut off the leg; both cases have happened to me. This is the price at which you eat sugar in Europe. Yet when my mother sold me for ten patagons on the coast of Guinea, she said to me: 'My dear child, bless our fetiches, adore them for ever; they will make thee live happily; thou hast the honour of being the slave of our lords, the whites, which is making the fortune of thy father and mother.' Alas! I know not whether I have made their fortunes; this I know, that they have not made mine. Dogs, monkeys, and parrots are a thousand times less wretched than I. The Dutch fetiches, who have converted me, declare every Sunday that we are all of us children of Adam—blacks as well as whites. I am not a genealogist, but if these preachers tell truth, we are all second cousins. Now, you must agree, that it is impossible to treat one's relations in a more barbarous manner."

"Oh, Pangloss!" cried Candide, "thou hadst not guessed at this abomination; it is the end. I must at last renounce thy optimism."

"What is this optimism?" said Cacambo.

"Alas!" said Candide, "it is the madness of maintaining that everything is right when it is wrong."

Looking at the negro, he shed tears, and weeping, he entered Surinam.

The first thing they inquired after was whether there was a vessel in the harbour which could be sent to Buenos Ayres. The person to whom they applied was a Spanish sea-captain, who offered to agree with them upon reasonable terms. He appointed to meet them at a public-house, whither Candide and the faithful Cacambo went with their two sheep, and awaited his coming.

Candide, who had his heart upon his lips, told the Spaniard all his adventures, and avowed that he intended to elope with Miss Cunegonde.

"Then I will take good care not to carry you to Buenos Ayres," said the seaman. "I should be hanged, and so would you. The fair Cunegonde is my lord's favourite mistress."

This was a thunderclap for Candide: he wept for a long while. At last he drew Cacambo aside.

"Here, my dear friend," said he to him, "this thou must do. We have, each of us in his pocket, five or six millions in diamonds; you are more clever than I; you must go and bring Miss Cunegonde from Buenos Ayres. If the Governor makes any difficulty, give him a million; if he will not relinquish her, give him two; as you have not killed an Inquisitor, they will have no suspicion of you; I'll get another ship, and go and wait for you at Venice; that's a free country, where there is no danger either from Bulgarians, Abares, Jews, or Inquisitors."

Cacambo applauded this wise resolution. He despaired at parting from so good a master, who had become his intimate friend; but the pleasure of serving him prevailed over the pain of leaving him. They embraced with tears; Candide charged him not to forget the good old woman. Cacambo set out that very same day. This Cacambo was a very honest fellow.

Candide stayed some time longer in Surinam, waiting for another captain to carry him and the two remaining sheep to Italy. After he had hired domestics, and purchased everything necessary for a long voyage, Mynheer Vanderdendur, captain of a large vessel, came and offered his services.

"How much will you charge," said he to this man, "to carry me straight to Venice—me, my servants, my baggage, and these two sheep?"

The skipper asked ten thousand piastres. Candide did not hesitate.

"Oh! oh!" said the prudent Vanderdendur to himself, "this stranger gives ten thousand piastres unhesitatingly! He must be very rich."

Returning a little while after, he let him know that upon second consideration, he could not undertake the voyage for less than twenty thousand piastres.

"Well, you shall have them," said Candide.

"Ay!" said the skipper to himself, "this man agrees to pay twenty thousand piastres with as much ease as ten."

He went back to him again, and declared that he could not carry him to Venice for less than thirty thousand piastres.

"Then you shall have thirty thousand," replied Candide.

"Oh! oh!" said the Dutch skipper once more to himself, "thirty thousand piastres are a trifle to this man; surely these sheep must be laden with an immense treasure; let us say no more about it. First of all, let him pay down the thirty thousand piastres; then we shall see."

Candide sold two small diamonds, the least of which was worth more than what the skipper asked for his freight. He paid him in advance. The two sheep were put on board. Candide followed in a little boat to join the vessel in the roads. The skipper seized his opportunity, set sail, and put out to sea, the wind favouring him. Candide, dismayed and stupefied, soon lost sight of the vessel.

"Alas!" said he, "this is a trick worthy of the old world!"

He put back, overwhelmed with sorrow, for indeed he had lost sufficient to make the fortune of twenty monarchs. He waited upon the Dutch magistrate, and in his distress he knocked over loudly at the door. He entered and told his adventure, raising his voice with unnecessary vehemence. The magistrate began by fining him ten thousand piastres for making a noise; then he listened patiently, promised to examine into his affair at the skipper's return, and ordered him to pay ten thousand piastres for the expense of the hearing.

This drove Candide to despair; he had, indeed, endured misfortunes a thousand times worse; the coolness of the magistrate and of the skipper who had robbed him, roused his choler and flung him into a deep melancholy. The villainy of mankind presented itself before his imagination in all its deformity, and his mind was filled with gloomy ideas. At length hearing that a French vessel was ready to set sail for Bordeaux, as he had no sheep laden with diamonds to take along with him he hired a cabin at the usual price. He made it known in the town that he would pay the passage and board and give two thousand piastres to any honest man who would make the voyage with him, upon condition that this man was the most dissatisfied with his state, and the most unfortunate in the whole province.

Such a crowd of candidates presented themselves that a fleet of ships could hardly have held them. Candide being desirous of selecting from among the best, marked out about one-twentieth of them who seemed to be sociable men, and who all pretended to merit his preference. He assembled them at his inn, and gave them a supper on condition that each took an oath to relate his history faithfully, promising to choose him who appeared to be most justly discontented with his state, and to bestow some presents upon the rest.

They sat until four o'clock in the morning. Candide, in listening to all their adventures, was reminded of what the old woman had said to him in their voyage to Buenos Ayres, and of her wager that there was not a person on board the ship but had met with very great misfortunes. He dreamed of Pangloss at every adventure told to him.

"This Pangloss," said he, "would be puzzled to demonstrate his system. I wish that he were here. Certainly, if all things are good, it is in El Dorado and not in the rest of the world."

At length he made choice of a poor man of letters, who had worked ten years for the booksellers of Amsterdam. He judged that there was not in the whole world a trade which could disgust one more.

This philosopher was an honest man; but he had been robbed by his wife, beaten by his son, and abandoned by his daughter who got a Portuguese to run away with her. He had just been deprived of a small employment, on which he subsisted; and he was persecuted by the preachers of Surinam, who took him for a Socinian. We must allow that the others were at least as wretched as he; but Candide hoped that the philosopher would entertain him during the voyage. All the other candidates complained that Candide had done them great injustice; but he appeased them by giving one hundred piastres to each.

20

WHAT HAPPENED AT SEA TO CANDIDE AND MARTIN

The old philosopher, whose name was Martin, embarked then with Candide for Bordeaux. They had both seen and suffered a great deal; and if the vessel had sailed from Surinam to Japan, by the Cape of Good Hope, the subject of moral and natural evil would have enabled them to entertain one another during the whole voyage.

Candide, however, had one great advantage over Martin, in that he always hoped to see Miss Cunegonde; whereas Martin had nothing at all to hope. Besides, Candide was possessed of money and jewels, and though he had lost one hundred large red sheep, laden with the greatest treasure upon earth; though the knavery of the Dutch skipper still sat heavy upon his mind; yet when he reflected upon what he had still left, and when he mentioned the name of Cunegonde, especially towards the latter end of a repast, he inclined to Pangloss's doctrine.

"But you, Mr. Martin," said he to the philosopher, "what do you think of all this? what are your ideas on moral and natural evil?"

"Sir," answered Martin, "our priests accused me of being a Socinian, but the real fact is I am a Manichean."

"You jest," said Candide; "there are no longer Manicheans in the world."

"I am one," said Martin. "I cannot help it; I know not how to think otherwise."

"Surely you must be possessed by the devil," said Candide.

"He is so deeply concerned in the affairs of this world," answered Martin, "that he may very well be in me, as well as in everybody else; but I own to you that when I cast an eye on this globe, or rather on this little ball, I cannot help thinking that God has abandoned it to some malignant being. I except, always, El Dorado. I scarcely ever knew a city that did not desire the destruction of a neighbouring city, nor a family that did not wish to exterminate some other family. Everywhere the weak execrate the powerful, before whom they cringe; and the powerful beat them like sheep whose wool and flesh they sell. A million regimented assassins, from one extremity of Europe to the other, get their bread by disciplined depredation and murder, for want of more honest employment. Even in those cities which seem to enjoy peace, and where the arts flourish, the inhabitants are devoured by more envy, care, and uneasiness than are experienced by a besieged town. Secret griefs are more cruel than public calamities. In a word I have seen so much, and experienced so much that I am a Manichean."

"There are, however, some things good," said Candide.

"That may be," said Martin; "but I know them not."

In the middle of this dispute they heard the report of cannon; it redoubled every instant. Each took out his glass. They saw two ships in close fight about three miles off. The wind brought both so near to the French vessel that our travellers had the pleasure of seeing the fight at their ease. At length one let off a broadside, so low and so truly aimed, that the other sank to the bottom. Candide and Martin could plainly perceive a hundred men on the deck of the sinking vessel; they raised their hands to heaven and uttered terrible outcries, and the next moment were swallowed up by the sea.

"Well," said Martin, "this is how men treat one another."

"It is true," said Candide; "there is something diabolical in this affair."

While speaking, he saw he knew not what, of a shining red, swimming close to the vessel. They put out the long-boat to see what it could be: it was one of his sheep! Candide was more rejoiced at the recovery of this one sheep than he had been grieved at the loss of the hundred laden with the large diamonds of El Dorado.

The French captain soon saw that the captain of the victorious vessel was a Spaniard, and that the other was a Dutch pirate, and the very same one who had robbed Candide. The immense plunder which this villain had amassed, was buried with him in the sea, and out of the whole only one sheep was saved.

"You see," said Candide to Martin, "that crime is sometimes punished. This rogue of a Dutch skipper has met with the fate he deserved."

"Yes," said Martin; "but why should the passengers be doomed also to destruction? God has punished the knave, and the devil has drowned the rest."

The French and Spanish ships continued their course, and Candide continued his conversation with Martin. They disputed fifteen successive days, and on the last of those fifteen days, they were as far advanced as on the first. But, however, they chatted, they communicated ideas, they consoled each other. Candide caressed his sheep.

"Since I have found thee again," said he, "I may likewise chance to find my Cunegonde."

21

CANDIDE AND MARTIN, REASONING, DRAW NEAR THE COAST OF FRANCE

At length they descried the coast of France.

"Were you ever in France, Mr. Martin?" said Candide.

"Yes," said Martin, "I have been in several provinces. In some one-half of the people are fools, in others they are too cunning; in some they are weak and simple, in others they affect to be witty; in all, the principal occupation is love, the next is slander, and the third is talking nonsense."

"But, Mr. Martin, have you seen Paris?"

"Yes, I have. All these kinds are found there. It is a chaos—a confused multitude, where everybody seeks pleasure and scarcely any one finds it, at least as it appeared to me. I made a short stay there. On my arrival I was robbed of all I had by pickpockets at the fair of St. Germain. I myself was taken for a robber and was imprisoned for eight days, after which I served as corrector of the press to gain the money necessary for my return to Holland on foot. I knew the whole scribbling rabble, the party rabble, the fanatic rabble. It is said that there are very polite people in that city, and I wish to believe it."

"For my part, I have no curiosity to see France," said Candide. "You may easily imagine that after spending a month at El Dorado I can desire to behold nothing upon earth but Miss Cunegonde. I go to await her at Venice. We shall pass through France on our way to Italy. Will you bear me company?"

"With all my heart," said Martin. "It is said that Venice is fit only for its own nobility, but that strangers meet with a very good reception if they have a good deal of money. I have none of it; you have, therefore I will follow you all over the world."

"But do you believe," said Candide, "that the earth was originally a sea, as we find it asserted in that large book belonging to the captain?"

"I do not believe a word of it," said Martin, "any more than I do of the many ravings which have been published lately."

"But for what end, then, has this world been formed?" said Candide.

"To plague us to death," answered Martin.

"Are you not greatly surprised," continued Candide, "at the love which these two girls of the Oreillons had for those monkeys, of which I have already told you?"

"Not at all," said Martin. "I do not see that that passion was strange. I have seen so many extraordinary things that I have ceased to be surprised."

"Do you believe," said Candide, "that men have always massacred each other as they do to-day, that they have always been liars, cheats, traitors, ingrates, brigands, idiots, thieves, scoundrels, gluttons, drunkards, misers, envious, ambitious, bloody-minded, calumniators, debauchees, fanatics, hypocrites, and fools?"

"Do you believe," said Martin, "that hawks have always eaten pigeons when they have found them?"

"Yes, without doubt," said Candide.

"Well, then," said Martin, "if hawks have always had the same character why should you imagine that men may have changed theirs?"

"Oh!" said Candide, "there is a vast deal of difference, for free will——"

And reasoning thus they arrived at Bordeaux.

22

WHAT HAPPENED IN FRANCE TO CANDIDE AND MARTIN

Candide stayed in Bordeaux no longer than was necessary for the selling of a few of the pebbles of El Dorado, and for hiring a good chaise to hold two passengers; for he could not travel without his Philosopher Martin. He was only vexed at parting with his sheep, which he left to the Bordeaux Academy of Sciences, who set as a subject for that year's prize, "to find why this sheep's wool was red;" and the prize was awarded to a learned man of the North, who demonstrated by A plus B minus C divided by Z, that the sheep must be red, and die of the rot.

Meanwhile, all the travellers whom Candide met in the inns along his route, said to him, "We go to Paris." This general eagerness at length gave him, too, a desire to see this capital; and it was not so very great a *détour* from the road to Venice.

He entered Paris by the suburb of St. Marceau, and fancied that he was in the dirtiest village of Westphalia.

Scarcely was Candide arrived at his inn, than he found himself attacked by a slight illness, caused by fatigue. As he had a very large diamond on his finger, and the people of the inn had taken notice of a prodigiously heavy box among his baggage, there were two physicians to attend him, though he had never sent for them, and two devotees who warmed his broths.

"I remember," Martin said, "also to have been sick at Paris in my first voyage; I was very poor, thus I had neither friends, devotees, nor doctors, and I recovered."

However, what with physic and bleeding, Candide's illness became serious. A parson of the neighborhood came with great meekness to ask for a bill for the other world payable to the bearer. Candide would do nothing for him; but the devotees assured him it was the new fashion. He answered that he was not a man of fashion. Martin wished to throw the priest out of the window. The priest swore that they would not bury Candide. Martin swore that he would bury the priest if he continued to be troublesome. The quarrel grew heated. Martin took him by the shoulders and roughly turned him out of doors; which occasioned great scandal and a law-suit.

Candide got well again, and during his convalescence he had very good company to sup with him. They played high. Candide wondered why it was that the ace never came to him; but Martin was not at all astonished.

Among those who did him the honours of the town was a little Abbé of Perigord, one of those busybodies who are ever alert, officious, forward, fawning, and complaisant; who watch for strangers in their passage through the capital, tell them the scandalous history of the town, and offer them pleasure at all prices. He first took Candide and Martin to La Comédie, where they played a new tragedy. Candide happened to be seated near some of the fashionable wits. This did not prevent his shedding tears at the well-acted scenes. One of these critics at his side said to him between the acts:

"Your tears are misplaced; that is a shocking actress; the actor who plays with her is yet worse; and the play is still worse than the actors. The author does not know a word of Arabic, yet the scene is in Arabia; moreover he is a man that does not believe in innate ideas; and I will bring you, to-morrow, twenty pamphlets written against him."

"How many dramas have you in France, sir?" said Candide to the Abbé.

"Five or six thousand."

"What a number!" said Candide. "How many good?"

"Fifteen or sixteen," replied the other.

"What a number!" said Martin.

Candide was very pleased with an actress who played Queen Elizabeth in a somewhat insipid tragedy sometimes acted.

"That actress," said he to Martin, "pleases me much; she has a likeness to Miss Cunegonde; I should be very glad to wait upon her."

The Perigordian Abbé offered to introduce him. Candide, brought up in Germany, asked what was the etiquette, and how they treated queens of England in France.

"It is necessary to make distinctions," said the Abbé. "In the provinces one takes them to the inn; in Paris, one respects them when they are beautiful, and throws them on the highway when they are dead."

"Queens on the highway!" said Candide.

"Yes, truly," said Martin, "the Abbé is right. I was in Paris when Miss Monime passed, as the saying is, from this life to the other. She was refused what people call the *honours of sepulture*—that is to say, of rotting with all the beggars of the neighbourhood in an ugly cemetery; she was interred all alone by her company at the corner of the Rue de Bourgogne, which ought to trouble her much, for she thought nobly."

"That was very uncivil," said Candide.

"What would you have?" said Martin; "these people are made thus. Imagine all contradictions, all possible incompatibilities—you will find them in the government, in the law-courts, in the churches, in the public shows of this droll nation."

"Is it true that they always laugh in Paris?" said Candide.

"Yes," said the Abbé, "but it means nothing, for they complain of everything with great fits of laughter; they even do the most detestable things while laughing."

"Who," said Candide, "is that great pig who spoke so ill of the piece at which I wept, and of the actors who gave me so much pleasure?"

"He is a bad character," answered the Abbé, "who gains his livelihood by saying evil of all plays and of all books. He hates whatever succeeds, as the eunuchs hate those who enjoy; he is one of the serpents of literature who nourish themselves on dirt and spite; he is a *folliculaire*."

"What is a *folliculaire*?" said Candide.

"It is," said the Abbé, "a pamphleteer—a Fréron."

Thus Candide, Martin, and the Perigordian conversed on the staircase, while watching every one go out after the performance.

"Although I am eager to see Cunegonde again," said Candide, "I should like to sup with Miss Clairon, for she appears to me admirable."

The Abbé was not the man to approach Miss Clairon, who saw only good company.

"She is engaged for this evening," he said, "but I shall have the honour to take you to the house of a lady of quality, and there you will know Paris as if you had lived in it for years."

Candide, who was naturally curious, let himself be taken to this lady's house, at the end of the Faubourg St. Honoré. The company was occupied in playing faro; a dozen melancholy punters held each in his hand a little pack of cards; a bad record of his misfortunes. Profound silence reigned; pallor was on the faces of the punters, anxiety on that of the banker, and the hostess, sitting near the unpitying banker, noticed with lynx-eyes all the doubled and other increased stakes, as each player dog's-eared his cards; she made them turn down the edges again with severe, but polite attention; she showed no vexation for fear of losing her customers. The lady insisted upon being called the Marchioness of Parolignac. Her daughter, aged fifteen, was among the punters, and notified with a covert glance the cheatings of the poor people who tried to repair the cruelties of fate. The Perigordian Abbé, Candide and Martin entered; no one rose, no one saluted them, no one looked at them; all were profoundly occupied with their cards.

"The Baroness of Thunder-ten-Tronckh was more polite," said Candide.

However, the Abbé whispered to the Marchioness, who half rose, honoured Candide with a gracious smile, and Martin with a condescending nod; she gave a seat and a pack of cards to Candide, who lost fifty thousand francs in two deals, after which they supped very gaily, and every one was astonished that Candide was not moved by his loss; the servants said among themselves, in the language of servants:—

"Some English lord is here this evening."

The supper passed at first like most Parisian suppers, in silence, followed by a noise of words which could not be distinguished, then with pleasantries of which most were insipid, with false news, with bad reasoning, a little politics, and much evil speaking; they also discussed new books.

"Have you seen," said the Perigordian Abbé, "the romance of Sieur Gauchat, doctor of divinity?"

"Yes," answered one of the guests, "but I have not been able to finish it. We have a crowd of silly writings, but all together do not approach the impertinence of 'Gauchat, Doctor of Divinity.' I am so satiated with the great number of detestable books with which we are inundated that I am reduced to punting at faro."

"And the *Mélanges* of Archdeacon Trublet, what do you say of that?" said the Abbé.

"Ah!" said the Marchioness of Parolignac, "the wearisome mortal! How curiously he repeats to you all that the world knows! How heavily he discusses that which is not worth the trouble of lightly remarking upon! How, without wit, he appropriates the wit of others! How he spoils what he steals! How he disgusts me! But he will disgust me no longer—it is enough to have read a few of the Archdeacon's pages."

There was at table a wise man of taste, who supported the

Marchioness. They spoke afterwards of tragedies; the lady asked why there were tragedies which were sometimes played and which could not be read. The man of taste explained very well how a piece could have some interest, and have almost no merit; he proved in few words that it was not enough to introduce one or two of those situations which one finds in all romances, and which always seduce the spectator, but that it was necessary to be new without being odd, often sublime and always natural, to know the human heart and to make it speak; to be a great poet without allowing any person in the piece to appear to be a poet; to know language perfectly—to speak it with purity, with continuous harmony and without rhythm ever taking anything from sense.

"Whoever," added he, "does not observe all these rules can produce one or two tragedies, applauded at a theatre, but he will never be counted in the ranks of good writers. There are very few good tragedies; some are idylls in dialogue, well written and well rhymed, others political reasonings which lull to sleep, or amplifications which repel; others demoniac dreams in barbarous style, interrupted in sequence, with long apostrophes to the gods, because they do not know how to speak to men, with false maxims, with bombastic commonplaces!"

Candide listened with attention to this discourse, and conceived a great idea of the speaker, and as the Marchioness had taken care to place him beside her, he leaned towards her and took the liberty of asking who was the man who had spoken so well.

"He is a scholar," said the lady, "who does not play, whom the Abbé sometimes brings to supper; he is perfectly at home among tragedies and books, and he has written a tragedy which was hissed, and a book of which nothing has ever been seen outside his bookseller's shop excepting the copy which he dedicated to me."

"The great man!" said Candide. "He is another Pangloss!"

Then, turning towards him, he said:

"Sir, you think doubtless that all is for the best in the moral and physical world, and that nothing could be otherwise than it is?"

"I, sir!" answered the scholar, "I know nothing of all that; I find that all goes awry with me; that no one knows either what is his rank, nor what is his condition, what he does nor what he ought to do; and that except supper, which is always gay, and where there appears to be enough concord, all the rest of the time is passed in impertinent quarrels; Jansenist against Molinist, Parliament against the Church, men of letters against men of letters, courtesans against courtesans, financiers against the people, wives against husbands, relatives against relatives—it is eternal war."

"I have seen the worst," Candide replied. "But a wise man, who since has had the misfortune to be hanged, taught me that all is marvellously well; these are but the shadows on a beautiful picture."

"Your hanged man mocked the world," said Martin. "The shadows are horrible blots."

"They are men who make the blots," said Candide, "and they cannot be dispensed with."

"It is not their fault then," said Martin.

Most of the punters, who understood nothing of this language, drank, and Martin reasoned with the scholar, and Candide related some of his adventures to his hostess.

After supper the Marchioness took Candide into her boudoir, and made him sit upon a sofa.

"Ah, well!" said she to him, "you love desperately Miss Cunegonde of Thunder-ten-Tronckh?"

"Yes, madame," answered Candide.

The Marchioness replied to him with a tender smile:

"You answer me like a young man from Westphalia. A Frenchman would have said, 'It is true that I have loved Miss Cunegonde, but seeing you, madame, I think I no longer love her.'"

"Alas! madame," said Candide, "I will answer you as you wish."

"Your passion for her," said the Marchioness, "commenced by picking up her handkerchief. I wish that you would pick up my garter."

"With all my heart," said Candide. And he picked it up.

"But I wish that you would put it on," said the lady.

And Candide put it on.

"You see," said she, "you are a foreigner. I sometimes make my Parisian lovers languish for fifteen days, but I give myself to you the first night because one must do the honours of one's country to a young man from Westphalia."

The lady having perceived two enormous diamonds upon the hands of the young foreigner praised them with such good faith that from Candide's fingers they passed to her own.

Candide, returning with the Perigordian Abbé, felt some remorse in having been unfaithful to Miss Cunegonde. The Abbé sympathised in his trouble; he had had but a light part of the fifty thousand francs lost at play and of the value of the two brilliants, half given, half extorted. His design was to profit as much as he could by the advantages which the acquaintance of Candide could procure for him. He spoke much of Cunegonde, and Candide told him that he should ask forgiveness of that beautiful one for his infidelity when he should see her in Venice.

The Abbé redoubled his politeness and attentions, and took a tender interest in all that Candide said, in all that he did, in all that he wished to do.

"And so, sir, you have a rendezvous at Venice?"

"Yes, monsieur Abbé," answered Candide. "It is absolutely necessary that I go to meet Miss Cunegonde."

And then the pleasure of talking of that which he loved induced him to relate, according to his custom, part of his adventures with the fair Westphalian.

"I believe," said the Abbé, "that Miss Cunegonde has a great deal of wit, and that she writes charming letters?"

"I have never received any from her," said Candide, "for being expelled from the castle on her account I had not an opportunity for writing to her. Soon after that I heard she was dead; then I found her alive; then I lost her again; and last of all, I sent an express to her two thousand five hundred leagues from here, and I wait for an answer."

The Abbé listened attentively, and seemed to be in a brown study. He soon took his leave of the two foreigners after a most tender embrace. The following day Candide received, on awaking, a letter couched in these terms:

"My very dear love, for eight days I have been ill in this town. I learn that you are here. I would fly to your arms if I could but move. I was informed of your passage at Bordeaux, where I left faithful Cacambo and the old woman, who are to follow me very soon. The Governor of Buenos Ayres has taken all, but there remains to me your heart. Come! your presence will either give me life or kill me with pleasure."

This charming, this unhoped-for letter transported Candide with an inexpressible joy, and the illness of his dear Cunegonde overwhelmed him with grief. Divided between those two passions, he took his gold and his diamonds and hurried away, with Martin, to the hotel where Miss Cunegonde was lodged. He entered her room trembling, his heart palpitating, his voice sobbing; he wished to open the curtains of the bed, and asked for a light.

"Take care what you do," said the servant-maid; "the light hurts her," and immediately she drew the curtain again.

"My dear Cunegonde," said Candide, weeping, "how are you? If you cannot see me, at least speak to me."

"She cannot speak," said the maid.

The lady then put a plump hand out from the bed, and Candide bathed it with his tears and afterwards filled it with diamonds, leaving a bag of gold upon the easy chair.

In the midst of these transports in came an officer, followed by the Abbé and a file of soldiers.

"There," said he, "are the two suspected foreigners," and at the same time he ordered them to be seized and carried to prison.

"Travellers are not treated thus in El Dorado," said Candide.

"I am more a Manichean now than ever," said Martin.

"But pray, sir, where are you going to carry us?" said Candide.

"To a dungeon," answered the officer.

Martin, having recovered himself a little, judged that the lady who acted the part of Cunegonde was a cheat, that the Perigordian Abbé was a knave who had imposed upon the honest simplicity of Candide, and that the officer was another knave whom they might easily silence.

Candide, advised by Martin and impatient to see the real Cunegonde, rather than expose himself before a court of justice, proposed to the officer to give him three small diamonds, each worth about three thousand pistoles.

"Ah, sir," said the man with the ivory baton, "had you committed all the imaginable crimes you would be to me the most honest man in the world. Three diamonds! Each worth three thousand pistoles! Sir, instead of carrying you to jail I would lose my life to serve you. There are orders for arresting all foreigners, but leave it to me. I have a brother at Dieppe in Normandy! I'll conduct you thither, and if you have a diamond to give him he'll take as much care of you as I would."

"And why," said Candide, "should all foreigners be arrested?"

"It is," the Perigordian Abbé then made answer, "because a poor beggar of the country of Atrébatie heard some foolish things said. This induced him to commit a parricide, not such as that of 1610 in the month of May, but such as that of 1594 in the month of December, and such as others which have been committed in other years and other months by other poor devils who had heard nonsense spoken."

The officer then explained what the Abbé meant.

"Ah, the monsters!" cried Candide. "What horrors among a people who dance and sing! Is there no way of getting quickly out of this country where monkeys provoke tigers? I have seen no bears in my country, but *men* I have beheld nowhere except in El Dorado. In the name of God, sir, conduct me to Venice, where I am to await Miss Cunegonde."

"I can conduct you no further than lower Normandy," said the officer.

Immediately he ordered his irons to be struck off, acknowledged himself mistaken, sent away his men, set out with Candide and Martin for Dieppe, and left them in the care of his brother.

There was then a small Dutch ship in the harbour. The Norman, who by the virtue of three more diamonds had become the most subservient of men, put Candide and his attendants on board a vessel that was just ready to set sail for Portsmouth in England.

This was not the way to Venice, but Candide thought he had made his way out of hell, and reckoned that he would soon have an opportunity for resuming his journey.

23

CANDIDE AND MARTIN TOUCHED UPON THE COAST OF ENGLAND, AND WHAT THEY SAW THERE

"Ah, Pangloss! Pangloss! Ah, Martin! Martin! Ah, my dear Cunegonde, what sort of a world is this?" said Candide on board the Dutch ship.

"Something very foolish and abominable," said Martin.

"You know England? Are they as foolish there as in France?"

"It is another kind of folly," said Martin. "You know that these two nations are at war for a few acres of snow in Canada, and that they spend over this beautiful war much more than Canada is worth. To tell you exactly, whether there are more people fit to send to a madhouse in one country than the other, is what my imperfect intelligence will not permit. I only know in general that the people we are going to see are very atrabilious."

Talking thus they arrived at Portsmouth. The coast was lined with crowds of people, whose eyes were fixed on a fine man kneeling, with his eyes bandaged, on board one of the men of war in the harbour. Four soldiers stood opposite to this man; each of them fired three balls at his head, with all the calmness in the world; and the whole assembly went away very well satisfied.

"What is all this?" said Candide; "and what demon is it that exercises his empire in this country?"

He then asked who was that fine man who had been killed with so much ceremony. They answered, he was an Admiral.

"And why kill this Admiral?"

"It is because he did not kill a sufficient number of men himself. He gave battle to a French Admiral; and it has been proved that he was not near enough to him."

"But," replied Candide, "the French Admiral was as far from the English Admiral."

"There is no doubt of it; but in this country it is found good, from time to time, to kill one Admiral to encourage the others."

Candide was so shocked and bewildered by what he saw and heard, that he would not set foot on shore, and he made a bargain with the Dutch skipper (were he even to rob him like the Surinam captain) to conduct him without delay to Venice.

The skipper was ready in two days. They coasted France; they passed in sight of Lisbon, and Candide trembled. They passed through the Straits, and entered the Mediterranean. At last they landed at Venice.

"God be praised!" said Candide, embracing Martin. "It is here that I shall see again my beautiful Cunegonde. I trust Cacambo as myself. All is well, all will be well, all goes as well as possible."

24

OF PAQUETTE AND FRIAR GIROFLÉE

Upon their arrival at Venice, Candide went to search for Cacambo at every inn and coffee-house, and among all the ladies of pleasure, but to no purpose. He sent every day to inquire on all the ships that came in. But there was no news of Cacambo.

"What!" said he to Martin, "I have had time to voyage from Surinam to Bordeaux, to go from Bordeaux to Paris, from Paris to Dieppe, from Dieppe to Portsmouth, to coast along Portugal and Spain, to cross the whole Mediterranean, to spend some months, and yet the beautiful Cunegonde has not arrived! Instead of her I have only met a Parisian wench and a Perigordian Abbé. Cunegonde is dead without doubt, and there is nothing for me but to die. Alas! how much better it would have been for me to have remained in the paradise of El Dorado than to come back to this cursed Europe! You are in the right, my dear Martin: all is misery and illusion."

He fell into a deep melancholy, and neither went to see the opera, nor any of the other diversions of the Carnival; nay, he was proof against the temptations of all the ladies.

"You are in truth very simple," said Martin to him, "if you imagine that a mongrel valet, who has five or six millions in his pocket, will go to the other end of the world to seek your mistress and bring her to you to Venice. If he find her, he will keep her to himself; if he do not find her he will get another. I advise you to forget your valet Cacambo and your mistress Cunegonde."

Martin was not consoling. Candide's melancholy increased; and Martin continued to prove to him that there was very little virtue or happiness upon earth, except perhaps in El Dorado, where nobody could gain admittance.

While they were disputing on this important subject and waiting for Cunegonde, Candide saw a young Theatin friar in St. Mark's Piazza, holding a girl on his arm. The Theatin looked fresh coloured, plump, and vigorous; his eyes were sparkling, his air assured, his look lofty, and his step bold. The girl was very pretty, and sang; she looked amorously at her Theatin, and from time to time pinched his fat cheeks.

"At least you will allow me," said Candide to Martin, "that these two are happy. Hitherto I have met with none but unfortunate people in the whole habitable globe, except in El Dorado; but as to this pair, I would venture to lay a wager that they are very happy."

"I lay you they are not," said Martin.

"We need only ask them to dine with us," said Candide, "and you will see whether I am mistaken."

Immediately he accosted them, presented his compliments, and invited them to his inn to eat some macaroni, with Lombard partridges, and caviare, and to drink some Montepulciano, Lachrymæ Christi, Cyprus and Samos wine. The girl blushed, the Theatin accepted the invitation and she followed him, casting her eyes on Candide with confusion and surprise, and dropping a few tears. No sooner had she set foot in Candide's apartment than she cried out:

"Ah! Mr. Candide does not know Paquette again."

Candide had not viewed her as yet with attention, his thoughts being entirely taken up with Cunegonde; but recollecting her as she spoke.

"Alas!" said he, "my poor child, it is you who reduced Doctor Pangloss to the beautiful condition in which I saw him?"

"Alas! it was I, sir, indeed," answered Paquette. "I see that you have heard all. I have been informed of the frightful disasters that befell the family of my lady Baroness, and the fair Cunegonde. I swear to you that my fate has been scarcely less sad. I was very innocent when you knew me. A Grey Friar, who was my confessor, easily seduced me. The consequences were terrible. I was obliged to quit the castle some time after the Baron had sent you away with kicks on the backside. If a famous surgeon had not taken compassion on me, I should have died. For some time I was this surgeon's mistress, merely out of gratitude. His wife, who was mad with jealousy, beat me every day unmercifully; she was a fury. The surgeon was one of the ugliest of men, and I the most wretched of women, to be continually beaten for a man I did not love. You know, sir, what a dangerous thing it is for an ill-natured woman to be married to a doctor. Incensed at the behaviour of his wife, he one day gave her so effectual a remedy to cure her of a slight cold, that she died two hours after, in most horrid convulsions. The wife's relations prosecuted the husband; he took flight, and I was thrown into jail. My innocence would not have saved me if I had not been good-looking. The judge set me free, on condition that he succeeded the surgeon. I was soon supplanted by a rival, turned out of doors quite destitute, and obliged to continue this abominable trade, which appears so pleasant to you men, while to us women it is the utmost abyss of misery. I have come to exercise the profession at Venice. Ah! sir, if you could only imagine what it is to be obliged to caress indifferently an old merchant, a lawyer, a monk, a gondolier, an abbé, to be exposed to abuse and insults; to be often reduced to borrowing a petticoat, only to go and have it raised by a disagreeable man; to be robbed by one of what one has earned from another; to be subject to the extortions of the officers of justice; and to have in prospect only a frightful old age, a hospital, and a dung-hill; you would conclude that I am one of the most unhappy creatures in the world."

Paquette thus opened her heart to honest Candide, in the presence of Martin, who said to his friend:

"You see that already I have won half the wager."

Friar Giroflée stayed in the dining-room, and drank a glass or two of wine while he was waiting for dinner.

"But," said Candide to Paquette, "you looked so gay and content when I met you; you sang and you behaved so lovingly to the Theatin, that you seemed to me as happy as you pretend to be now the reverse."

"Ah! sir," answered Paquette, "this is one of the miseries of the trade. Yesterday I was robbed and beaten by an officer; yet to-day I must put on good humour to please a friar."

Candide wanted no more convincing; he owned that Martin was in the right. They sat down to table with Paquette and the Theatin; the repast was entertaining; and towards the end they conversed with all confidence.

"Father," said Candide to the Friar, "you appear to me to enjoy a state that all the world might envy; the flower of health shines in your face, your expression makes plain your happiness; you have a very pretty girl for your recreation, and you seem well satisfied with your state as a Theatin."

"My faith, sir," said Friar Giroflée, "I wish that all the Theatins were at the bottom of the sea. I have been tempted a hundred times to set fire to the convent, and go and become a Turk. My parents forced me at the age of fifteen to put on this detestable habit, to increase the fortune of a cursed elder brother, whom God confound. Jealousy, discord, and fury, dwell in the convent. It is true I have preached a few bad sermons that have brought me in a little money, of which the prior stole half, while the rest serves to maintain my girls; but when I return at night to the monastery, I am ready to dash my head against the walls of the dormitory; and all my fellows are in the same case."

Martin turned towards Candide with his usual coolness.

"Well," said he, "have I not won the whole wager?"

Candide gave two thousand piastres to Paquette, and one thousand to Friar Giroflée.

"I'll answer for it," said he, "that with this they will be happy."

"I do not believe it at all," said Martin; "you will, perhaps, with these piastres only render them the more unhappy."

"Let that be as it may," said Candide, "but one thing consoles me. I see that we often meet with those whom we expected never to see more; so that, perhaps, as I have found my red sheep and Paquette, it may well be that I shall also find Cunegonde."

"I wish," said Martin, "she may one day make you very happy; but I doubt it very much."

"You are very hard of belief," said Candide.

"I have lived," said Martin.

"You see those gondoliers," said Candide, "are they not perpetually singing?"

"You do not see them," said Martin, "at home with their wives and brats. The Doge has his troubles, the gondoliers have theirs. It is true that, all things considered, the life of a gondolier is preferable to that of a Doge; but I believe the difference to be so trifling that it is not worth the trouble of examining."

"People talk," said Candide, "of the Senator Pococurante, who lives in that fine palace on the Brenta, where he entertains foreigners in the politest manner. They pretend that this man has never felt any uneasiness."

"I should be glad to see such a rarity," said Martin.

Candide immediately sent to ask the Lord Pococurante permission to wait upon him the next day.

25

THE VISIT TO LORD POCOCURANTE, A NOBLE VENETIAN

Candide and Martin went in a gondola on the Brenta, and arrived at the palace of the noble Signor Pococurante. The gardens, laid out with taste, were adorned with fine marble statues. The palace was beautifully built. The master of the house was a man of sixty, and very rich. He received the two travellers with polite indifference, which put Candide a little out of countenance, but was not at all disagreeable to Martin.

First, two pretty girls, very neatly dressed, served them with chocolate, which was frothed exceedingly well. Candide could not refrain from commending their beauty, grace, and address.

"They are good enough creatures," said the Senator. "I make them lie with me sometimes, for I am very tired of the ladies of the town, of their coquetries, of their jealousies, of their quarrels, of their humours, of their pettinesses, of their prides, of their follies, and of the sonnets which one must make, or have made, for them. But after all, these two girls begin to weary me."

After breakfast, Candide walking into a long gallery was surprised by the beautiful pictures. He asked, by what master were the two first.

"They are by Raphael," said the Senator. "I bought them at a great price, out of vanity, some years ago. They are said to be the finest things in Italy, but they do not please me at all. The colours are too dark, the figures are not sufficiently rounded, nor in good relief; the draperies in no way resemble stuffs. In a word, whatever may be said, I do not find there a true imitation of nature. I only care for a picture when I think I see nature itself; and there are none of this sort. I have a great many pictures, but I prize them very little."

While they were waiting for dinner Pococurante ordered a concert. Candide found the music delicious.

"This noise," said the Senator, "may amuse one for half an hour; but if it were to last longer it would grow tiresome to everybody, though they durst not own it. Music, to-day, is only the art of executing difficult things, and that which is only difficult cannot please long. Perhaps I should be fonder of the opera if they had not found the secret of making of it a monster which shocks me. Let who will go to see bad tragedies set to music, where the scenes are contrived for no other end than to introduce two or three songs ridiculously out of place, to show off an actress's voice. Let who will, or who can, die away with pleasure at the sight of an eunuch quavering the *rôle* of Cæsar, or of Cato, and strutting awkwardly upon the stage. For my part I have long since renounced those paltry entertainments which constitute the glory of modern Italy, and are purchased so dearly by sovereigns."

Candide disputed the point a little, but with discretion. Martin was entirely of the Senator's opinion.

They sat down to table, and after an excellent dinner they went into the library. Candide, seeing a Homer magnificently bound, commended the virtuoso on his good taste.

"There," said he, "is a book that was once the delight of the great Pangloss, the best philosopher in Germany."

"It is not mine," answered Pococurante coolly. "They used at one time to make me believe that I took a pleasure in reading him. But that continual repetition of battles, so extremely like one another;

those gods that are always active without doing anything decisive; that Helen who is the cause of the war, and who yet scarcely appears in the piece; that Troy, so long besieged without being taken; all these together caused me great weariness. I have sometimes asked learned men whether they were not as weary as I of that work. Those who were sincere have owned to me that the poem made them fall asleep; yet it was necessary to have it in their library as a monument of antiquity, or like those rusty medals which are no longer of use in commerce."

"But your Excellency does not think thus of Virgil?" said Candide.

"I grant," said the Senator, "that the second, fourth, and sixth books of his *Æneid* are excellent, but as for his pious Æneas, his strong Cloanthus, his friend Achates, his little Ascanius, his silly King Latinus, his bourgeois Amata, his insipid Lavinia, I think there can be nothing more flat and disagreeable. I prefer Tasso a good deal, or even the soporific tales of Ariosto."

"May I presume to ask you, sir," said Candide, "whether you do not receive a great deal of pleasure from reading Horace?"

"There are maxims in this writer," answered Pococurante, "from which a man of the world may reap great benefit, and being written in energetic verse they are more easily impressed upon the memory. But I care little for his journey to Brundusium, and his account of a bad dinner, or of his low quarrel between one Rupilius whose words he says were full of poisonous filth, and another whose language was imbued with vinegar. I have read with much distaste his indelicate verses against old women and witches, nor do I see any merit in telling his friend Mæcenas that if he will but rank him in the choir of lyric poets, his lofty head shall touch the stars. Fools admire everything in an author of reputation. For my part, I read only to please myself. I like only that which serves my purpose."

Candide, having been educated never to judge for himself, was much surprised at what he heard. Martin found there was a good deal of reason in Pococurante's remarks.

"Oh! here is Cicero," said Candide. "Here is the great man whom I fancy you are never tired of reading."

"I never read him," replied the Venetian. "What is it to me whether he pleads for Rabirius or Cluentius? I try causes enough myself; his philosophical works seem to me better, but when I found that he doubted of everything, I concluded that I knew as much as he, and that I had no need of a guide to learn ignorance."

"Ha! here are four-score volumes of the Academy of Sciences," cried Martin. "Perhaps there is something valuable in this collection."

"There might be," said Pococurante, "if only one of those rakers of rubbish had shown how to make pins; but in all these volumes there is nothing but chimerical systems, and not a single useful thing."

"And what dramatic works I see here," said Candide, "in Italian, Spanish, and French."

"Yes," replied the Senator, "there are three thousand, and not three dozen of them good for anything. As to those collections of sermons, which altogether are not worth a single page of Seneca, and those huge volumes of theology, you may well imagine that neither I nor any one else ever opens them."

Martin saw some shelves filled with English books.

"I have a notion," said he, "that a Republican must be greatly pleased with most of these books, which are written with a spirit of freedom."

"Yes," answered Pococurante, "it is noble to write as one thinks; this is the privilege of humanity. In all our Italy we write only what we do not think; those who inhabit the country of the Cæsars and the Antoninuses dare not acquire a single idea without the permission of a Dominican friar. I should be pleased with the liberty which inspires the English genius if passion and party spirit did not corrupt all that is estimable in this precious liberty."

Candide, observing a Milton, asked whether he did not look upon this author as a great man.

"Who?" said Pococurante, "that barbarian, who writes a long

commentary in ten books of harsh verse on the first chapter of Genesis; that coarse imitator of the Greeks, who disfigures the Creation, and who, while Moses represents the Eternal producing the world by a word, makes the Messiah take a great pair of compasses from the armoury of heaven to circumscribe His work? How can I have any esteem for a writer who has spoiled Tasso's hell and the devil, who transforms Lucifer sometimes into a toad and other times into a pigmy, who makes him repeat the same things a hundred times, who makes him dispute on theology, who, by a serious imitation of Ariosto's comic invention of firearms, represents the devils cannonading in heaven? Neither I nor any man in Italy could take pleasure in those melancholy extravagances; and the marriage of Sin and Death, and the snakes brought forth by Sin, are enough to turn the stomach of any one with the least taste, [and his long description of a pest-house is good only for a grave-digger]. This obscure, whimsical, and disagreeable poem was despised upon its first publication, and I only treat it now as it was treated in its own country by contemporaries. For the matter of that I say what I think, and I care very little whether others think as I do."

Candide was grieved at this speech, for he had a respect for Homer and was fond of Milton.

"Alas!" said he softly to Martin, "I am afraid that this man holds our German poets in very great contempt."

"There would not be much harm in that," said Martin.

"Oh! what a superior man," said Candide below his breath. "What a great genius is this Pococurante! Nothing can please him."

After their survey of the library they went down into the garden, where Candide praised its several beauties.

"I know of nothing in so bad a taste," said the master. "All you see here is merely trifling. After to-morrow I will have it planted with a nobler design."

"Well," said Candide to Martin when they had taken their leave, "you will agree that this is the happiest of mortals, for he is above everything he possesses."

"But do you not see," answered Martin, "that he is disgusted with all he possesses? Plato observed a long while ago that those stomachs are not the best that reject all sorts of food."

"But is there not a pleasure," said Candide, "in criticising everything, in pointing out faults where others see nothing but beauties?"

"That is to say," replied Martin, "that there is some pleasure in having no pleasure."

"Well, well," said Candide, "I find that I shall be the only happy man when I am blessed with the sight of my dear Cunegonde."

"It is always well to hope," said Martin.

However, the days and the weeks passed. Cacambo did not come, and Candide was so overwhelmed with grief that he did not even reflect that Paquette and Friar Giroflée did not return to thank him.

26

OF A SUPPER WHICH CANDIDE AND MARTIN TOOK WITH SIX STRANGERS, AND WHO THEY WERE

One evening that Candide and Martin were going to sit down to supper with some foreigners who lodged in the same inn, a man whose complexion was as black as soot, came behind Candide, and taking him by the arm, said:

"Get yourself ready to go along with us; do not fail."

Upon this he turned round and saw—Cacambo! Nothing but the sight of Cunegonde could have astonished and delighted him more. He was on the point of going mad with joy. He embraced his dear friend.

"Cunegonde is here, without doubt; where is she? Take me to her that I may die of joy in her company."

"Cunegonde is not here," said Cacambo, "she is at Constantinople."

"Oh, heavens! at Constantinople! But were she in China I would fly thither; let us be off."

"We shall set out after supper," replied Cacambo. "I can tell you nothing more; I am a slave, my master awaits me, I must serve him at table; speak not a word, eat, and then get ready."

Candide, distracted between joy and grief, delighted at seeing his faithful agent again, astonished at finding him a slave, filled with the fresh hope of recovering his mistress, his heart palpitating, his understanding confused, sat down to table with Martin, who saw all these scenes quite unconcerned, and with six strangers who had come to spend the Carnival at Venice.

Cacambo waited at table upon one of the strangers; towards the end of the entertainment he drew near his master, and whispered in his ear:

"Sire, your Majesty may start when you please, the vessel is ready."

On saying these words he went out. The company in great surprise looked at one another without speaking a word, when another domestic approached his master and said to him:

"Sire, your Majesty's chaise is at Padua, and the boat is ready."

The master gave a nod and the servant went away. The company all stared at one another again, and their surprise redoubled. A third valet came up to a third stranger, saying:

"Sire, believe me, your Majesty ought not to stay here any longer. I am going to get everything ready."

And immediately he disappeared. Candide and Martin did not doubt that this was a masquerade of the Carnival. Then a fourth domestic said to a fourth master:

"Your Majesty may depart when you please."

Saying this he went away like the rest. The fifth valet said the same thing to the fifth master. But the sixth valet spoke differently to the sixth stranger, who sat near Candide. He said to him:

"Faith, Sire, they will no longer give credit to your Majesty nor to me, and we may perhaps both of us be put in jail this very night. Therefore I will take care of myself. Adieu."

The servants being all gone, the six strangers, with Candide and Martin, remained in a profound silence. At length Candide broke it.

"Gentlemen," said he, "this is a very good joke indeed, but why should you all be kings? For me I own that neither Martin nor I is a king."

Cacambo's master then gravely answered in Italian:

"I am not at all joking. My name is Achmet III. I was Grand Sultan many years. I dethroned my brother; my nephew dethroned me, my viziers were beheaded, and I am condemned to end my days in the old Seraglio. My nephew, the great Sultan Mahmoud, permits me to travel sometimes for my health, and I am come to spend the Carnival at Venice."

A young man who sat next to Achmet, spoke then as follows:

"My name is Ivan. I was once Emperor of all the Russias, but was dethroned in my cradle. My parents were confined in prison and I was educated there; yet I am sometimes allowed to travel in company with persons who act as guards; and I am come to spend the Carnival at Venice."

The third said:

"I am Charles Edward, King of England; my father has resigned all his legal rights to me. I have fought in defence of them; and above eight hundred of my adherents have been hanged, drawn, and quartered. I have been confined in prison; I am going to Rome, to pay a visit to the King, my father, who was dethroned as well as myself and my grandfather, and I am come to spend the Carnival at Venice."

The fourth spoke thus in his turn:

"I am the King of Poland; the fortune of war has stripped me of my hereditary dominions; my father underwent the same vicissitudes; I resign myself to Providence in the same manner as Sultan Achmet, the Emperor Ivan, and King Charles Edward, whom God long preserve; and I am come to the Carnival at Venice."

The fifth said:

"I am King of Poland also; I have been twice dethroned; but

Providence has given me another country, where I have done more good than all the Sarmatian kings were ever capable of doing on the banks of the Vistula; I resign myself likewise to Providence, and am come to pass the Carnival at Venice."

It was now the sixth monarch's turn to speak:

"Gentlemen," said he, "I am not so great a prince as any of you; however, I am a king. I am Theodore, elected King of Corsica; I had the title of Majesty, and now I am scarcely treated as a gentleman. I have coined money, and now am not worth a farthing; I have had two secretaries of state, and now I have scarce a valet; I have seen myself on a throne, and I have seen myself upon straw in a common jail in London. I am afraid that I shall meet with the same treatment here though, like your majesties, I am come to see the Carnival at Venice."

The other five kings listened to this speech with generous compassion. Each of them gave twenty sequins to King Theodore to buy him clothes and linen; and Candide made him a present of a diamond worth two thousand sequins.

"Who can this private person be," said the five kings to one another, "who is able to give, and really has given, a hundred times as much as any of us?"

Just as they rose from table, in came four Serene Highnesses, who had also been stripped of their territories by the fortune of war, and were come to spend the Carnival at Venice. But Candide paid no regard to these newcomers, his thoughts were entirely employed on his voyage to Constantinople, in search of his beloved Cunegonde.

27

CANDIDE'S VOYAGE TO CONSTANTINOPLE

The faithful Cacambo had already prevailed upon the Turkish skipper, who was to conduct the Sultan Achmet to Constantinople, to receive Candide and Martin on his ship. They both embarked after having made their obeisance to his miserable Highness.

"You see," said Candide to Martin on the way, "we supped with six dethroned kings, and of those six there was one to whom I gave charity. Perhaps there are many other princes yet more unfortunate. For my part, I have only lost a hundred sheep; and now I am flying into Cunegonde's arms. My dear Martin, yet once more Pangloss was right: all is for the best."

"I wish it," answered Martin.

"But," said Candide, "it was a very strange adventure we met with at Venice. It has never before been seen or heard that six dethroned kings have supped together at a public inn."

"It is not more extraordinary," said Martin, "than most of the things that have happened to us. It is a very common thing for kings to be dethroned; and as for the honour we have had of supping in their company, it is a trifle not worth our attention."

No sooner had Candide got on board the vessel than he flew to his old valet and friend Cacambo, and tenderly embraced him.

"Well," said he, "what news of Cunegonde? Is she still a prodigy of beauty? Does she love me still? How is she? Thou hast doubtless bought her a palace at Constantinople?"

"My dear master," answered Cacambo, "Cunegonde washes dishes on the banks of the Propontis, in the service of a prince, who has very few dishes to wash; she is a slave in the family of an ancient sovereign named Ragotsky, to whom the Grand Turk allows three crowns a day in his exile. But what is worse still is, that she has lost her beauty and has become horribly ugly."

"Well, handsome or ugly," replied Candide, "I am a man of honour, and it is my duty to love her still. But how came she to be reduced to so abject a state with the five or six millions that you took to her?"

"Ah!" said Cacambo, "was I not to give two millions to Senor Don Fernando d'Ibaraa, y Figueora, y Mascarenes, y Lampourdos, y Souza, Governor of Buenos Ayres, for permitting Miss Cunegonde to come away? And did not a corsair bravely rob us of all the rest? Did not this corsair carry us to Cape Matapan, to Milo, to Nicaria, to Samos, to Petra, to the Dardanelles, to Marmora, to Scutari? Cunegonde and the old woman serve the prince I now mentioned to you, and I am slave to the dethroned Sultan."

"What a series of shocking calamities!" cried Candide. "But after all, I have some diamonds left; and I may easily pay Cunegonde's ransom. Yet it is a pity that she is grown so ugly."

Then, turning towards Martin: "Who do you think," said he, "is most to be pitied—the Sultan Achmet, the Emperor Ivan, King Charles Edward, or I?"

"How should I know!" answered Martin. "I must see into your hearts to be able to tell."

"Ah!" said Candide, "if Pangloss were here, he could tell."

"I know not," said Martin, "in what sort of scales your Pangloss would weigh the misfortunes of mankind and set a just estimate on their sorrows. All that I can presume to say is, that there are millions of people upon earth who have a hundred times more to complain of than King Charles Edward, the Emperor Ivan, or the Sultan Achmet."

"That may well be," said Candide.

In a few days they reached the Bosphorus, and Candide began by paying a very high ransom for Cacambo. Then without losing time, he and his companions went on board a galley, in order to search on the banks of the Propontis for his Cunegonde, however ugly she might have become.

Among the crew there were two slaves who rowed very badly, and to whose bare shoulders the Levantine captain would now and then apply blows from a bull's pizzle. Candide, from a natural impulse, looked at these two slaves more attentively than at the other oarsmen, and approached them with pity. Their features though greatly disfigured, had a slight resemblance to those of Pangloss and the unhappy Jesuit and Westphalian Baron, brother to Miss Cunegonde. This moved and saddened him. He looked at them still more attentively.

"Indeed," said he to Cacambo, "if I had not seen Master Pangloss hanged, and if I had not had the misfortune to kill the Baron, I should think it was they that were rowing."

At the names of the Baron and of Pangloss, the two galley-slaves uttered a loud cry, held fast by the seat, and let drop their oars. The captain ran up to them and redoubled his blows with the bull's pizzle.

"Stop! stop! sir," cried Candide. "I will give you what money you please."

"What! it is Candide!" said one of the slaves.

"What! it is Candide!" said the other.

"Do I dream?" cried Candide; "am I awake? or am I on board a galley? Is this the Baron whom I killed? Is this Master Pangloss whom I saw hanged?"

"It is we! it is we!" answered they.

"Well! is this the great philosopher?" said Martin.

"Ah! captain," said Candide, "what ransom will you take for Monsieur de Thunder-ten-Tronckh, one of the first barons of the empire, and for Monsieur Pangloss, the profoundest metaphysician in Germany?"

"Dog of a Christian," answered the Levantine captain, "since these two dogs of Christian slaves are barons and metaphysicians, which I doubt not are high dignities in their country, you shall give me fifty thousand sequins."

"You shall have them, sir. Carry me back at once to Constantinople, and you shall receive the money directly. But no; carry me first to Miss Cunegonde."

Upon the first proposal made by Candide, however, the Levantine captain had already tacked about, and made the crew ply their oars quicker than a bird cleaves the air.

Candide embraced the Baron and Pangloss a hundred times.

"And how happened it, my dear Baron, that I did not kill you? And, my dear Pangloss, how came you to life again after being hanged? And why are you both in a Turkish galley?"

"And it is true that my dear sister is in this country?" said the Baron.

"Yes," answered Cacambo.

"Then I behold, once more, my dear Candide," cried Pangloss.

Candide presented Martin and Cacambo to them; they embraced each other, and all spoke at once. The galley flew; they were already in the port. Instantly Candide sent for a Jew, to whom he sold for fifty thousand sequins a diamond worth a hundred thousand, though the fellow swore to him by Abraham that he could give him no more. He immediately paid the ransom for the Baron and Pangloss. The latter threw himself at the feet of his deliverer, and bathed them with his tears; the former thanked him with a nod, and promised to return him the money on the first opportunity.

"But is it indeed possible that my sister can be in Turkey?" said he.

"Nothing is more possible," said Cacambo, "since she scours the dishes in the service of a Transylvanian prince."

Candide sent directly for two Jews and sold them some more diamonds, and then they all set out together in another galley to deliver Cunegonde from slavery.

28

WHAT HAPPENED TO CANDIDE, CUNEGONDE, PANGLOSS, MARTIN, ETC

"I ask your pardon once more," said Candide to the Baron, "your pardon, reverend father, for having run you through the body."

"Say no more about it," answered the Baron. "I was a little too hasty, I own, but since you wish to know by what fatality I came to be a galley-slave I will inform you. After I had been cured by the surgeon of the college of the wound you gave me, I was attacked and carried off by a party of Spanish troops, who confined me in prison at Buenos Ayres at the very time my sister was setting out thence. I asked leave to return to Rome to the General of my Order. I was appointed chaplain to the French Ambassador at Constantinople. I had not been eight days in this employment when one evening I met with a young Ichoglan, who was a very handsome fellow. The weather was warm. The young man wanted to bathe, and I took this opportunity of bathing also. I did not know that it was a capital crime for a Christian to be found naked with a young Mussulman. A cadi ordered me a hundred blows on the soles of the feet, and condemned me to the galleys. I do not think there ever was a greater act of injustice. But I should be glad to know how my sister came to be scullion to a Transylvanian prince who has taken shelter among the Turks."

"But you, my dear Pangloss," said Candide, "how can it be that I behold you again?"

"It is true," said Pangloss, "that you saw me hanged. I should have been burnt, but you may remember it rained exceedingly hard when they were going to roast me; the storm was so violent that they despaired of lighting the fire, so I was hanged because they could do no better. A surgeon purchased my body, carried me home, and dissected me. He began with making a crucial incision on me from the navel to the clavicula. One could not have been worse hanged than I was. The executioner of the Holy Inquisition was a sub-deacon, and knew how to burn people marvellously well, but he was not accustomed to hanging. The cord was wet and did not slip properly, and besides it was badly tied; in short, I still drew my breath, when the crucial incision made me give such a frightful scream that my surgeon fell flat upon his back, and imagining that he had been dissecting the devil he ran away, dying with fear, and fell down the staircase in his flight. His wife, hearing the noise, flew from the next room. She saw me stretched out upon the table with my crucial incision. She was seized with yet greater fear than her husband, fled, and tumbled over him. When they came to themselves a little, I heard the wife say to her husband: 'My dear, how could you take it into your head to dissect a heretic? Do you not know that these people always have the devil in their bodies? I will go and fetch a priest this minute to exorcise him.' At this proposal I shuddered, and mustering up what little courage I had still remaining I cried out aloud, 'Have mercy on me!' At length the Portuguese barber plucked up his spirits. He sewed up my wounds; his wife even nursed me. I was upon my legs at the end of fifteen days. The barber found me a place as lackey to a knight of Malta who was going to Venice, but finding that my master had no money to pay me my wages I entered the service of a Venetian merchant, and went with him to Constantinople. One day I took it into my head to step into a mosque, where I saw an old Iman and a very pretty young devotee who was saying her paternosters. Her bosom was uncovered, and between her breasts she had a beautiful bouquet of tulips, roses, anemones, ranunculus, hyacinths, and auriculas. She dropped her bouquet; I picked it up, and presented it to her with a profound reverence. I was so long in delivering it that the Iman began to get angry, and seeing that I was a Christian he called out for help. They carried me before the cadi, who ordered me a hundred lashes on the soles of the feet and sent me to the galleys. I was chained to the very same galley and the same bench as the young Baron. On board this galley there were four young men from Marseilles, five Neapolitan priests, and two monks from Corfu, who told us similar adventures happened daily. The Baron maintained that he had suffered greater injustice than I, and I insisted that it was far more innocent to take up a bouquet and place it again on a woman's bosom than to be found stark naked with an Ichoglan. We were continually disputing, and received twenty lashes with a bull's pizzle when the concatenation of universal events brought you to our galley, and you were good enough to ransom us."

"Well, my dear Pangloss," said Candide to him, "when you had been hanged, dissected, whipped, and were tugging at the oar, did you always think that everything happens for the best?"

"I am still of my first opinion," answered Pangloss, "for I am a philosopher and I cannot retract, especially as Leibnitz could never be wrong; and besides, the pre-established harmony is the finest thing in the world, and so is his *plenum* and *materia subtilis*."

29

HOW CANDIDE FOUND CUNEGONDE AND THE OLD WOMAN AGAIN

While Candide, the Baron, Pangloss, Martin, and Cacambo were relating their several adventures, were reasoning on the contingent or non-contingent events of the universe, disputing on effects and causes, on moral and physical evil, on liberty and necessity, and on the consolations a slave may feel even on a Turkish galley, they arrived at the house of the Transylvanian prince on the banks of the Propontis. The first objects which met their sight were Cunegonde and the old woman hanging towels out to dry.

The Baron paled at this sight. The tender, loving Candide, seeing his beautiful Cunegonde embrowned, with blood-shot eyes, withered neck, wrinkled cheeks, and rough, red arms, recoiled three paces, seized with horror, and then advanced out of good manners. She embraced Candide and her brother; they embraced the old woman, and Candide ransomed them both.

There was a small farm in the neighbourhood which the old woman proposed to Candide to make a shift with till the company could be provided for in a better manner. Cunegonde did not know she had grown ugly, for nobody had told her of it; and she reminded Candide of his promise in so positive a tone that the good man durst not refuse her. He therefore intimated to the Baron that he intended marrying his sister.

"I will not suffer," said the Baron, "such meanness on her part, and such insolence on yours; I will never be reproached with this scandalous thing; my sister's children would never be able to enter the church in Germany. No; my sister shall only marry a baron of the empire."

Cunegonde flung herself at his feet, and bathed them with her tears; still he was inflexible.

"Thou foolish fellow," said Candide; "I have delivered thee out of the galleys, I have paid thy ransom, and thy sister's also; she was a scullion, and is very ugly, yet I am so condescending as to marry her; and dost thou pretend to oppose the match? I should kill thee again, were I only to consult my anger."

"Thou mayest kill me again," said the Baron, "but thou shalt not marry my sister, at least whilst I am living."

30

THE CONCLUSION

At the bottom of his heart Candide had no wish to marry Cunegonde. But the extreme impertinence of the Baron determined him to conclude the match, and Cunegonde pressed him so strongly that he could not go from his word. He consulted Pangloss, Martin, and the faithful Cacambo. Pangloss drew up an excellent memorial, wherein he proved that the Baron had no right over his sister, and that according to all the laws of the empire, she might marry Candide with her left hand. Martin was for throwing the Baron into the sea; Cacambo decided that it would be better to deliver him up again to the captain of the galley, after which they thought to send him back to the General Father of the Order at Rome by the first ship. This advice was well received, the old woman approved it; they said not a word to his sister; the thing was executed for a little money, and they had the double pleasure of entrapping a Jesuit, and punishing the pride of a German baron.

It is natural to imagine that after so many disasters Candide married, and living with the philosopher Pangloss, the philosopher Martin, the prudent Cacambo, and the old woman, having besides brought so many diamonds from the country of the ancient Incas, must have led a very happy life. But he was so much imposed upon by the Jews that he had nothing left except his small farm; his wife became uglier every day, more peevish and unsupportable; the old woman was infirm and even more fretful than Cunegonde. Cacambo, who worked in the garden, and took vegetables for sale to Constantinople, was fatigued with hard work, and cursed his destiny. Pangloss was in despair at not shining in some German university. For Martin, he was firmly persuaded that he would be as badly off elsewhere, and therefore bore things patiently. Candide, Martin, and Pangloss sometimes disputed about morals and metaphysics. They often saw passing under the windows of their farm boats full of Effendis, Pashas, and Cadis, who were going into banishment to Lemnos, Mitylene, or Erzeroum. And they saw other Cadis, Pashas, and Effendis coming to supply the place of the exiles, and afterwards exiled in their turn. They saw heads decently impaled for presentation to the Sublime Porte. Such spectacles as these increased the number of their dissertations; and when they did not dispute time hung so heavily upon their hands, that one day the old woman ventured to say to them:

"I want to know which is worse, to be ravished a hundred times by negro pirates, to have a buttock cut off, to run the gauntlet among the Bulgarians, to be whipped and hanged at an *auto-da-fé*, to be dissected, to row in the galleys—in short, to go through all the miseries we have undergone, or to stay here and have nothing to do?"

"It is a great question," said Candide.

This discourse gave rise to new reflections, and Martin especially concluded that man was born to live either in a state of distracting inquietude or of lethargic disgust. Candide did not quite agree to that, but he affirmed nothing. Pangloss owned that he had always suffered horribly, but as he had once asserted that everything went wonderfully well, he asserted it still, though he no longer believed it.

What helped to confirm Martin in his detestable principles, to stagger Candide more than ever, and to puzzle Pangloss, was that one day they saw Paquette and Friar Giroflée land at the farm in extreme misery. They had soon squandered their three thousand piastres, parted, were reconciled, quarrelled again, were thrown into gaol, had escaped, and Friar Giroflée had at length become Turk. Paquette continued her trade wherever she went, but made nothing of it.

"I foresaw," said Martin to Candide, "that your presents would soon be dissipated, and only make them the more miserable. You have rolled in millions of money, you and Cacambo; and yet you are not happier than Friar Giroflée and Paquette."

"Ha!" said Pangloss to Paquette, "Providence has then brought you amongst us again, my poor child! Do you know that you cost me the tip of my nose, an eye, and an ear, as you may see? What a world is this!"

And now this new adventure set them philosophising more than ever.

In the neighbourhood there lived a very famous Dervish who was esteemed the best philosopher in all Turkey, and they went to consult him. Pangloss was the speaker.

"Master," said he, "we come to beg you to tell why so strange an animal as man was made."

"With what meddlest thou?" said the Dervish; "is it thy business?"

"But, reverend father," said Candide, "there is horrible evil in this world."

"What signifies it," said the Dervish, "whether there be evil or good? When his highness sends a ship to Egypt, does he trouble his head whether the mice on board are at their ease or not?"

"What, then, must we do?" said Pangloss.

"Hold your tongue," answered the Dervish.

"I was in hopes," said Pangloss, "that I should reason with you a little about causes and effects, about the best of possible worlds, the origin of evil, the nature of the soul, and the pre-established harmony."

At these words, the Dervish shut the door in their faces.

During this conversation, the news was spread that two Viziers and the Mufti had been strangled at Constantinople, and that several of their friends had been impaled. This catastrophe made a great noise for some hours. Pangloss, Candide, and Martin, returning to the little farm, saw a good old man taking the fresh air at his door under an orange bower. Pangloss, who was as inquisitive as he was argumentative, asked the old man what was the name of the strangled Mufti.

"I do not know," answered the worthy man, "and I have not known the name of any Mufti, nor of any Vizier. I am entirely ignorant of the event you mention; I presume in general that they who meddle with the administration of public affairs die sometimes miserably, and that they deserve it; but I never trouble my head about what is transacting at Constantinople; I content myself with sending there for sale the fruits of the garden which I cultivate."

Having said these words, he invited the strangers into his house; his two sons and two daughters presented them with several sorts of sherbet, which they made themselves, with Kaimak enriched with the candied-peel of citrons, with oranges, lemons, pine-apples, pistachio-nuts, and Mocha coffee unadulterated with the bad coffee of Batavia or the American islands. After which the two daughters of the honest Mussulman perfumed the strangers' beards.

"You must have a vast and magnificent estate," said Candide to the Turk.

"I have only twenty acres," replied the old man; "I and my children cultivate them; our labour preserves us from three great evils—weariness, vice, and want."

Candide, on his way home, made profound reflections on the old man's conversation.

"This honest Turk," said he to Pangloss and Martin, "seems to be in a situation far preferable to that of the six kings with whom we had the honour of supping."

"Grandeur," said Pangloss, "is extremely dangerous according to the testimony of philosophers. For, in short, Eglon, King of Moab, was assassinated by Ehud; Absalom was hung by his hair, and pierced with three darts; King Nadab, the son of Jeroboam, was killed by Baasa; King Ela by Zimri; Ahaziah by Jehu; Athaliah by Jehoiada; the Kings Jehoiakim, Jeconiah, and Zedekiah, were led into captivity. You know how perished Crœsus, Astyages, Darius, Dionysius of Syracuse, Pyrrhus, Perseus, Hannibal, Jugurtha, Ariovistus, Cæsar, Pompey, Nero, Otho, Vitellius, Domitian, Richard II. of England, Edward II., Henry VI., Richard III., Mary Stuart, Charles I., the three Henrys of France, the Emperor Henry IV.! You know———"

"I know also," said Candide, "that we must cultivate our garden."

"You are right," said Pangloss, "for when man was first placed in the Garden of Eden, he was put there *ut operaretur eum*, that he might cultivate it; which shows that man was not born to be idle."

"Let us work," said Martin, "without disputing; it is the only way to render life tolerable."

The whole little society entered into this laudable design, according to their different abilities. Their little plot of land produced plentiful crops. Cunegonde was, indeed, very ugly, but she became an excellent pastry cook; Paquette worked at embroidery; the old woman looked after the linen. They were all, not excepting Friar Giroflée, of some service or other; for he made a good joiner, and became a very honest man.

Pangloss sometimes said to Candide:

"There is a concatenation of events in this best of all possible worlds: for if you had not been kicked out of a magnificent castle for love of Miss Cunegonde: if you had not been put into the Inquisition: if you had not walked over America: if you had not stabbed the Baron: if you had not lost all your sheep from the fine country of El Dorado: you would not be here eating preserved citrons and pistachio-nuts."

"All that is very well," answered Candide, "but let us cultivate our garden."

ZADIG

OR THE BOOK OF FATE

An Oriental History
Translated from the French Original of Mr Voltaire

THE DEDICATION TO THE SULTANA SHERAA BY SADI

The 18th of the Month Scheval, in the Year of the Hegira, 837

Thou Joy of ev'ry Eye! Thou Torment of every Heart! Thou Intellectual Light! I do not kiss the Dust of thy Feet; because thou seldom art seen out of the Seraglio, and when thou art, thou walkest only on the Carpets of Iran, or on Beds of Roses.

I here present you with a Translation of the Work of an ancient Sage, who having the Happiness of living free from all Avocations, thought proper, by Way of Amusement, to write the History of Zadig; a Performance, that comprehends in it more Instruction than, 'tis possible, you may at first be aware of. I beg you would indulge me so far as to read it over, and then pass your impartial Judgment upon it: For notwithstanding you are in the Bloom of your Life; tho' ev'ry Pleasure courts you; tho' you are Nature's Darling, and have internal Qualities in proportion to your Beauty; tho' the World resounds your Praises from Morning till Night, and consequently you must have a just Title to a superior Degree of Understanding than the rest of your Sex; Yet your Wit is no ways flashy; Your Taste is refin'd, and I have had the Honour to hear you talk more learnedly than the wisest Dervise, with his venerable Beard, and pointed Bonnet: You are discreet, and yet not mistrustful; you are easy, but not weak; you are beneficent with Discretion; you love your Friends, and create yourself no Enemies. Your most sprightly Flights borrow no Graces from Detraction;

you never speak a misbecoming Word, nor do an ill-natur'd Action, tho' 'tis always in your Power. In a Word, your Soul is as spotless as your Person. You have, moreover, a little Fund of Philosophy, which gives me just Grounds to hope that you'll relish this Historical Performance better than any other Lady of your Quality would do.

It was originally compos'd in the Chaldean Language, to which both you and my self are perfect Strangers. It was translated, however, into Arabic, for the Amusement of the celebrated Sultan Ouloug-beg. It first appear'd in Public, when the Arabian and Persian Tales of One Thousand and One Nights, and One Thousand and One Days, were most in Vogue: Ouloug chose rather to entertain himself with the Adventures of Zadig. The Sultanas indeed were more fond of the former. How can you, said the judicious Ouloug, be so partial, as to prefer a Set of Tales, that are no ways interesting or instructive, to a Work, that has a Variety of Beauties to recommend it? Oh! replied the Sultanas, the less Sense there is in them, the more they are in Taste; and the less their Merit, the greater their Commendation.

I flatter my self, thou Patroness of Wisdom, that thou wilt not copy after those thoughtless Sultanas, but give into the Sentiments of Ouloug. I am in hopes likewise, when you are tir'd with the Conversation of such as make those senseless Romances abovemention'd their favourite Amusements, you will vouchsafe to listen for one Minute or two, to the Dictates of solid Sense. Had you been Thalestris in the Days of Scander, the Son of Philip; had you been the Queen of Sheba, in the Reign of Solomon, those Kings would have been proud to have taken a Tour to visit you.

May the Celestial Virtues grant, that your Pleasures may meet with no Interruption; your Charms know no Decay; and may your Felicity be everlasting!

—Sadi

THE APPROBATION

I, Who have subscrib'd my Name hereto, ambitious of being thought a Man of Wit and Learning, have perus'd this Manuscript, which I find, to my great Mortification, amusing, moral, philosophical, and fit to be read, even by those who have an utter Aversion to Romances; for which Reason, I have depretiated it, as it deserves, and have in direct Terms told the Cadi-Lesquier, that 'tis a most detestable Performance.

1
THE BLIND EYE

In the Reign of King Moabdar, there was a young Man, a Native of Babylon, by name Zadig; who was not only endowed by Nature with an uncommon Genius, but born of illustrious Parents, who bestowed on him an Education no ways inferior to his Birth. Tho' rich and young, he knew how to give a Check to his Passions; he was no ways self-conceited; he didn't always act up to the strictest Rules of Reason himself, and knew how to look on the Foibles of others, with an Eye of Indulgence. Every one was surpriz'd to find, that notwithstanding he had such a Fund of Wit, he never insulted; nay, never so much as rallied any of his Companions, for that Tittle Tattle, which was so vague and empty, so noisy and confus'd; for those rash Reflections, those illiterate Conclusions, and those insipid Jokes; and, in short, for that Flow of unmeaning Words, which was call'd polite Conversation in Babylon. He had learned from the first Book of Zoroaster, that Self-love is like a Bladder full blown, which when once prick'd, discharges a kind of petty Tempest. Zadig, in particular, never boasted of his Contempt of the Fair Sex, or of his Facility to make Conquests amongst them. He was of a generous Spirit; insomuch, that he was not afraid of obliging even an ungrateful Man; strictly adhering to that wise Maxim of Zoroaster. When you are eating, throw an Offal to the Dogs that are under the Table, lest they should be tempted to bite you. He was as wise as he could well be wish'd; since he was fond of no Company, but such as were distinguish'd for Men of Sense. As he was well-grounded, in all the Sciences of the antient Chaldeans, he was no Stranger to those Principles of Natural Philosophy, which were then known:

And understood as much of Metaphysics as any one in all Ages after him; that is to say, he knew little or nothing of the Matter. He was firmly convinc'd, that the Year consisted of 365 Days and an half, tho' directly repugnant to the new Philosophy of the Age he liv'd in; and that the Sun was situated in the Center of the Earth; And when the Chief Magi told him, with an imperious Air, that he maintain'd erroneous Principles; and that it was an Indignity offered to the Government under which he liv'd, to imagine the Sun should roll round its own Axis, and that the Year consisted of twelve Months, he knew how to sit still and quiet, without shewing the least Tokens of Resentment or Contempt.

As Zadig was immensely rich, and had consequently Friends without Number; and as he was a Gentleman of a robust Constitution, and remarkably handsome; as he was endowed with a plentiful Share of ready and inoffensive Wit: And, in a Word, as his Heart was perfectly sincere and open, he imagin'd himself, in some Measure, qualified to be perfectly happy. For which Purpose he determin'd to marry a gay young Lady (one Semira by name) whose Beauty, Birth and Fortune, render'd her the most desirable Person in all Babylon. He had a sincere Affection for her, grounded on Honour, and Semira conceiv'd as tender a Passion for him. They were just upon the critical Minute of a mutual Conjunction in the Bands of Matrimony, when, as they were walking Hand in Hand together towards one of the Gates of Babylon, under the Shade of a Row of Palm-trees, that grew on the Banks of the River Euphrates, they were beset by a Band of Ruffians, arm'd with Sabres, Bows and Arrows. They were the Guards, it seems, of young Orçan (Nephew of a certain Minister of State) whom the Parasites, kept by his Uncle, had buoy'd up with a Permission to do, with Impunity, whatever he thought proper. This young Rival, tho' he had none of those internal Qualities to boast of that Zadig had, yet he imagin'd himself a Man of more Power; and for that Reason, was perfectly outrageous to see the other preferr'd before him. This Fit of Jealousy, the Result of mere Vanity, prompted him to think that he was deeply in Love with the fair Semira; and fir'd with that amorous Notion, he was determin'd to take her away from Zadig, by Dint of Arms. The Ravishers rush'd rudely upon her, and in the Transport of their Rage, drew the Blood of a Beauty, the Sight of whose Charms would have soften'd the very Tigers of Mount Imaüs. The injur'd Lady rent the very Heavens with her Exclamations. Where's my dear Husband, she cried? They have torn me from the Arms of the only Man whom I adore. She never reflected on the Danger to which she was expos'd; her sole Concern was for her beloved Zadig. At the same Time, he defended her, like a Lover, and a Man of Integrity and Courage. With the Assistance only of two domestic Servants, he put those Sons of Violence to Flight, and conducted Semira, bloody as she was, and in fainting Fits, to her own House. No sooner was she come to her self, but she fix'd her lovely Eyes on her Dear Deliverer. O Zadig, said she, I love thee as affectionately, as if I were actually thy Bride: I love thee, as the Man, to whom I owe my Life, and what is dearer to me, the Preservation of my Honour. No Heart sure could be more deeply smitten than that of Semira. Never did the Lips of the fairest Creature living utter softer Sounds; never did the most enamoured Lady breathe such tender Sentiments of Love and Gratitude for his signal Service; never, in short, did the most affectionate Bride express such Transports of Joy for the fondest Husband. Her Wounds, however, were but very superficial, and she was soon recover'd. Zadig receiv'd a Wound that was much more dangerous: An unlucky Arrow had graz'd one of his Eyes, and the Orifice was deep. Semira was incessant in her Prayers to the Gods that they might restore her Zadig. Her Eyes were Night and Day overwhelm'd with Tears. She waited with Impatience for the happy Moment, when those of Zadig might dart their Fires upon her; but alas! the wounded Eye grew so inflam'd and swell'd, that she was terrified to the last Degree. She sent as far as Memphis for Hermes, the celebrated Physician there, who instantly attended his new Patient with a numerous Retinue. Upon his first Visit, he peremptorily declared that Zadig would lose his Eye; and foretold not only the Day, but the very Hour when that woful Disaster would befal him. Had it been, said that Great Man, his right Eye, I could have administred an infallible Specific; but as it is, his Misfortune is beyond the Art of Man to cure. Tho' all Babylon pitied the hard Case of Zadig, they equally stood astonish'd at the profound Penetration of Hermes. Two Days after the Imposthume broke, without any Application, and Zadig soon after was perfectly recover'd. Hermes thereupon wrote a very long and elaborate Treatise, to prove that his Wound ought not to have been heal'd. Zadig, however, never thought it worth his while to peruse his learned Lucubrations; but, as soon as ever he could get abroad, determin'd to pay the Lady a Visit, who had testified such uncommon Concern for his Welfare, and for whose Sake alone he wish'd for the Restoration of his Sight. Semira he found had been out of Town for three Days; but was inform'd, by the bye, that his intended Spouse, having conceived an implacable Aversion to a one-ey'd Man, was that very Night to be married to Orcan. At this unexpected ill News, poor Zadig was perfectly thunder-struck: He laid his Disappointment so far to Heart, that in a short Time he was become a mere Skeleton, and was sick almost to death for some Months afterwards. At last, however, by Dint of Reflection, he got the better of his Distemper; and the Acuteness of the Pain he underwent, in some Measure, contributed towards his Consolation.

Since I have met with such an unexpected Repulse, said he, from a capricious Court-Lady, I am determin'd to marry some substantial Citizen's Daughter. He pitch'd accordingly upon Azora, a young Gentlewoman extremely well-bred, an excellent Oeconomist, and one, whose Parents were very rich.

Their Nuptials accordingly were soon after solemniz'd, and for a whole Month successively, no two Turtles were ever more fond of each other. In Process of Time, however, he perceiv'd she was a little Coquettish, and too much inclin'd to think, that the handsomest young Fellows were always the most virtuous and the greatest Wits.

2

THE NOSE

One Day Azora, as she was just return'd home from taking a short Country airing, threw herself into a violent Passion, and swell'd with Invectives. What, in God's Name, my Dear, said Zadig, has thus ruffled your Temper? What can be the Meaning of all these warm Exclamations? Alas! said she, you would have been disgusted as much as I am, had you been an Eye-witness of that Scene of Female Falshood, as I was Yesterday. I went, you must know, to visit the disconsolate Widow Cosrou, who has been these two Days erecting a Monument to the Memory of her young deceased Husband, near the Brook that runs on one side of her Meadow. She made the most solemn Vow, in the Height of her Affliction, never to stir from that Tomb, as long as ever that Rivulet took its usual Course.— Well! and wherein, pray, said Zadig, is the good Woman so much to blame? Is it not an incontestable Mark of her superior Merit and Conjugal-Affection? But, Zadig, said Azora, was you to know how her Thoughts were employ'd when I made my Visit, you'd never forget or forgive her. Pray, my dearest Azora, what then was she about? Why, the Creature, said Azora, was studying, to be sure, to find out Ways and Means to turn the Current of the River.

Azora, in short, harangu'd so long, and, was so big with her Invectives against the young Widow, that her too affected, vain Shew of Virtue, gave Zadig a secret Disgust.

Zadig had an intimate Friend, one Cador by Name, whose Spouse was perfectly honest, and had in reality a greater Regard for him, than all Mankind besides: This Friend Zadig made his Confident, and bound him to keep a Project of his entirely a Secret, by a Promise of some valuable Token of his Respect. Azora had been visiting a Female Companion for two Days together in the Country, and on the third was returning home: No sooner, however, was she in Sight of the House, but the Servants ran to meet her with Tears in their Eyes, and told her, that their Master dy'd suddenly the Night before; that they durstn't carry her the doleful Tidings, but were going to bury Zadig in the Sepulchre of his Ancestors, at the Bottom of the Garden. She burst into a Flood of Tears; tore her Hair; and vow'd to die by his Side. As soon as it was dark, young Cador came, and begg'd the Favour of being introduc'd to the Widow. He was so, and they wept together very cordially. Next Day the Storm was somewhat abated, and they din'd together; Cador inform'd her, that his Friend had left him the much greater Part of his Effects, and gave her to understand, that he should think himself the happiest Creature in the World, if she would condescend to be his Partner in that Demise. The Widow wept, sobb'd, and began to melt. More Time was spent in Supper than at Dinner. They discoursed together with a little more Freedom. Azora was lavish of her Encomiums on Zadig; but then, 'twas true, she said, he had some secret Infirmities to which Cador was a Stranger. In the Midst of their Midnight Entertainment, Cador all on a sudden complain'd that he was taken with a most violent pleuretic Fit, and was ready to swoon away. Our Lady being extremely concern'd, and over-officious, flew to her Closet of Cordials, and brought down every Thing she could think of that might be of Service on this emergent Occasion. She was extremely sorry that the famous Hermes was gone from Babylon, and condescended to lay her warm Hand upon the Part affected, in which he felt such an agonizing Pain. Pray Sir, said she, in a soft, languishing Tone, are you subject to this tormenting Malady? Sometimes, Madam, said Cador, so strong, that they bring me almost to Death's Door; and there is but one Thing can infallibly cure me; and that is, the Application of a dead Man's Nose to the part affected. An odd Remedy truly, said Azora. Not stranger, Madam, said he, than the Great Arnon's (There was at this Time in Babylon, a famous Doctor, nam'd Arnon, who both cur'd Apoplectic Fits, and prevented them from affecting his Patients, as was frequently advertiz'd in the Gazettes, by a little never-failing Purse that he hung round their Necks.) infallible Apoplectic Necklaces.

This Assurance of Success, together with Cador's personal Merit, determin'd Azora in his Favour. After all, said she, when my Husband shall be about to cross the Bridge Tchimavar, from this World of Yesterday, to the other, of To-morrow, will the Angel Asrael, think you, make any Scruple about his Passage, should his Nose prove something shorter in the next Life than 'twas in this? She would venture, however, and taking up a sharp Razor, repair'd to her Husband's Tomb; water'd it first with her Tears, and then intended to perform the innocent Operation, as he lay extended breathless, as she thought, in his Coffin. Zadig mounted in a Moment; secur'd his Nose with one Hand, and the Incision-Knife with the other. Madam, said he, never more exclaim against the Widow Cosrou. The Scheme for cutting my Nose off was much closer laid than hers of throwing the River into a new Channel.

3

THE DOG AND THE HORSE

Zadig found, by Experience, that the first thirty Days of Matrimony (as 'tis written in the Book of Zend) is Honey-Moon; but the second is all Wormwood. He was oblig'd, in short, as Azora grew such a Termagant, to sue out a Bill of Divorce, and to seek his Consolation for the future, in the Study of Nature. Who is happier, said he, than the Philosopher, who peruses with Understanding that spacious Book, which the supreme Being has laid open before his Eyes? The Truths he discovers there, are of infinite Service to him. He thereby cultivates and improves his Mind. He lives in Peace and Tranquility all his Days; he is afraid of Nobody, and he has no tender, indulgent Wife to shorten his Nose for him.

Wrapped up in these Contemplations, he retir'd to a little Country House on the Banks of the Euphrates; there he never spent his Time in calculating how many Inches of Water run thro' the Arch of a Bridge in a second of Time, or in enquiring if a Cube Line of Rain falls more in the Mouse-Month, than in that of the Ram. He form'd no Projects for making Silk Gloves and Stockings out of Spiders Webbs, nor of China-Ware out of broken Glass-Bottles; but he pry'd into the Nature and Properties of Animals and Plants, and soon, by his strict and repeated Enquiries, he was capable of discerning a Thousand Variations in visible Objects, that others, less curious, imagin'd were all alike.

One Day, as he was taking a solitary Walk by the Side of a Thicket, he espy'd one of the Queen's Eunuchs, with several of his Attendants, coming towards him, hunting about, in deep Concern, both here and there, like Persons almost in Despair, and seeking, with Impatience, for something lost of the utmost Importance. Young Man, said the Queen's chief Eunuch, have not you seen, pray, her Majesty's Dog? Zadig very cooly replied, you mean her Bitch, I presume. You say very right Sir, said the Eunuch, 'tis a Spaniel-Bitch indeed.—And very small said Zadig: She has had Puppies too lately; she's a little lame with her left Forefoot, and has long Ears. By your exact Description, Sir, you must doubtless have seen her, said the Eunuch, almost out of Breath. But I have not Sir, notwithstanding, neither did I know, but by you, that the Queen ever had such a favourite Bitch.

Just at this critical Juncture, so various are the Turns of Fortune's Wheel! the best Palfrey in all the King's Stable had broke loose from the Groom, and got upon the Plains of Babylon. The Head Huntsman with all his inferior Officers, were in Pursuit after him, with as much Concern, as the Eunuch about the Bitch. The Head Huntsman address'd himself to Zadig, and ask'd him, whether he hadn't seen the King's Palfrey run by him. No Horse, said Zadig, ever gallop'd smoother; he is about five Foot high, his Hoofs are very small; his Tail is about three Foot six Inches long; the studs of his Bit are of pure Gold, about 23 Carats; and his Shoes are of Silver, about Eleven penny Weight a-piece. What Course did he take, pray, Sir? Whereabouts is he, said the Huntsman? I never sat

Eyes on him, reply'd Zadig, not I, neither did I ever hear before now, that his Majesty had such a Palfrey.

The Head Huntsman, as well as the Head Eunuch, upon his answering their Interrogatories so very exactly, not doubting in the least, but that Zadig had clandestinely convey'd both the Bitch and the Horse away, secur'd him, and carried him before the grand Desterham, who condemn'd him to the Knout, and to be confin'd for Life in some remote and lonely Part of Siberia. No sooner had the Sentence been pronounc'd, but the Horse and Bitch were both found. The Judges were in some Perplexity in this odd Affair, and yet thought it absolutely necessary, as the Man was innocent, to recal their Decree. However, they laid a Fine upon him of Four Hundred Ounces of Gold, for his false Declaration of his not having seen, what doubtless he did: And the Fine was order'd to be deposited in Court accordingly: On the Payment whereof, he was permitted to bring his Cause on to a Hearing before the grand Desterham.

On the Day appointed for that Purpose he open'd the Cause himself, in Terms to this or the like Effect.

Ye bright Stars of Justice, ye profound Abyss of universal Knowledge, ye Mirrors of Eqity, who have in you the Solidity of Lead, the Hardness of Steel, the Lustre of a Diamond, and the Resemblance of the purest Gold! Since ye have condescended so far, as to admit of my Address to this August Assembly, I here, in the most solemn Manner, swear to you by Orosmades, that I never saw the Queen's illustrious Bitch, nor the sacred Palfrey of the King of Kings. I'll be ingenuous, however, and declare the Truth, and nothing but the Truth. As I was walking by the Thicket's Side, where I met with her Majesty's most venerable chief Eunuch, and the King's most illustrious chief Huntsman, I perceiv'd upon the Sand the Footsteps of an Animal, and I easily inferr'd that it must be a little one. The several small, tho' long Ridges of Land between the Footsteps of the Creature, gave me just Grounds to imagine it was a Bitch whose Teats hung down; and for that Reason, I concluded she had but lately pupp'd. As I observ'd likewise some other Traces, in some Degree different, which seem'd to have graz'd all the Way upon the Surface of the Sand, on the Side of the fore-Feet, I knew well enough she must have had long Ears. And forasmuch as I discern'd; with some Degree of Curiosity, that the Sand was every where less hollow'd by one Foot in particular, than by the other three, I conceiv'd that the Bitch of our most august Queen was somewhat lamish, if I may presume to say so.

As to the Palfrey of the King of Kings, give me leave to inform you, that as I was walking down the Lane by the Thicket-side, I took particular Notice of the Prints made upon the Sand by a Horse's Shoes; and found that their Distances were in exact Proportion; from that Observation, I concluded the Palfrey gallop'd well. In the next Place, the Dust of some Trees in a narrow Lane, which was but seven Foot broad, was here and there swept off, both on the Right and on the Left, about three Feet and six Inches from the Middle of the Road. For which Reason I pronounc'd the Tail of the Palfrey to be three Foot and a half long, with which he had whisk'd off the Dust on both Sides as he ran along. Again, I perceiv'd under the Trees, which form'd a Kind of Bower of five Feet high, some Leaves that had been lately fallen on the Ground, and I was sensible the Horse must have shook them off; from whence I conjectur'd he was five Foot high. As to the Bits of his Bridle, I knew they must be of Gold, and of the Value I mention'd; for he had rubb'd the Studs upon a certain Stone, which I knew to be a Touch-stone, by an Experiment that I had made of it. To conclude, by the Prints which his Shoes had left of some Flint-Stones of another Nature, I concluded his Shoes were Silver, and of eleven penny Weight Fineness, as I before mention'd.

The whole Bench of Judges stood astonish'd at the Profundity of Zadig's nice Discernment. The News was soon carried to the King and the Queen. Zadig was not only the whole Subject of the Court's Conversation; but his Name was mention'd with the utmost Veneration in the King's Chambers, and his Privy-Council. And notwithstanding several of their Magi declar'd he ought to be burnt for a Sorcerer; yet the King thought proper, that the Fine he had deposited in Court, should be peremptorily restor'd. The Clerk of the Court, the Tipstaffs, and other petty Officers, waited on him in their proper Habit, in order to refund the four Hundred Ounces of Gold, pursuant to the King's express Order; modestly reserving only three Hundred and ninety Ounces, part thereof, to defray the Fees of the Court. And the Domesticks swarm'd about him likewise, in Hopes of some small Consideration.

Zadig, upon winding up of the Bottom, was fully convinc'd, that it was very dangerous to be over-wise; and was determin'd to set a Watch before the Door of his Lips for the future.

An Opportunity soon offer'd for the Trial of his Resolution. A Prisoner of State had just made his Escape, and pass'd under the Window of Zadig's House. Zadig was examin'd thereupon, but was absolutely dumb. However, as it was plainly prov'd upon him, that he did look out of the Window at the same Time, he was sentenc'd to pay five Hundred Ounces of Gold for that Misdemeanor; and moreover, was oblig'd to thank the Court for their Indulgence; a Compliment which the Magistrates of Babylon expect to be paid them. Good God! said he, to himself, have I not substantial Reason to complain, that my impropitious Stars should direct me to walk by a Wood's-Side, where the Queen's Bitch and the King's Palfrey should happen to pass by? How dangerous is it to pop one's Head out of one's Window? And, in a Word, how difficult is it for a Man to be happy on this Side the Grave?

4

THE ENVIOUS MAN

As Zadig had met with such a Series of Misfortunes, he was determin'd to ease the Weight of them by the Study of Philosophy, and the Conversation of select Friends. He was still possess'd of a little pretty Box in the Out-parts of Babylon, which was furnish'd in a good Taste; where every Artist was welcome, and wherein he enjoy'd all the rational Pleasures that a virtuous Man could well wish for. In the Morning, his Library was always open for the Use of the Learned; at Night his Table was fill'd with the most agreeable Companions; but he was soon sensible, by Experience, how dangerous it was to keep learned Men Company. A warm Dispute arose about a certain Law of Zoroaster; which prohibited the Eating of Griffins: But to what Purpose said some of the Company, was that Prohibition, since there is no such Animal in Nature? Some again insisted that there must; for otherwise Zoroaster could never have been so weak as to give his Pupils such a Caution. Zadig, in order to compromize the Matter, said; Gentlemen, If there are such Creatures in Being, let us never touch them; and if there are not, we are well assur'd we can't touch them; so in either Case we shall comply with the Commandment.

A learned Man at the upper End of the Table, who had compos'd thirteen Volumes, expatiating on every Property of the Griffin, took this Affair in a very serious Light, which would greatly have embarrass'd Zadig, but for the Credit of a Magus, who was Brother to his Friend Cador. From that Day forward, Zadig ever distinguish'd and preferr'd good, before learned Company: He associated with the most conversible Men, and the most amiable Ladies in all Babylon; he made elegant Entertainments, which were frequently preceded by a Concert of Musick, and enliven'd by the most facetious Conversation, in which, as he had felt the Smart of it, he had laid aside all Thoughts of shewing his Wit, which is not only the surest Proof that a Man has none, but the most infallible Means to spoil all good Company.

Neither the Choice of his Friends, nor that of his Dishes, was the Result of Pride or Ostentation. He took Delight in appearing to be, what he actually was, and not in seeming to be what he was not; and by that Means, got a greater real Character than he actually aim'd at.

Directly opposite to his House liv'd Arimazes, one puff'd up with Pride, who not meeting with Success in the World, sought his Revenge in railing against all Mankind. Rich as he was, it was almost more than he could accomplish, to procure ev'n any Parasites about him. Tho' the rattling of the Chariots which stopp'd at Zadig's Door was a perfect Nuisance to him; yet the good Character which every Body gave him was still a higher Provocation. He would sometimes intrude himself upon Zadig, and set down at his Table without any Invitation; when there, he would most certainly interrupt the Mirth of the Company, as Harpies, they say, infect the very Carrion that they eat.

Arimazes took it in his Head one Day to invite a young Lady to an Entertainment; but she, instead of accepting of his Offer, spent the Evening at Zadig's. Another Time, as Zadig and he were chatting together at Court, a Minister of State came up to them, and invited Zadig to Supper, but took no Notice of Arimazes. The most implacable Aversions have frequently no better Foundations. This Gentleman, who was call'd the *envious Man*, would have taken away the Life of Zadig if he could because most People distinguish'd him by the Title of the Happy Man. "An Opportunity of doing Mischief, says Zoroaster, offers itself a hundred Times a Day; but that of doing a Friend a good Office but once a Year."

Arimazes went one Day to Zadig's House, when he was walking in his Garden with two Friends, and a young Lady, to whom he said Abundance of fine Things, with no other Design but the innocent Pleasure of saying them. Their Conversation turn'd on a War that the King had happily put an End to, between him and his Vassal, the Prince of Hyrcania. Zadig having signaliz'd himself in that short War, commended his Majesty very highly, but was more lavish of his Compliments on the Lady. He took out his Pocket Book, and wrote four extempore Verses on that Occasion, and gave them the Lady to read. The Gentlemen then present begg'd to be oblig'd with a Sight of them, as well as the Lady, But either thro' Modesty, or rather a self-Consciousness that he hadn't happily succeeded, he gave them a flat Denial. He was sensible, that a sudden poetic Flight must prove insipid to every one but the Person in whose Favour it is written, whereupon he snapt the Table in two whereon the Lines were wrote, and threw both Pieces into a Rose-bush, where they were hunted for, but to no Purpose. Soon after it happened to rain, and all the Company flew into the House, but Arimazes. Notwithstanding the Shower, he continued in the Garden, and never quitted it, till he had found one Moiety of the Tablet, which was unfortunately broke in such a Manner, that even the half Lines were good sense, and good Metre, tho' very short. But what was still more remarkably unfortunate, they appear'd at first View, to be a severe satyr upon the King: The Words were these:

> To flagrant Crimes
> His Crown he owes;
> To peaceful Times
> The worst of Foes.

This was the first Moment that ever Arimazes was happy. He had it now in his Power to ruin the most virtuous and innocent of Men. Big with his execrable Joy, he flew to his Majesty with this virulent Satyr of Zadig's under his own Hand. Not only Zadig, but his two Friends and the Lady were immediately close confin'd. His Cause was soon over; for the Judges turn'd a deaf Ear to what he had to say. When Sentence of Condemnation was pass'd upon him, Arimazes, still spiteful, was heard to say, as he went out of Court, with an Air of Contempt, that Zadig's Lines were Treason indeed, but nothing more. Tho' Zadig didn't value himself on Account of his Genius for Poetry; yet he was almost distracted to find himself condemn'd for the worst of Traitors, and his two Friends and the Lady lock'd up in a Dungeon for a Crime, of which he was no ways guilty. He wasn't permitted to speak one Word for himself. His Pocket-Book was sufficient Evidence against him. So strict were the Laws of Babylon! He was carried to the Place of Execution, through a Croud of Spectators, who durstn't condole with him, and who flock'd about him, to observe whether his Countenance chang'd, or whether he died with a good Grace. His Relations were the only real Mourners; for there was no Estate in Reversion for them; three Parts of his Effects were confiscated for the King's Use, and the fourth was devoted, as a Reward, to the use of the Informer.

Just at the Time that he was preparing himself for Death, the King's Parrot flew from her Balcony, into Zadig's Garden, and alighted on a Rose-bush. A Peach, that had been blown down, and drove by the Wind from an adjacent Tree, just under the Bush, was glew'd, as it were, to the other Moiety of the Tablet. Away flew the Parrot with her Booty, and return'd to the King's Lap. The Monarch, being somewhat curious, read the Words on the broken Tablet, which had no Meaning in them as he could perceive, but seem'd to be the broken Parts of a Tetrastick. He was a great Admirer of Poetry; and the odd Adventure of his Parrot, put him upon Reflection. The Queen who recollected full well the Lines that were wrote on the Fragment of Zadig's Tablet, order'd that Part of it to be produc'd: Both the broken Pieces being put together, they answered exactly the Indentures; and then the Verses which Zadig had written, in a Flight of Loyalty, ran thus,

> Tyrants are prone to flagrant Crimes;
> To Clemency his Crown he owes;
> To Concord and to peaceful Times,
> Love only is the worst of Foes.

Upon this the King order'd Zadig to be instantly brought before him; and his two Friends and the Lady to be that Moment discharg'd. Zadig, as he stood before the King and Queen, fix'd his Eyes upon the Ground, and begg'd their Majesty's Pardon for his little worthless, poetical Attempt. He spoke, however, with such a becoming Grace, and with so much Modesty and good Sense, that the King and the Queen, ordered him to be brought before them once again. He was brought accordingly, and he pleas'd them still more and more. In short, they gave him all the immense Estate of Arimazes, who had so unjustly accus'd him; but Zadig generously return'd the wicked Informer the Whole to a Farthing. The envious Man, however, was no ways affected, but with the Restoration of his Effects. Zadig every Day grew more and more in Favour at Court. He was made a Party in all the King's Pleasures, and nothing was done in the Privy-Council without him. The Queen, from that very Hour, shew'd him so much Respect, and spoke to him in such soft and endearing Terms, that in Process of Time, it prov'd of fatal Consequence to herself, her Royal Consort, to Zadig, and the whole Kingdom. Zadig now began to think it was not so difficult a Thing to be happy as at first he imagin'd.

5

THE FORCE OF GENEROSITY

The Time now drew near for the Celebration of a grand Festival, which was kept but once in five Years. 'Twas a constant Custom in Babylon at the Expiration of the Term abovemention'd, to distinguish that Citizen from all the Rest, in the most solemn Manner, who had done the most generous Action; and the Grandees and Magi always sat as Judges. The Satrap inform'd them of every praise-worthy Deed that occurr'd within his District. All were put to the Vote, and the King himself pronounc'd the Definitive Sentence. People of all Ranks and Degrees came from the remotest Part of the Kingdom to be present at this Solemnity. The Victor, whoever he was, receiv'd from the King's own Hand a golden Cup, enrich'd with precious Stones, and upon the Delivery, the King made use of the following Salutation. Receive this Reward of your Generosity, and may the Gods grant me Thousands of such valuable Subjects!

Upon this memorable Day, the King appear'd in all the Pomp imaginable on his Throne of State, surrounded by his Grandees, the Magi, and the Deputies, from all the surrounding Nations, of every Province that attended these public Sports, where Honour was to be acquir'd, not by the Velocity of the best Race-Horse, or by bodily Strength, but by intrinsic Merit. The principal Satrap proclaim'd, with an audible Voice, such Actions as would entitle the Victor to the inestimable Prize; but never mention'd one Word of Zadig's Greatness of Soul, in returning his invidious Neighbour all his Estate, notwithstanding he would have taken away his Life: That was but a Trifle, and not worth speaking of.

The first that was set up for the Prize, was a Judge, that had occasion'd a Citizen to lose a very considerable Cause, through some Mistake, for which he was no ways responsible, and made him Restitution out of his private Purse.

The next Candidate was a Youth, that tho' violently in Love with one that he intended shortly to make his Spouse, yet resign'd her to his Friend, who was just expiring at her Feet; and moreover, gave her a Portion at the same Time.

After this appear'd a Soldier, who, in the Hyrcanian War, had done a much more glorious Action than the Lover. A Gang of Hyrcanians having taken his Mistress from him, he fought them bravely, and rescued her out of their Hands: Soon after, he was inform'd, that another Band of the same Party had hurried away his Mother to a Place not far distant; he left his Mistress, all drown'd in Tears, and ran to his Mother's Assistance: After that Skirmish was over, he returned to his Sweet-heart, and found her just expiring. He would fain have plung'd a Dagger into his Heart that Moment; but his Mother remonstrated to him, that, should he die, she should be entirely helpless, and upon that Account only he had Courage to live a little longer.

The Judges seem'd very much inclin'd to give their Votes for the Soldier; but the King prevented them, by saying, that the Soldier's Action was praise-worthy enough, and so were those of the rest, but none of them give me any Surprize. What Zadig did Yesterday perfectly struck me with Astonishment. I'll mention another Instance. I had some few Days ago, as a Testimony of my Resentment, banish'd my Prime-Minister, and Favourite Coreb from the Court. I complain'd of his Conduct in the warmest Terms; and all my Sycophants about me, told me that I was too merciful; and loaded him with the sharpest Invectives. I ask'd Zadig what his Opinion was of Coreb; and he dar'd to give him the best of Characters. I must confess, I have read in our publick Records, indeed, of Instances where Restitution have been generally made, for Injuries committed by Mistake; where a Mistress has been resign'd; and where a Mother has been preferr'd to a Mistress; but I never read of a Courtier, that would speak to the Advantage of a Minister in Disgrace, and against whom the Sovereign was highly incens'd. I'll give 20,000 Pieces of Gold to every Candidate that has been this Day proclaim'd, but I'll give the Cup to no one but Zadig.

Sire, said Zadig, 'tis your Majesty alone, that deserves the Cup; 'tis you alone who have done an Action of Generosity, never heard of before; since you, who are King of Kings, wasn't exasperated against your Slave, when he contradicted you in the Heat of your Passion. Every Body gaz'd with Eyes of Admiration on the King and Zadig. The Judge, who had generously made Restitution for his Error; the Lover, who had married his Mistress to his Friend; the Soldier, who had preferr'd the Welfare of his Mother to that of his Mistress; received the promis'd Donation from the Monarch, and saw their Names register'd in the Book of Fame: But Zadig had the Cup. The King got the universal Character of a good Prince, which he did not long preserve. This joyful Day was solemniz'd with Festivals beyond the Time by Law establish'd. Tragedies were acted there that drew Tears from the Spectators; and Comedies that made them laugh; Entertainments, that the Babylonians were perfect Strangers to: The Commemoration of it is still preserv'd in Asia. Now, said Zadig, I am happy at last; but he was grosly mistaken.

6

THE JUDGMENTS

Young as Zadig was, he was constituted chief Judge of all the Tribunals throughout the Empire. He fill'd the Place, like one, whom the Gods had endow'd with the strictest Justice, and the most solid Wisdom. It was to him, the Nations round about were indebted for that generous Maxim; that 'tis much more Prudence to acquit two Persons, tho' actually guilty, than to pass Sentence of Condemnation in one that is virtuous and innocent. It was his firm Opinion, that the Laws were intended to be a Praise to those who did well, as much as to be a Terror to Evildoers. It was his peculiar Talent to render Truth as obvious as possible: Whereas most Men study to render it intricate and obscure. On the very first Day of his Entrance into his High Office, he exerted this peculiar Talent. A rich Merchant, and a Native of Babylon, died in the Indies. He had made his Will, and appointed his two Sons Joint-Heirs of his Estate, as soon as they had settled their Sister, and married her with their mutual Approbation. Moreover, he left a specific Legacy of 30,000 Pieces of Gold to that Son, who should, after his Decease, be prov'd to love him best. The Eldest erected to his Memory a very costly Monument: The Youngest appropriated a considerable Part of his Bequest to the Augmentation of his Sister's Fortune: Every one, without Hesitation, gave the Preference to the Elder, allowing the Younger to have the greatest Affection for his Sister. The Legacy therefore was doubtless due to the Eldest.

Their Cause came before Zadig, and he examin'd them apart. To the former, said Zadig, Your Father, Sir, is not dead, as is reported, but being happily recover'd, is on his Return to Babylon. God be praised, said the young Man! but I hope the Expence I have been at in raising this superb Monument will be consider'd. After this, Zadig repeated the same Story to the Younger. God be praised, said he! I will immediately restore all that he has left me; but I hope my

Father will not recal the little Present I have made my Sister. You have nothing to restore, Sir; you shall have the Legacy of the thirty thousand Pieces; for 'tis you that have the greatest Veneration for your deceased Father.

A young Lady that was very rich, had entred into a Marriage-Contract with two Magis; and having receiv'd Instructions from both Parties for some Months, she prov'd with Child. They were both ready and willing to marry her. But, said she, he shall be my Husband, that has put me into a Capacity of serving my Country, by adding one to it. 'Tis I, Madam, that have answered that valuable End, said one; but the other insisted 'twas his Operation. Well! said she, since this is a Moot-point, I'll acknowledge him for the Father of the Child, that will give him the most liberal Education. In a short Time after, my Lady was brought to Bed of a hopeful Boy. Each of them insisted on being Tutor, and the Cause was brought before Zadig. The two Magi were order'd to appear in Court. Pray Sir, said Zadig to the first, what Method of Instruction do you propose to pursue for the Improvement of your young Pupil? He shall first be grounded, said this learned Pedagogue, in the Eight Parts of Speech; then I'll teach him Logic, Astrology, Magick, the wide Difference between the Terms Substance and Accident, Abstract and Concrete, &c. &c. As for my Part, Sir, I shall take another Course, said the second; I'll do my utmost to make him an honest Man, and acceptable to his Friends. Upon this, Zadig said, you, Sir, shall marry the Mother, let who will be the Father.

There came daily Complaints to Court against the Itimadoulet of Media, whose Name was Irax. He was a Person of Quality, who was possess'd of a very considerable Estate, notwithstanding he had squander'd away a great Part of it, by indulging himself in all Manner of expensive Pleasures. It was but seldom that an Inferior was suffer'd to speak to him; but not a Soul durst contradict him: No Peacock was more gay; no Turtle more amorous; and no Tortoise more indolent and inactive. He made false Glory and false Pleasures his sole Pursuit.

Zadig, undertaking to cure him, sent him forthwith, as by express Order from the King, a Musick-Master with twelve Voices, and 24 Violins, as his Attendants; a Head Steward, with six Men Cooks, and 4 Chamberlains, who were never to be out of his Sight. The King issued out his Writ for the punctual Observance of his Royal Will; and thus the Affair proceeded.

The first Morning, as soon as the voluptuous Irax had open'd his Eyes, his Musick-Master, with the Voices and Violins, entred his Apartment. They sang a Cantata, that lasted two Hours and three Minutes. Every three Minutes the Chorus, or Burthen of the Song, was to this Effect.

Tisn't in Words to speak your Praise;
What mighty Honours are your Due!
To worth like yours we Altars raise,
No Monarch's happier, Sir, than you.

After the Cantata was over, the Chamberlain address'd him in a formal Harangue for three Quarters of an Hour without ceasing; wherein he took Occasion to extol every Virtue to which he was a perfect Stranger; when the Oration was over, he was conducted to Dinner, where the Musicians were all in waiting, and play'd, as soon as he was seated at his Table. Dinner lasted three Hours before he condescended to speak a Word. When he did; you say Right, Sir, said the chief Chamberlain; scarce had he utter'd four Words more, but Right, Sir, said the second. The other two Chamberlain's Time was taken up in laughing with Admiration at Irax's Smart Repartees, or at least such as he ought to have made. After the Cloth was taken away, the adulating Chorus was repeated.

This first Day Irax was all in Raptures; he imagin'd, that this Honour done him by the King of Kings, was the sole Result of his exalted Merit. The second wasn't altogether so agreeable; The third prov'd somewhat troublesome; the fourth insupportable; the fifth was tormenting; and at last, he was perfectly outrageous at the continual Peal in his Ears of No Monarch's happier Sir, than you, You say right, &c. and at being daily harangu'd at the same Hour. Whereupon he wrote to Court, and begg'd of his Majesty to recal his Chamberlain, his Musick-Master, and all his Retinue, his Head Steward and his Cooks, and promis'd, in the most submissive Manner, to be less vain, and more industrious for the future. Tho' he didn't require so much Adulations, nor such grand Entertainments, he was much more happy; for, as Sadder has it, One continued Scene of Pleasure, is no Pleasure at all.

Zadig every Day gave incontestable Proofs of his wondrous Penetration, and the Goodness of his Heart; he was ador'd by the People, and was the Darling of the King. The little Difficulties that he met with in the first Stage of his Life, serv'd only to augment his present Felicity. Every Night, however, he had some unlucky Dream or another, that gave him some Disturbance. One while, he imagin'd himself extended on a Bed of wither'd Plants, amongst which there were some that were sharp pointed, and made him very restless and uneasy; another Time, he fancied himself repos'd on a Bed of Roses, out of which rush'd a Serpent, that stung him to the Heart with his envenom'd Tongue. Alas! said he, waking, I was one while upon a Bed of hard and nauseous Plants, and just this Moment repos'd on a Bed of Roses. But then the Serpent.

7

THE FORCE OF JEALOUSY

The Misfortunes that attended Zadig proceeded, in a great Measure, from his Preferment; but more from his intrinsic Merit. Every Day he had familiar Converse with the King, his Royal Master, and his august Consort, Astarte. And the Pleasure arising from thence was greatly enhanc'd from an innate Ambition of pleasing, which, in regard to Wit, is the same, as Dress is to Beauty. His Youth, and graceful Deportment, had a greater Influence on Astarte, than she was at first aware of. Tho' her Affection for him daily encreas'd;

yet she was perfectly innocent. Astarte would say, without the least Reserve or Apprehension of Fear, that she was extreamly pleas'd with the Company of one, who was, not only a Favourite of her Husband, but the Darling of the whole Empire. She was continually speaking in his Commendation before the King: He was the Subject of her whole Discourse amongst her Ladies of Honour, who were as lavish of their Praises as herself. Such repeated Discourses, however innocent, made a deeper Impression on her Heart, than she at that Time apprehended. She would every now and then send Zadig some little Present or another; which he construed as the Result of a greater Value for him than she intended. She said no more of him, as she thought, than a Queen might innocently do, who was perfectly assur'd of his Attachment to her Husband; sometimes, indeed, she would express her self with an Air of Tenderness and Affection.

Astarte was much handsomer than either his Mistress Semira, who had such a natural Antipathy to a one-eyed Lord, or Azora, his late loving Spouse, that would innocently have cut his Nose off. The Freedoms which Astarte took, her tender Expressions, at which she began to blush, the Glances of her Eye, which she would turn away, if perceiv'd, and which she fix'd upon his, kindled in the Heart of Zadig a Fire, which struck him with Amazement. He did all he could to smother it; he call'd up all the Philosophy he was Master of to his Aid; but all in vain, for no Consolation arose from those Reflections.

Duty, Gratitude, and an injur'd Monarch, presented themselves before his Eyes, as avenging Deities: He bravely struggled; he triumph'd indeed; but this Conquest over his Passions, which he was oblig'd to check every Moment, cost him many a deep Sigh and Tear. He durst not talk with the Queen any more, with that Freedom which was too engaging on both Sides; his Eyes were obnubilated; his Discourse was forc'd and unconnected; he turn'd his Eyes another Way; and when, against his Inclination, they met with those of the Queen, he found, that tho' drown'd in Tears, they darted Flames of Fire: They seem'd in Silence to intimate, that they were afraid of being in love with each other; and that both burn'd with a Fire which both condemn'd.

Zadig flew from her Presence, like one beside himself, and in Despair; his Heart was over-charg'd with a Burthen, too great for him to bear: In the Heat of his Conflicts, he disclos'd the Secrets of his Heart to his trusty Friend Cador, as one, who, having long groan'd under the Weight of an inexpressible Anguish of Mind, at once makes known the Cause of his Torments by the Groans, as it were, extorted from him, and by the Drops of a cold Sweat, that trickled down his Cheeks.

Cador said to him; 'tis now some considerable Time since, I have discover'd that secret Passion which you have foster'd in your Bosom, and yet endeavour'd to conceal even from your self. The Passions carry along with them such strong Impressions, that they cannot be conceal'd. Tell me ingenuously Zadig; and be your own Accuser, whether or no, since I have made this Discovery, the King has not shewn some visible Marks of his Resentment. He has no other Foible, but that of being the most jealous Mortal breathing. You take more Pains to check the Violence of your Passion, than the Queen herself does; because you are a Philosopher; because, in short, you are Zadig; Astarte is but a weak Woman; and tho' her Eyes speak too visibly, and with too much Imprudence; yet she does not think her self blame-worthy. Being conscious of her Innocence, to her own Misfortune, as well as yours, she is too unguarded. I tremble for her; because I am sensible her Conscience acquits her. Were you both agreed, you might conceal your Regard for each other from all the World: A rising Passion, that is smother'd, breaks out into a Flame; Love, when once gratified, knows how to conceal itself with Art. Zadig shudder'd at the Proposition of ungratefully violating the Bed of his Royal Benefactor; and never was there a more loyal Subject to a Prince, tho' guilty of an involuntary Crime. The Queen, however, repeated the Name of Zadig so often, and her Cheeks glow'd with such a red, when ever she utter'd it; she was one while so transported, and at another, so dejected, when the Discourse turn'd upon him in the King's Presence; she was in such a Reverie, so confus'd and stupid, when he went out of the Presence, that her Deportment made the King extremely uneasy. He was convinc'd of every Thing he saw, and form'd in his Mind an Idea of a thousand Things he did not see. He observ'd, particularly, that Astarte's Sandals were blue; so Zadig's were blue likewise; that as the Queen wore yellow Ribbands, Zadig's Turbet was of the same Colour: These were shocking Circumstances for a Monarch of his Cast of Mind to reflect on! To a Mind, in short, so distemper'd as his was, Suspicions were converted into real Facts.

All Court Slaves, and Sycophants, are so many Spies on Kings and Queens: They soon discover'd that Astarte was fond, and Moabdar jealous. Arimazius, his envious Foe, who was as incorrigible as ever; for Flints will never soften; and Creatures, that are by Nature venemous, forever retain their Poison. Arimazius, I say, wrote an anonymous Letter to Moabdar, the infamous Recourse of sordid Spirits, who are the Objects of universal Contempt; but in this Case, an Affair of the last Importance; because this Letter tallied with the baneful Suggestions that Monarch had conceiv'd. In short, his Thoughts were now wholly bent upon Revenge. He determin'd to poison Astarte on a certain Night, and to have Zadig strangled by Break of Day. Orders for that Purpose were expressly given to a merciless, inhuman Eunuch, the ready Executioner of his Vengeance. At that critical Conjuncture, there happen'd to be a Dwarf, who was dumb, but not deaf, in the King's Apartment. Nobody regarded him: He was an Eye and Ear-witness of all that pass'd, and yet no more suspected than any irrational Domestic Animal. This little Dwarf had conceiv'd a peculiar Regard for Astarte and Zadig: He heard, with equal Horror and Surprize, the King's Orders to destroy them both. But how to prevent those Orders from being put into Execution, as the Time was so short, was all his Concern. He could not write, 'tis true, but he had luckily learnt to draw, and take a Likeness. He spent a good Part of the Night in delineating with Crayons, on a Piece of Paper, the imminent Danger that thus attended the Queen. In one Corner, he represented the King highly incens'd, and giving his cruel Eunuch the fatal Orders; in another, a Bowl and a Cord upon a Table; in the Center was the Queen, expiring in the Arms of her Maids of Honour, with Zadig strangled, and laid dead at her Feet. In the Horizon was the rising Sun, to denote, that this execrable Scene was to be exhibited by Break of Day. No sooner was his Design finish'd, but he ran with it to one of Astarte's Female Favourites, then in waiting, call'd her up, and gave her to understand, that she must carry the Draught to Astarte that very Moment.

In the mean Time, the Queen's Attendants, tho' it was Dead of Night, knock'd at the Door of Zadig's Apartment, wak'd him, and deliver'd into his Hands a Billet from the Queen. At first he could not well tell whether he was only in a Dream or not, but soon read the Letter, with a trembling Hand, and a heavy Heart: Words can't express his Surprise, and the Agonies of Despair which he was in upon his perusal of the Contents. Fly, said she, Dear Zadig, this very Moment; for your Life's in the utmost Danger: Fly, Dear Zadig, I conjure you, in the Name of that fatal Passion, with which I have long struggled, and which I now venture to discover, as I am to make Atonement for it, in a few Moments, by the Loss of my Life. Tho' I am conscious to myself of my Innocence, I find I am to feel the Weight of my Husband's Resentment, and die the Death of a Traitor.

Zadig was scarce able to speak. He order'd his Friend Cador to be instantly call'd, and gave him the Letter the Moment he came, without opening his Lips. Cador press'd him to regard the Contents, and to make the best of his Way to Memphis. If you presume, said he, to have an Interview with her Majesty first, you inevitably hasten her Execution; or if you wait upon the King, the fatal Consequence will be the same: I'll prevent her unhappy Fate, if possible; you follow but your own: I'll give it out, that you are gone to the Indies: I'll wait on you as soon as the Hurricane is blown over, and I'll let you know all that occurs material in Babylon.

Cador, that Instant, order'd two of the fleetest Dromedaries that could be got, to be in readiness at a private Back-Door belonging to the Court; he help'd Zadig to mount his Beast, tho' ready to drop into the Earth. He had but one trusty Servant to attend him, and Cador, overwhelm'd with Grief, soon lost Sight of his dearly beloved Friend.

This illustrious Fugitive soon reach'd the Summit of a little Hill, that afforded him a fair Prospect of the whole City of Babylon: But turning his Eyes back towards the Queen's Palace, he fainted away; and when he had recover'd his Senses, he drown'd his Eyes in a Flood of Tears, and with Impatience wish'd for Death. To conclude, after he had reflected, with Horror, on the deplorable Fate of the most amiable Creature in the Universe, and of the most meritorious Queen that ever liv'd; he for a Moment commanded his Passion, and with a Sigh, made the following Exclamations: What is this mortal Life! O Virtue, Virtue, of what Service hast thou been to me! Two young Ladies, a Mistress, and a Wife, have prov'd false to me; a third, who is perfectly innocent, and ten thousand Times handsomer than either of them, has suffer'd Death, 'tis probable, before this, on my Account! All the Acts of Benevolence which I have shewn, have been the Foundation of my Sorrows, and I have been only rais'd to the highest Spoke of Fortune's Wheel, for no other Purpose than to be tumbled down with the greater Force. Had I been as abandon'd as some Miscreants are, I had like them been happy. His Head thus overwhelm'd with these melancholy Reflections, his Eyes thus sunk in his Head, and his meagre Cheeks all pale and languid; and, in a Word, his very Soul thus plung'd in the Abyss of deep Despair, he pursu'd his Journey towards Egypt.

8

THE THRASH'D WIFE

Zadig steer'd his Course by the Stars that shone over his Head. The Constellation of Orion, and the radiant Dog-star directed him towards the Pole of Canope. He reflected with Admiration on those immense Globes of Light, which appear'd to the naked Eye no more than little twinkling Lights; whereas the Earth he was then traversing, which, in Reality, is no more than an imperceptible Point in Nature, seem'd, according to the selfish Idea we generally entertain of it, something very immense, and very magnificent. He then reflected on the whole Race of Mankind, and look'd upon them, as they are in Fact, a Parcel of Insects, or Reptiles, devouring one another on a small Atom of Clay. This just Idea of them greatly alleviated his Misfortunes, recollecting the Nothingness, if we may be allow'd the Expression, of his own Being, and even of Babylon itself. His capacious Soul now soar'd into Infinity, and he contemplated, with the same Freedom, as if she was disencumber'd from her earthly Partner, on the immutable Order of the Universe. But as soon as she cower'd her Wings, and resumed her native Seat, he began to consider that Astarte might possibly have lost her Life for his Sake; upon which, his Thoughts of the Universe vanish'd all at once, and no other Objects appear'd before his distemper'd Eyes, but his Astarte giving up the Ghost, and himself overwhelm'd with a Sea of Troubles: As he gave himself up to this Flux and Reflux of sublime Philosophy and Anxiety of Mind, he was insensibly arriv'd on the Frontiers of Egypt: And his trusty Attendant had, unknown to him, stept into the first Village, and sought out for a proper Apartment for his Master and himself. Zadig in the mean Time made the best of his Way to the adjacent Gardens; where he saw, not far distant from the High-way, a young Lady, all drown'd in Tears, calling upon Heaven and Earth for Succour in her Distress, and a Man, fir'd with Rage and Resentment, in pursuit after her. He had now just overtaken her, and she fell prostrate at his Feet imploring his Forgiveness. He loaded her with a thousand Reproaches; nor did he spare to chastise her in the most outrageous Manner. By the Egyptian's cruel Deportment towards her, he concluded that the Man was a jealous Husband, and that the Lady was an Inconstant, and had defil'd his Bed: But when he reflected, that the Woman was a perfect Beauty, and to his thinking something like the unfortunate Astarte, he perceiv'd his Heart yearn with Compassion towards the Lady, and swell with Indignation against her Tyrant. For Heaven's sake, Sir, assist me, said she, to Zadig, sobbing as if her Heart would break, Oh! deliver me out of the Hands of this Barbarian: Save, Sir, O save my Life. Upon these her shocking Outcries, Zadig threw himself between the injur'd Lady and the inexorable Brute. And as he had some smattering of the Egyptian Tongue, he expostulated with him in his own Dialect, and said: Dear Sir, if you are endow'd with the least Spark of Humanity, let me conjure you to have some Pity and Remorse for so beautiful a Creature; have some Regard, Sir, to the Weakness of her Sex. How can you treat a Lady, who is one of Nature's Master-pieces, in such a rude and outrageous Manner, one who lies weeping at your Feet for Forgiveness, and one who has no other Recourse than her Tears for her Defence? Oh! Oh! said the jealous-pated Fellow in a Fury to Zadig, What! You are one of her Gallants, I suppose. I'll be reveng'd of thee, thou Villain, this Moment. No sooner were the Words out of his Mouth, but he quits hold of the Lady, in whose Hair he had twisted his Fingers before, takes up his Lance in a Fury, and endeavours to the utmost of his Pow'r to plunge it in the Stranger's Heart: Zadig, however, being cool, warded the intended Blow with Ease. He laid fast hold of his Lance towards the Point. One strove to recover it, and the other to snatch it away by Force. They broke it between them. Whereupon the Egyptian drew his Sword. Zadig drew his: They fought: The former made a hundred rash Passes one after another, which the latter parried with the utmost Dexterity. The Lady sat herself upon a Grass-plat, adjusting her Head-dress, and looking on the Combatants. The Egyptian was too strong for Zadig, but Zadig was more nimble and active. The latter fought as a Man whose Hand was guided by his Head; the former as a Mad-man who dealt about his Blows at random. Zadig took the Advantage, made a Plunge at him, and disarm'd him. And forasmuch as he found that the Egyptian was hotter than ever, and endeavour'd all he could to throw him down by Dint of Strength, Zadig laid fast hold of him, flew upon him, and tripp'd up his Heels: After that, holding the Point of his Sword to his Breast, like a Man of Honour, gave him his Life. The Egyptian, fir'd with Rage, and having no Command of his Passion, drew his Dagger, and wounded Zadig like a Coward, whilst the Victor generously forgave him. Upon that unexpected Action, Zadig, being incens'd to the last Degree, plung'd his Sword deep into his Bosom. The Egyptian fetch'd a hideous Groan, and died upon the Spot. Zadig then approach'd the Lady, and with a kind of Concern, in the softest Terms told her, that he was oblig'd to kill her Insulter, tho' against his Inclinations. I have aveng'd your Cause, and deliver'd you out of the merciless Hands of the most outrageous Man I ever saw. Now, Madam, let me know your farther Will and Pleasure with me. You shall die, you Villain! You have murder'd my Love. Oh! I could tear your Heart out. Indeed, Madam, said Zadig, you had one of the most hot-headed, oddest Lovers I ever saw. He beat you most unmercifully, and would have taken away my Life because you call'd me in to your Assistance. Would to God he was but alive to beat me again, said she, blubbering and roaring; I deserv'd to be beat. I gave him too just Occasion to be jealous of me. Would to God that he had beat me, and you had died in his Stead! Zadig more astonish'd, and more exasperated than ever he was in all his Life, said to her: Really, Madam, you put on such extravagant Airs, that you tempt me, pretty as you are, to thresh you most cordially in my Turn; but I scorn to concern my self any more about you. Upon this, he remounted his Dromedary, and made the best of his Way towards the Village: But before he had got near a hundred Yards, he return'd upon an Out-cry that was made by four Couriers from Babylon. They rode full Speed. One of them, spying the young Widow, cried out. There she is, That's she. She answers in every Respect to the Description we had of her. They never took the least Notice of her dead Gallant, but secur'd her directly. Oh! Sir, cried she to Zadig, again and again, dear Sir, most generous Stranger, once more deliver me from a Pack of Villains. I most humbly beg your Pardon for my late Conduct and unjust Complaint of you. Do but stand my Friend, at this critical Conjuncture, and I'll be your most obedient Vassal till Death. Zadig had now no Inclination to fight for one so undeserving any more. Find some other to be your Fool now, Madam; you shan't impose upon me a second Time. I'll assure you, Madam, I know better Things. Besides he was wounded; and bled so fast that he wanted Assistance himself: And 'tis very probable, that the Sight of the Babylonian Couriers, who were dispatch'd from King Moabdar, might discompose him very much. He made all the Haste he could towards the Village, not being able to conceive what should be the real Cause of the young Lady's being secur'd by those Babylonish Officers, and as much at a Loss, at the same Time, what to think of such a Termagant and a Coquet.

9

THE CAPTIVE

No sooner was Zadig arriv'd at the Egyptian Village before-mention'd, but he found himself surrounded by a Croud. The People one and all cried out! See! See! there's the Man that ran away with the beauteous Lady Missouf, and murder'd Cletofis. Gentlemen, said he, God forbid that I should ever entertain a Thought of running away with the Lady you speak of: She is too much of a Coquet: And as to Cletofis, I did not murder him, but kill'd him in my own Defence. He endeavour'd all he could to take my Life away, because I entreated him to take some Pity and Compassion on the beauteous Missouf, whom he beat most unmercifully. I am a Stranger, who am fled hither for Shelter, and 'tis highly improbable, that upon my first Entrance into a Country, where I came for Safety and Protection, I should be guilty of two such enormous Crimes, as that of running away with another Man's Partner, and that of clandestinely murdering him on her Account.

The Egyptians at that Time were just and humane. The Populace, tis true, hurried Zadig to the Town-Goal; but they took care in the first Place to stop the Bleeding of his Wounds, and afterwards examin'd the suppos'd Delinquents apart, in order to discover, if possible, the real Truth. They acquitted Zadig of the Charge of wilful and premeditated Murder; but as he had taken a Subject's Life away, tho' in his own Defence, he was sentenc'd to be a Slave, as the Law directed. His two Beasts were sold in open Market, for the Service of the Hamlet; What Money he had was distributed amongst the Inhabitants; and he and his Attendant were expos'd in the Market-place to public Sale. An Arabian Merchant, Setoc by Name, purcha'd them both; but as the Valet, or Attendant, was a robust Man, and better cut out for hard Labour than the Master, he fetch'd the most Money. There was no Comparison to be made between them. Zadig therefore was a Slave subordinate to his Valet; they secur'd them both, however, by a Chain upon their Legs; and so link'd they accompanied their Master home. Zadig, as they were on the Road, comforted his Fellow-Slave, and exhorted him to bear his Misfortunes with Patience: But, according to Custom, he made several Reflections on the Vicissitudes of human Life. I am now sensible, said he, that my impropitious Fortune has some malignant Influence over thine; every Occurrence of my Life hitherto has prov'd strangely odd and unaccountable. In the first Place, I was sentenc'd to die at Babylon, for writing a short Panegyrick on the King, my Master. In the next, I narrowly escap'd being strangled, for the Queen his Royal Consort's speaking a little too much in my Favour; and here I am a joint-Slave with thy self; because a turbulent Fellow of a Gallant would beat his Lady. However, Comrade, let us march on boldly; let not our Courage be cast down; all this may possibly have a happier Issue than we expect. 'Tis absolutely necessary that these Arabian Merchants should have Slaves, and why should not you and I, as we are but Men, be Slaves as Thousands of others are? This Master of ours may not prove inexorable. He must treat his Slaves with some Thought and Consideration, if he expects them to do his Work. This was his Discourse to his Comrade; but his Mind was more attentive to the Misfortunes of the Queen of Babylon.

Two Days afterwards Setoc set out with his two Slaves and his Camels, for Arabia Deserta. His Tribe liv'd near the Desert of Horeb. The Way was long and tedious. Setoc, during the Journey, paid a much greater Regard to Zadig's Valet, than to himself; because the former was the most able to load the Camels; and therefore what little Distinctions were made, they were in his Favour. It so happen'd that one of the Camels died upon the Road: The Load which the Beast carried was immediately divided, and thrown upon the Shoulders of the two Slaves; Zadig had his Share. Setoc, couldn't forbear laughing to see his two Slaves crouching under their Burthen. Zadig took the Liberty to explain the Reason thereof; and convinc'd him of the Laws of the Equilibrium. The Merchant was a little startled at his philosophical Discourse, and look'd upon him with a more favourable Eye than at first. Zadig, perceiving he had rais'd his Curiosity, redoubled it, by instructing him in several material Points, which were in some Measure, advantageous to him in his Way of Business: Such as, the specific Weight of Metals, and other Commodities of various Kinds, of an equal Bulk; the Properties of several useful Animals, and the best Ways and Means to make Such as were wild, tame by Degrees, and fit for Service: In short, Zadig was look'd upon by his Master, as a perfect Oracle. Setoc now thought the Master the much better Man of the two. He us'd him courteously, and had no Room to repent of his Indulgence towards him.

Being got to their Journey's End, the first Step that Setoc took was to claim a Debt of five hundred Ounces of Silver of a Jew, who had borrow'd it in the Presence of two Witnesses; but both of them were dead; and as the Jew was conscious he couldn't be cast for Want of Evidence, appropriated the Merchant's Money to his own Use, and thank'd God that it lay in his Power for once to bite an Arabian with Impunity. Setoc discover'd to Zadig the unhappy Situation of his Case, as he was now become his Confident. Where was it, pray, said Zadig, that you lent this large Sum to that ungrateful

Infidel? Upon a large Stone, said the Merchant, at the Foot of Mount Horeb. What sort of a Man is your Debtor, said Zadig? Oh! he is as errand a Rogue as ever breath'd, reply'd Setoc. That I take for granted; but, says Zadig, is he a lively, active Man, or is he a dull heavy-headed Fellow? He is one of the worst of Pay-masters in the World, but the merriest, most sprightly Fellow I ever met with. Very well! said Zadig, let me be one of your Council when your Cause comes to be heard. In short, he summon'd the Jew to attend the Court; where, when the Judge was sat, Zadig open'd the Cause: Thou impartial Judge of this Court of Equity, I am come here, in behalf of my Master, to demand of the Defendant five hundred Ounces of Silver, which he refuses to pay, and would fain traverse the Debt. Have you, Friend, your Witnesses ready to prove the Loan, said the Judge? No, they are dead; but there is a large Stone still subsisting, on which the Money was deposited; and if your Excellence, will be pleas'd to order the Stone to be brought in Court, I don't doubt but the Evidence it will give, will be Proof sufficient of the Fact. I hope your Excellence will order, that the Jew and myself shall be oblig'd to attend the Court, till the Stone comes, and I'll dispatch a special Messenger to fetch it, at my Master's Expence. Your Request is very reasonable, said the Judge. Do as you propose; and so call'd another Cause.

When the Court was ready to break up, Well! said the Judge to Zadig, is your Stone come yet? The Jew, with a Sneer, replied, your Excellence may wait here till this Time To-morrow, before the Stone will appear in Court; for 'tis above six Mile off, and it will require fifteen Men to remove it from its Place. 'Tis well! replied Zadig. I told your Excellence that the Stone would be a very material Evidence. Since the Defendant can point out the Place where the Stone lies, he tacitly confesses, that it was upon that Stone the Money was deposited. The Jew thus unexpectedly confuted, was soon oblig'd to acknowledge the Debt. The Judge order'd that the Jew should be tied fast to the Stone, without Victuals or Drink, till he should advance the five hundred Ounces of Silver, which were soon paid accordingly, and the Jew releas'd. The Slave Zadig, and this remarkable Stone-Witness, were in great Repute all over Arabia.

10

THE FUNERAL PILE

Setoc, transported with his good Success, of a Slave made Zadig his Favourite Companion and Confident; he found him as necessary in the Conduct of his Affairs, as the King of Babylon had before done in the Administration of his Government; and lucky it was for Zadig that Setoc had no Wife.

He discover'd, that his Master was in his Temper benevolent, strictly honest, and a Man of good natural Parts. Zadig was very much concern'd, that One of so much Sense should pay divine Adoration to a whole Host of created, tho' Celestial Beings, that is to say, the Sun, Moon, and Stars, according to the antient Custom of the Arabians. He talk'd, at first, to his Master, with great Precaution on so important a Topick. But at last told him, in direct Terms, that they were created Bodies, as others, tho' of less Lustre, and that there was no more Adoration due to them, than to a Stock or a Stone. But, said Setoc, they are eternal Beings to whom we are indebted for all the Blessings we enjoy; they animate Nature; they regulate the Seasons; they are, in a Word, at such an infinite Distance from us, that it would be downright impious not to adore them. You are more indebted, said Zadig, to the Waters of the Red Sea, which transport so many valuable Commodities into the Indies. Why, pray, may not they be deem'd as antient as the Stars? And if you are so fond of paying your Adoration on Account of their vast Distance; why don't you adore the Land of the Gangarides, which lies in the utmost Extremities of the Earth. No, said Setoc, there is something so surprisingly more brilliant in the Stars than what you speak of; that a Man must adore them whether he will or not.

At the Close of the Evening, Zadig planted a long Range of Candles in the Front of his Tent, where Setoc and he were to sup that Night: And as soon as he perceiv'd his Patron to be at the Door, he fell prostrate on his Knees before the Wax-Lights. O ye everlasting, ever-shining Luminaries, be always propitious to your Votary, said Zadig. Having repeated these Words so loud as Setoc might hear them, he sat down to Table, without taking the least Notice of Setoc. What! said Setoc, somewhat startled at his Conduct, art thou at thy Prayers before Supper? I act just as inconsistently, Sir, as you do; I worship these Candles; without reflecting on their Makers, or yourself, who are my most beneficent Patron.

Setoc took the Hint, and was conscious of the Reproof that was conceal'd so genteely under a Vail. The superior Wisdom of his Slave enlightned his Mind; and from that Hour he was less lavish than ever he had been, of his Incense to those created Beings, and for the future, paid his Adoration to the eternal God who made them.

At that Time there was a most hideous Custom in high Repute all over Arabia, which came originally from Scythia; but having met with the Sanction of the bigotted Brachmans, threatn'd to spread its Infection all over the East. When a married Man happen'd to die, if his dearly beloved Widow ever expected to be esteem'd a Saint, she must throw herself headlong upon her Husband's Funeral-Pile. This was look'd upon as a solemn Festival, and was call'd the Widow's Sacrifice. That Tribe which could boast of the greatest Number of burnt-Widows, was look'd upon as the most meritorious. An Arabian, who was of the Tribe of Setoc, happen'd just at that Juncture, to be dead, and his Widow (Almona by Name) who was a noted Devotee, publish'd the Day, nay, the Hour, that she propos'd to throw herself (according to Custom) on her deceased Husband's Funeral Pile, and be attended by a Concert of Drums and Trumpets. Zadig remonstrated to Setoc, what a shocking Custom this was, and how directly repugnant to human Nature; by permitting young Widows, almost every Day, to become wilful Self-Murderers; when they might be of Service to their Country, either by the Addition of new Subjects, or by the Education of such as demanded their Maternal Indulgence. And, by arguing seriously with Setoc for some Time, he forc'd from him at last, an ingenuous Confession, that the barbarous Custom then subsisting, ought, if possible, to be abolish'd. 'Tis now, replied Setoc, above a thousand Years since the Widows of Arabia have been indulg'd with this Privilege of dying with their Husbands; and how shall any one dare to abrogate a Law that has been establish'd Time out of Mind? Is there any Thing more inviolable than even an antient Error? But, replied Zadig, Reason is of more antient Date than the Custom you plead for. Do you communicate these Sentiments to the Sovereigns of your Tribes, and in the mean while I'll go, and sound the Widow's Inclinations.

Accordingly he paid her a Visit, and having insinuated himself into her Favour, by a few Compliments on her Beauty, after urging what a pity it was, that a young Widow, Mistress of so many Charms, should make away with herself for no other reason but to mingle her Ashes with a Husband that was dead; he, notwithstanding, applauded her for her heroic Constancy and Courage. I perceive, Madam, said he, you was excessively fond of your deceased Spouse. Not I truly, reply'd the young Arabian Devotee. He was a Brute, infected with a groundless Jealousy of my Virtue; and, in short, a perfect Tyrant. But, notwithstanding all this, I am determin'd to comply with our Custom. Surely then, Madam, there's a Sort of secret Pleasure in being burnt alive. Alas! with a Sigh, cried Almona, 'tis a Shock indeed to Nature; but must be complied with for all that. I am a profess'd Devotee, and should I shew the least Reluctance, my Reputation would be lost for ever; all the World would laugh at me, should I not burn myself on this Occasion: Zadig having forc'd her ingenuously to confess, that she parted with her Life more out of Regard to what the World would say of her, and out of Pride and Ostentation, than any real Love for the deceas'd, he talk'd to her for some considerable Time so rationally, and us'd so many prevailing Arguments with her to justify her due Regard for the Life which she was going to throw away, that she began to wave the Thought, and entertain a secret Affection for her friendly Monitor. Pray, Madam, tell me, said Zadig, how would you dispose of yourself, upon the Supposition, that you could shake off this vain and barbarous Notion? Why, said Dame, with an amorous Glance, I think verily I should accept of yourself for a second Bed-fellow.

The Memory of Astarte had made too strong an Impression on his Mind, to close with this warm Declaration: He took his leave, however, that Moment, and waited on the Chiefs. He communicated to them the Substance of their private Conversation, and prevailed with them to make it a Law for the future, that no Widow should be allow'd to fall a Victim to a deceased Husband, till after she had admitted some young Man to converse with her in private for a whole Hour together. The Law was pass'd accordingly, and not one Widow in all Arabia, from that Day to this, ever observ'd the Custom. 'Twas to Zadig alone that the Arabian Dames were indebted for the Abolition, in one Hour, of a Custom so very inhuman, that had been practis'd for such a Number of Ages. Zadig, therefore, with the strictest Justice, was look'd upon by all the Fair Sex in Arabia, as their most bountiful Benefactor.

11

THE EVENING'S ENTERTAINMENT

Setoc, who would never stir out without his Bosom-Friend (in whom alone, as he thought, all Wisdom center'd) resolv'd to take him with him to Balzora Fair, whither the richest Merchants round the whole habitable Globe, us'd annually to resort. Zadig was delighted to see such a Concourse of substantial Tradesmen from all Countries, assembled together in one Place. It appear'd to him, as if the whole Universe was but one large Family, and all happily met together at Balzora. On the second Day of the Fair, he sat down to Table with an Egyptian, an Indian, that liv'd on the Banks of the River Ganges, an

Inhabitant of Cathay, a Grecian, a Celt, and several other Foreigners, who by their frequent Voyages towards the Arabian Gulf, were so far conversant with the Arabic Language, as to be able to discourse freely, and be mutually understood. The Egyptian began to fly into a Passion; what a scandalous Place is this Balzora, said he, where they refuse to lend me a thousand Ounces of Gold, upon the best Security that can possibly be offer'd. Pray, said Setoc, what may the Commodity be that you would deposit as a Pledge for the Sum you mention. Why, the Corpse of my deceased Aunt, said he, who was one of the finest Women in all Egypt. She was my constant Companion; but unhappily died upon the Road. I have taken so much Care, that no Mummy whatever can equal it: And was I in my own Country, I could be furnish'd with what Sum soever I pleas'd, were I dispos'd to mortgage it. 'Tis a strange Thing that Nobody here will advance so small a Sum upon so valuable a Commodity. No sooner had he express'd his Resentment, but he was going to cut up a fine boil'd Pullet, in order to make a Meal on't, when an Indian laid hold of his Hand, and with deep Concern, cried out, For God's Sake what are you about? Why, said the Egyptian, I design to make a Wing of this Fowl one Part of my Supper. Pray, good Sir, consider what you are doing, said the Indian. 'Tis very possible, that the Soul of the deceas'd Lady may have taken its Residence in that Fowl. And you wouldn't surely run the Risque of eating up your Aunt? To boil a Fowl is, doubtless, a most shameful Outrage done to Nature. Pshaw! What a Pother you make about the boiling of a Fowl, and flying in the Face of Nature, replied the Egyptian in a Pet; tho' we Egyptians pay divine Adoration to the Ox; yet we can make a hearty Meal of a Piece of roast Beef for all that. Is it possible, Sir, that your Country-men should act so absurdly, as to pay an Ox the Tribute of divine Worship, said the Indian? Absurd as you think it, said the other, the Ox has been the principal Object of Adoration all over Egypt, for these hundred and thirty five thousand Years, and the most abandon'd Egyptian has never been as yet so impious as to gain-say it. Ay, Sir, an hundred thirty five thousand Years, say you, surely you must be out a little in your Calculation. 'Tis but about fourscore thousand Years, since India was first inhabited. Sure I am, we are a more antient People than you are, and our Brama prohibited the eating of Beef long before your Nation ever erected an Altar in Honour of the Ox, or ever put one upon a Spit. What a Racket you make about your Brama! Is he able to stand the least in Competition with our Apis, said the Egyptian? Let us hear, pray, what mighty Feats have been done by your boasted Brama? Why, replied the Bramin, he first taught his Votaries to write and read; and 'tis to him alone, all the World is indebted for the Invention of the noble Game of Chess. You are quite out, Sir, in your Notion, said a Chaldean, who sat within Hearing: All these invaluable Blessings were deriv'd from the Fish Oannés; and 'tis that alone to which the Tribute of divine Adoration is justly due. All the World will tell you, that 'twas a divine Being whose Tail was pure Gold, whose Head resembled that of a Man, tho' indeed the Features were much more beautiful; and that he condescended to visit the Earth three Hours every Day, for the Instruction of Mankind. He had a numerous Issue, as is very well known, and all of them were powerful Monarchs. I have a Picture of it at Home, to which, as in Duty I ought, I Say my Prayers at Night before I go to Bed, and every Morning that I rise. There is no Harm, Sir, as I can conceive, in partaking of a Piece of roast Beef; but, doubtless, 'tis a mortal Sin, a Crime of the blackest Dye, to touch a Piece of Fish. Besides, you cannot justly boast of so illustrious an Origin, and you are both of you mere Moderns, in Comparison to us Chaldeans, You Egyptians lay claim to no more than 135,000 Years, and you Indians, but of 80,000. Whereas we have Almanacks that are dated 4000 Centuries backwards. Take my Word for it; I speak nothing but Truth; renounce your Errors, and I'll make each of you a Present of a fine Portrait of our Oannés.

A Native of Cambalu, entring into the Debate, said, I have a very great Veneration, not only for the Egyptians, Chaldeans, Greeks, and Celtæ; but for Brama, Apis, and the Oannés, but in my humble Opinion, the *Li, * The Chinese Term, Li, signifies, properly speaking, natural Light, or Reason; and Tien, the Heavens, or the supreme Being. or as 'tis by some call'd, the *Tien, is an Object more deserving of divine Adoration than any Ox, or Fish, how much soever you may boast of their respective Perfections. All I shall say, in regard to my native Country, 'tis of much greater Extent, than all Egypt, Chaldea, and the Indies put together. I shall lay no Stress on the Antiquity of my Country; for I imagine 'tis of much greater Importance to be the happiest People, than the most antient under the Sun. However, since you were talking of the Almanacks, I must beg the Liberty to tell you, that ours are look'd upon to be the best all over Asia; and that we had several very correct ones before the Art of Arithmetick was ever heard of in Chaldea.

You are all of you a Parcel of illiterate, ignorant Bigots, cry'd a Grecian: 'Tis plain, you know nothing of the Chaos, and that the World, as it now stands, is owing wholly to Matter and Form. The Greek ran on for a considerable Time; but was at last interrupted by a Celt, who having drank deep, during the whole Time of this Debate, thought himself ten Times wiser than any of his Antagonists; and wrapping out a great Oath, insisted, that all their Gods were nothing, if set in Competition with the Teutath or the Misletoe on the Oak. As for my part, said he, I carry some of it always in my Pocket: As to my Ancestors, they were Scythians, and the only Men worth talking of in the whole World: 'Tis true, indeed, they would now and then make a Meal of their Country-men, but that ought not to be urg'd as any Objection to his Country; and, in short, if any one of you, or all of you, shall dare to say any thing disrespectful of Teutath, I'll defend its Cause to the last Drop of my Blood. The Quarrel grew warmer and warmer, and Setoc expected that the Table would be overset, and that Blood-shed would ensue. Zadig, who hadn't once open'd his Lips during the whole Controversy, at last rose up, and address'd himself to the Celt, in the first Place, as being the most noisy and outrageous. Sir, said he, Your Notions in this Affair are very just: Good Sir, oblige me with a Bit of your Misletoe. Then turning about, he expatiated on the Eloquence of the Grecian, and in a Word, soften'd in the most artful Manner all the contending Parties. He said but little indeed to the Cathayian; because he was more cool, and sedate than any of the others. To conclude, he address'd them all in general Terms, to this or the like Effect: My dear Friends, You have been contesting all this while about an important Topick, in which 'tis evident, you are all unanimously agreed. Agreed, quotha! they all cried, in an angry Tone, How so, pray? Why said he to the hot, testy Celt, is it not true, that you do not in effect adore this Misletoe, but that Being who created that Misletoe and the Oak, to which it is so closely united? Doubtless, Sir, reply'd the Celt. And you, Sir, said he, to the Egyptian, You revere, thro' your venerable Apis, the great Author of every Ox's Being. We do so, said the Egyptian. The mighty Oannés, tho' the Sovereign of the Sea, continued he, must give Precedence to that Power, who made both the Sea, and every Fish that dwells therein. We allow it, said the Chaldean. The Indian, adds he, and the Cathayan, acknowledge one supreme Being, or first Cause, as well as you. As to what that profound worthy Gentleman the Grecian has advanc'd, is, I must own, a little above my weak Comprehension, but I am fully persuaded, that he will allow there is a supreme Being on whom his favourite Matter and Form are entirely dependent. The Grecian, who was look'd upon as a Sage amongst them, said, with Abundance of Gravity, that Zadig, had made a very just Construction of his Meaning. Now, Gentlemen, I appeal to you all, said Zadig, whether you are not unanimous to a Man, in the Debate upon the Carpet, and whether there are any just Grounds for the least Divisions or Animosities amongst you. The whole Company, cool at once, caress'd him; and Setoc, after he had sold off all his Goods and Merchandize at a round Price, took his Friend Zadig Home with him to the Land of Horeb. Zadig, upon his first Arrival was inform'd, that a Prosecution had been carried on against him during his Absence, and that the Sentence pronounc'd against him was, that he should be burnt alive before a slow Fire.

12

THE RENDEZVOUS

Whilst Zadig attended his Friend Setoc to Balzora, the Priests of the Stars were determin'd to punish him. As all the costly Jewels, and other valuable Decorations, in which every young Widow that sacrificed her self on her Husband's Funeral-pile, were their customary Fees, 'tis no great Wonder, indeed, that they were inclin'd to burn poor Zadig, for playing them such a scurvy Trick. Zadig therefore, was accus'd of holding heretical and damnable Tenets, in regard to the Celestial Host: They depos'd, and swore point-blank, that he had been heard to aver, that the Stars never sat in the Sea. This horrid blasphemous Declaration thunder-struck all the Judges, and they were ready to rend their Mantles at the Sound of such an impious Assertion; and they would have made Zadig, had he been a Man of Substance, paid very severely for his heretical Notions. But in the Height of their Pity and Compassion for even such an Infidel, they would lay no Fine upon him; but content themselves with seeing him roasted alive before a slow Fire. Setoc, tho' without Hopes of Success, us'd all the Interest he had to save his bosom Friend from so shocking a Death; but they turn'd a deaf Ear to all his Remonstrances, and oblig'd him to hold his Tongue. The young Widow Almona, who by this Time was not only reconcil'd to living a little longer, but had some Taste for the Pleasures of Life, and knew that she was entirely indebted to Zadig for it, resolv'd, if possible, to free her Benefactor from being burnt, as he had before convinc'd her of the Folly of it in her Case. She ponder'd upon this weighty Affair very seriously; but said nothing to any one whomsoever. Zadig was to be executed the next Day; and she had only a few Hours left to carry her Project into Execution. Now the Reader shall hear with how much Benevolence and Discretion this amiable Widow behav'd on this emergent Occasion.

In the first Place, she made use of the most costly Perfumes;

and drest herself to the utmost Advantage to render her Charms as conspicuous as possible; And thus gaily attir'd, demanded a private Audience of the High Priest of the Stars. Upon her first Admittance into his august and venerable Presence, she address'd herself in the following Terms. O thou first-born and well-beloved Son of the Great Bear, Brother of the Bull, and first Cousin to the Dog, (these you must know were the Pontiff's high Titles) I come to confess myself before you: My Conscience is my Accuser, and I am terribly afraid I have been guilty of a mortal Sin, by declining the stated Custom of burning my self on my Husband's Funeral-pile? What could tempt me, in short, to a Prolongation of my Life, I can't imagine, I, who am grown a perfect Skeleton, all wrinkled and deform'd. She paus'd, and pulling off, with a negligent but artful Air, her long silk Gloves; She display'd a soft, plump, naked Arm, and white as Snow: You see, Sir, said she, that all my Charms are blasted. Blasted, Madam, said the luscious Pontiff; No! Your Charms are still resistless: His Eyes, and his Mouth, with which he kiss'd her Hand, confirm'd their Power: Such an Arm, Madam, by the Great Orasmades, I never saw before. Alas! said the Widow, with a modest Blush; my Arm Sir, 'tis probable, may have the Advantage of any hidden Part; but see, good Father, what a Neck is here; as yellow as Saffron, an Object not worth regarding. Then she display'd such a snowy, panting Bosom, that Nature could not mend it. A Rose-Bud on an Ivory Apple, would, if set in Competition with her spotless Whiteness, make no better Appearance than common Madder upon a Shrub; and the whitest Wool, just out of the Laver, were she but by, would seem but of a light-brown Hue.

Her Neck, her large black, sparkling Eyes, that languishingly roll'd, and seem'd as 'twere, on Fire; her lovely Cheeks, glowing with White and Red, her Nose, that was not unlike the Tower of Mount Lebanon, her Lips, which were like two Borders of Coral, inclosing two Rows of the best Pearls in the Arabian Sea; such a Combination, I say, of Charms, made the old Pontiff judge she was scarce twenty Years of Age; and in a kind of Flutter, to make her a Declaration of his tender Regard for her. Almona, perceiving him enamour'd, begg'd his Interest in Favour of Zadig. Alas! my dear Charmer, my Interest alone, when you request the Favour, would be but a poor Compliment; I'll take care his Acquittance shall be signed by three more of my Brother Priests. Do you sign first, however, said Almona. With all my Soul, said the amorous Pontiff, provided—— you'll be kind, my dearest. You do me too much Honour, said Almona; but should you give your self the Trouble to pay me a Visit after Sunset, and as soon as the Star Sheat twinkles on the Horizon, you shall find me, most venerable Father, repos'd upon a rosy-colour'd silver Sopha, where you shall use your Pleasure with your humble Servant. With that she made him a low Courtesy; took up Zadig's general Release as soon as duely sign'd, and left the old Doatard all over Love, tho' somewhat diffident of his own Abilities. The Residue of the Day he spent in his Bagnio; he drank large enlivening Draughts of a Water distill'd from the Cinnamon of Ceilan, and the costly Spices of Tidor and Ternate, and waited with the utmost Impatience for the up-rising of the brilliant Sheat.

In the mean time Almona went to the second Pontiff. He assur'd her that the Sun, Moon, and all the starry Host of Heav'n, were but languid Fires to her bright Eyes. He put the Question to her, in short, at once, and agreed to sign upon her Compliance. She suffer'd herself to be over-persuaded, and made an Assignation to meet him at a certain Place, as soon as the Star Algenib should make its Appearance. From him she repair'd to the third and fourth Pontiff, taking care, wherever she went, to see Zadig's Acquittance duely sign'd, and made fresh Appointments at the Rising of Star after Star.

When she had carried her Point thus far, she sent a proper Message to the Judges of the Court, who had condemn'd Zadig, requesting that they would come to her House, that she might advise with them upon an Affair of the last Importance. They waited on her accordingly; she produc'd Zadig's Discharge duly sign'd by four several Hands, and told them the Definitive Treaty between all the contracting Parties. Each of the pontifical Gallants observ'd their

Summons to a Moment. Each was startled at the Sight of his Rival; but perfectly thunderstruck to see the Judges, before whom the Widow had laid open her Case. Zadig procur'd an absolute Pardon, and Setoc was so charm'd with the artful Address of Almona, that he married her the next Day. Zadig went afterwards to throw himself at the Feet of his fair Benefactress. Setoc and he took their Leave of each other with Tears in their Eyes, and vowing that an eternal mutual Friendship should be preserv'd between them; and, in short, should Fortune at any Time afterwards prove more propitious than could well be expected to either Party; the other should partake of an equal Share of his Success.

Zadig steer'd his Course towards Syria; forever pondering on the hard Fate of the justly-admir'd Astarte, and reflecting on his own Stars that so obstinately darted down their malignant Rays, and continu'd daily to torment him. What, said he! to pay four hundred Ounces of Gold for only seeing a Bitch pass by me; to be condemn'd to be beheaded for four witless Verses in Praise of the King; to be strangled to Death, because a Queen was pleas'd to look upon me; to be made a Prisoner, and sold as a Slave for saving a young Lady from being sorely abus'd by a Brute rather than a Man; and to be upon the Brink of being roasted alive, for no other Offence than saving for the future all the Widows in Arabia from becoming idle Burnt-Offerings, and mingling their Ashes with those of their deceased worthless Husbands.

13

THE FREE-BOOTER

Zadig, arriving at the Frontiers which separate Arabia Petræa from Syria, and passing by a very strong Castle, several arm'd Arabians rush'd out upon him, and surrounding him, cried out: Whatever you have belonging to you is our Property, but as for your Person, that is entirely at our Sovereign's Disposal. Zadig, instead of making any Reply, drew his Sword, and as his Attendant was a very couragious Fellow, he drew likewise. Those who laid hold on them, first fell a Sacrifice to their Fury: Their Numbers redoubled: Yet still, Both dauntless, determin'd to conquer or to die. When two Men defend themselves against a whole Gang, the Contest, doubtless, cannot last long. The Master of the Castle, one Arbogad by Name, having been an Eye-Witness from his Window, of the Intrepidity and surprising Exploits of Zadig, took a Fancy to him. He ran down therefore in Haste, and giving Orders himself to his Vassals to desist, deliver'd the two Travellers out of their Hands. Whatever Goods or Chattels, said he, come upon my Territories, are my Effects; and whatever I find likewise that is valuable upon the Premises of others, is my free Booty; but, as you appear, Sir, to me to be a Gentleman of uncommon Courage, you shall prove an Exception to my general Rule. Upon this, he invited Zadig into his magnificent Mansion, giving his inferior Officers strict Orders to use him with all due Respect; and at Night Arbogad was desirous of supping with Zadig. The Lord of the Mansion was one of those Arabians, that are call'd Free-booters; but a Man who now and then did good Actions amongst a Thousand bad ones. He plunder'd without Mercy; but was liberal in his Benefactions. When in Action, intrepid; but in Traffick, easy enough; a perfect Epicure in his Eating and Drinking, an absolute Debauchee, but very frank and open. Zadig pleas'd him extremely; his Conversation being very lively, prolong'd their Repast: At last, Arbogad said to him; I would advise you, Sir, to enlist yourself in my Troop; you cannot possibly do a better Thing: My Profession is none of the worst; and in Time, you may become perhaps as great a Man as myself. May I presume, Sir, to ask you one Question; how long may you have follow'd this honourable Calling? From my Youth upwards, replied his Host, I was only a Valet at first to an Arabian, who indeed was courteous enough; but Servitude was a State of Life I could not brook. It made me stark-mad to see, in a wide World, which ought to be divided fairly between Mankind, that Fate had reserv'd for me so scanty a Portion. I communicated my Grievance to an old Sage Arabian. Son, said he, never despair; once upon a Time, there was a Grain of Sand, that bemoan'd itself, as being nothing more than a worthless Atom of the Deserts. At the Expiration, however, of a few Years, it became that inestimable Diamond, which at this very Hour, is the richest, and most admir'd Ornament of the Indian Crown. The old Man's Discourse fir'd me with some Ambition; I was conscious to myself that I was at that Time the Atom he mention'd, but was determin'd, if possible, to become the Diamond. At my first setting out, I stole two Horses; then I got into a Gang; where we play'd at small Game, and stopp'd the small Caravans; thus I gradually lessen'd the wide Disproportion, which there was at first between me and the rest of Mankind: I enjoy'd not only my full Share of the good Things of this Life, but enjoy'd them with Usury. I was look'd upon as a Man of Consequence, and I procur'd this Castle by my military Atchievements. The Satrap of Syria had Thoughts of dispossessing me; but I was then too rich to be any Ways afraid of him; I gave the Satrap a certain Sum of Money, upon Condition that I kept quiet Possession of my Castle. And, moreover, I aggrandiz'd my Domains; for he constituted me, at the same Time, Treasurer of the Imports that Arabia Petræa paid to the King of Kings. I executed my Trust, in every Respect, as I ought, in the Capacity of a Collector; but I never did, nor never intended to balance my Accounts.

The grand Desterham of Babylon sent hither, in the Name of the King Moabdar, a petty Satrap, with a Commission to strangle me. He and his Attendants arriv'd here with his Royal Warrant. I was appriz'd of the whole Affair, and, accordingly, order'd his whole Retinue, consisting of four inferior Officers, to be strangled before his Face, after the same Manner as was intended for my Execution. After this, I ask'd him what he thought the Commission with which he was entrusted, might reasonably be valued at; he answer'd, that he presum'd his Premium (had he succeeded) might have amounted to about three Hundred Pieces of Gold. I made him sensible, that it would be for his Interest to be a commission'd Officer under me; I made him accordingly Deputy Free-booter. He is at this very Day not only the best Officer, but the richest I have in all my Court. If my Word may be credited, I'll raise your Fortune as I have done his. Never was Trade brisker in our Way; for Moabdar, is knock'd on the Head, and all Babylon in the utmost Confusion. Moabdar kill'd, said you! cry'd Zadig, and pray, Sir, what is become of his Royal Consort, Astarte? I know nothing at all of that Affair, replied Arbogad, all that I have to say, is, that Moabdar became a perfect Madman, and had his Brains beat out; that all the People in Babylon are cutting one another's Throats, and that the whole Empire is laid waste; that there is still an Opportunity for making several bold Pushes; and let me tell you, Sir, I have done my Part, and made the most on't. But the Queen, Sir, said Zadig; pray favour me so far, as to inform me, if you know any Thing of the Queen. I have heard great Talk, said he, of a certain Prince of Hyrcania; 'tis very possible, she may have listed herself amongst his Concubines, if she had the good Fortune to escape the Resentment of those popular Tumults; but my Head, Sir, is better turn'd for the Highway than for News; I have taken several Ladies Prisoners in the Course of my Excursions; I keep none of them for my Part; and as to such as are handsomer than ordinary, I make the best Market I can of them, without enquiring who they are. Their Quality or Titles will fetch no Price at all; a Queen, if she be homely, is worth nothing. 'Tis probable, Sir, I have dispos'd of the Lady myself; and 'tis possible, likewise, she may be dead; 'tis no Concern of mine; and to my thinking, it should be an Affair of no Manner of Importance to you. After this Declaration, he drank so hard, and confounded his Ideas in such a Manner, that Zadig was not one whit the wiser. Upon which he was struck dumb, confounded, and stood as motionless as a Statue. Arbogad, in the mean while, swill'd down whole Bumpers, told a Hundred merry Tales, and swore a thousand Times over, that he was the happiest Creature upon God's Earth; persuading Zadig to be as merry, and thoughtless as himself. At last, being gradually overcome by the

Fumes of his Liquor, he fell fast asleep. Zadig spent the Remainder of the Night in deep Contemplation, and in all the Uneasiness of Mind imaginable. What, said he, the King first became crazy, and then was murder'd. I think I have just Grounds for Complaint. The whole Empire is in Confusion, and torn to Pieces, and this Freebooter is as happy as a King. O Fortune! O Fate! a Highwayman as happy as a Monarch! and the most amiable Creature that Nature ever fram'd has suffer'd perhaps, an ignominious Death, or perhaps, is in a State of Life a thousand Times worse than Death itself! O Astarte! Astarte! What art thou become?

As soon as it was Break of Day he went out, and ask'd every one he saw if they knew any Thing of her: But the whole Gang were too intent upon other Matters, to return him any Answer. By Virtue of their Night's Excursions, they had brought in some fresh Booty, and were busy in dividing the Spoil. All the Favour he could procure, in their Hurry and Tumult, was, to go away without the least Examination. He took the Advantage of their Remissness, and mov'd off the Premises, but more overwhelm'd with Grief and deep Reflection than ever.

Zadig, in his March, was very restless and uneasy. His Thoughts were forever rolling on the unfortunate Astarte, the King of Babylon, his Bosom-Friend Cador, the happy Free-booter, Arbogad, the fair Coquet, that was taken Prisoner on the Confines of Egypt, by the Babylonish Courier; in a Word, on the various Scenes of Misfortunes and Disappointments, which he had successively met with.

14

THE FISHERMAN

When Zadig had travelled some few Leagues from Arbogad's Castle, he found himself arriv'd at the Banks of a little River; incessantly deploring, as he went along, his unhappy Fate, and looking upon himself as the very Picture of ill Luck. He perceiv'd at a little Distance a Fisherman, reclin'd on a verdant Bank by the Riverside, trembling, scarce able to hold his Net in his Hand, (which he seem'd but little to regard) and with uplift Eyes, imploring Heaven's Assistance. I am, doubtless, said the poor Fisherman, the most unhappy Wretch that ever liv'd! No Merchant in all Babylon, it is very well known, was ever so noted for selling Cream-Cheeses as myself; and yet I am ruin'd to all Intents and Purposes. No Man of my Profession ever had a handsomer, more compleat Housewife, than my Dame was; but I have been treacherously depriv'd of her. I had still left a poor, pitiful Cottage, but that I saw plunder'd and destroy'd. I am cubb'd up here in a Cell; I have nothing to depend upon but my Fishery, and not one single Fish have I caught. Thou unfortunate Net! I'll never throw thee into the Water more: Much sooner will I throw myself in. No sooner were the Words out of his Mouth, but he started up, and ran to the River-side, like one that was resolutely bent to plunge in, and get rid of a miserable Life at once. Is it possible, said Zadig? Is there then the Man in Being more wretched than myself? His Benevolence, and good Will to save the poor Man's Life, was as quick as the Reflection he had just made! He ran to his Assistance; he laid hold of him; and ask'd him, with an Air of Pity and Concern, the Cause of his rash Intention. 'Tis an old saying, that a Person is less unhappy when he sees himself not singular in Misfortune. But if we will credit Zoroaster, this is not from a Principle of Malignity, but the Effect of a fatal Necessity. He was attracted, as it were, to any Person in Distress, as being One in the same unhappy Circumstances. The Transport of a happy Man, would be a Kind of Insult; but two Persons in bad Circumstances, are like two weak Shrubs, which, by propping up each other, are fenc'd against a Storm. Why are you thus cast down, said Zadig to the Fisherman? Never sink Man, under the Weight of your Burden. I can't help it, said the poor Fisherman; I have not the least Prospect of Redress. I was once, Sir, the tip-top Man of the whole Village of Derlbach, near Babylon, where I liv'd, and with the Help of my

Wife, made the best Cream-Cheeses that were ever eaten in the Persian Empire. Her Majesty, the Queen Astarte, and the famous Prime-Minister Zadig were very fond of them. I serv'd the Court with about six Hundred of them, I went the other Day in Hopes of being paid; but before I had well got into the Suburbs of Babylon, I was inform'd, that not only the Queen, but Zadig too had privately left the Court: Whereupon I ran directly to Zadig's House, tho' I never sat Eye on the Man in all my Life. There I found the Court-Marshals of the grand Desterham, plundering, by Virtue of his Majesty's Mandate, all his Effects, in the most loyal Manner. From thence I made the best of my Way to the Queen's Kitchin; where, applying my self to the Steward of her Household, and his inferior Officers; one of them told me she was dead; another, that she was confin'd in Prison; a third, indeed, said that she had made her Escape by Flight; all in general, however, assur'd me for my Comfort, that my Cheeses would never be paid for. From thence I went, with my Wife in my Hand, to Lord Orcan's; who was another of my Court-Customers; of whom we begg'd for Shelter and Protection: The Favour, I confess, was readily granted to my Wife; but as for my own Part, I was absolutely rejected. She was fairer, Sir, than the fairest Cheese I ever sold; from whence I date all my Misfortunes; and the red that adorn'd her blushing Cheeks was ten Times more lively than any Tyrian Scarlet. And between you and I, Sir, that was the main Cause of my Wife's Reception, and my Disgrace. Whereupon I wrote a doleful Letter to my Wife, in all the Agonies of one in the deepest Despair: 'Tis very well, said she, to the Messenger; I have some little Knowledge of the Man; I have heard say no one sells better Cream-Cheeses than he does; desire him, next Time he comes, to bring a small Parcel with him, and let him know, I'll take care he shall be punctually paid.

In the Height of my Misfortunes, I determin'd to seek Redress in a Court of Equity: I had but six Ounces of Gold left: Two whereof went for a Fee to my Counsellor; two to my Lawyer, who took my Cause in Hand, and the other two to the Judge's Clerk.

Notwithstanding what I had done, my Cause was not so much as commenc'd; and I had already disburs'd more Money than all my Cheeses and my Wife with them were worth. I return'd therefore to my Native Habitation, with a full Resolution to sell it for the Ransom of my Wife.

My little Cot, with the Appurtenances, were worth about threescore Ounces of Gold: But as the Purchasers found I was necessitous, and drove to my last Shifts; the first whom I apply'd to, offer'd me thirty Ounces; the second, twenty; and the third, but ten: Just as I had come to Terms of Accommodation with one of them, the Prince of Hyrcania came to Babylon, and swept all before him. My little Cottage, with all its Furniture, was first plunder'd of all that was valuable, and at last reduc'd to Ashes.

Having thus lost my Money, my Wife, and my House, I withdrew to this Desart, where you see me. I have since endeavour'd to get my Bread by Fishing; but the Fish, as well as all Mankind, desert me. I scarce catch one in a Day; I am half starv'd; and had it not been for your unexpected Benevolence and Generosity, I had been at the Bottom of the River before this.

This long Detail of Particulars, however, was not deliver'd without several Interruptions; for, said Zadig, with Abundance of Warmth and Confusion, Have you never heard, Sir, of what is become of the Queen Astarte? No Sir, not I, said the disconsolate Fisherman; but this I know, to my Sorrow, that neither the Queen, nor Zadig, ever paid me the least Consideration in the World for my Cream Cheeses; that my dear Spouse is taken from me; and that I am drove to the very Brink of Despair. I am verily persuaded, said Zadig, that you will not lose all your Money. I have heard much talk of that same Zadig; they say he is very honest, and that if ever he returns to Babylon, as 'tis to be hop'd he will, he'll discharge his Debts with Interest, like a Man of Honour. But, as for your Wife, who appears to me, to be no better than a Wag-tail, never take the Trouble, if you'll take my Advice, to hunt after her any more. Be rul'd, and make the best of your Way to Babylon. I shall be there before you, as I shall ride, and you will be on Foot. Make your Applications to the illustrious Cador; tell him you met his Friend upon the Road; and stay there still I come. Observe my Orders, and 'tis very probable it may turn out to your Advantage.

O puissant Orosmades, continu'd he, you have made me, 'tis true, an Instrument of Comfort to this poor Man; but what Friend will you raise for me, to alleviate my Sorrows? Having utter'd this short Expostulation, he gave the distrest Fisherman one full Moiety of all the Money he brought with him out of Arabia. The Fisherman, thunder-struck, and transported with Joy at so unexpected a Benefaction, kiss'd the Feet of Cador's Friend, and cried out, sure you are a Messenger of Heaven, sent down to be my Saviour!

In the mean Time, Zadig every now and then ask'd him Questions, and wept as he ask'd them. What! Sir, said the Fisherman, can you, who are so bountiful a Benefactor, be in Distress yourself? Alas! said he, Friend, I am a hundred Times more unhappy than thou art. But pray, Sir, said the good Man, how can it possibly be, that he, who is so lavish of his Favours, should be overwhelm'd with greater Misfortunes than the Man he so generously relieves? Your greatest Uneasiness, said he, arose from the Narrowness of your Circumstances; but mine proceeds from an internal, and much deeper Cause. Pray, Sir, said the Fisherman, has Orcan robb'd you of your Wife? This Interrogatory put Zadig in a Moment upon a Retrospection of all his past Adventures. He recollected the whole Series of his Misfortunes; commencing from that of the Eunuch and the Huntsman, to his Arrival at the Free-booter's Castle. Alas! said he, to the Fisherman, Orcan, 'tis true, deserves severely to be punish'd: But for the Generality, we find, such worthless Barbarians are the Favourites of Fortune. Be that, however, as it will, go as I bade you, to my Friend Cador, and wait there till I come. They took their Leave; the Fisherman blessing his propitious Stars, and Zadig cursing, every Step he went, the Hour he was born.

15

THE BASILISK

As Zadig was traversing a verdant Meadow, he perceiv'd several young Female Syrians, intent on searching for something very curious, that lay conceal'd, as they imagin'd, in the Grass. He took the Freedom to approach one of them, and ask her, in the most courteous Manner, if he might have the Honour to assist her in her Researches. Have a care, said she. What we are hunting after, Sir, is an Animal, that will not suffer itself to be touch'd by a Man. 'Tis somewhat surprizing, said Zadig. May I be so bold, pray, as to ask you what you are in Pursuit after, that shuns the Touch of any Thing but the Hands of the Fair Sex. 'Tis, Sir, said she, the Basilisk: A Basilisk, Madam, said he! And pray, if you will be so good as to inform me, with what View, are you searching after a Creature so very difficult to be met with? 'Tis, Sir, said she, for our Lord and Master Ogul, whose Castle, you see, situate on the River-side, at the Bottom of the Meadow. We are all his Vassals. Ogul, you must know, is in a very bad State of Health, and his first Physician has order'd him, as a Specific, to eat a Basilisk, boil'd in Rose water: And as that Animal is very hard to be catch'd, and will suffer nothing to approach it, but one of our Sex, our dying Sovereign Ogul has promis'd to honour her, that shall be so happy as to catch it for him, so far as to make her his Consort. The Case, being thus circumstantiated, Sir, I hope you will not interrupt me any longer, lest my Rivals here in the Field should happen to circumvent me.

Zadig withdrew, and left the Syrian Ladies in Quest of their imaginary Booty, in order to pursue his intended Journey. But as he came to the Banks of a Rivulet, at the remotest part of the Meadow, he perceiv'd another young Lady, reclin'd on the Grass, and entirely disengag'd. Her Stature seem'd majestic, but her Face was cover'd with a Vail; and her Eyes were fixt, as one at her Looking-glass, on the River. Every now and then a Sigh burst out, as if her Heart were breaking. In her Hand she held a little Wand or Rod, with which she was tracing out some Characters on the dry Sand, that lay between the flow'ry Bank she sat on, and the purling Current. Zadig's Curiosity induc'd him, unperceiv'd, to observe her Operations at some Distance. But approaching nearer, and perceiving very distinctly the first Character to be an Z. the next an A. and the third a D. he started; but when he saw the additional Capitals of I and G. his Astonishment was too great for Words to express. He stood for some Time perfectly thunder-struck, and as motionless as a Statue; At last, in a soft, faultring Tone, he broke Silence: O generous Lady, said he, forgive a Stranger, one overwhelm'd with Sorrows like yourself, if he asks you, by what amazing Accident he finds the Name of Zadig delineated by so angelick a Hand. Thus unexpectedly interrupted, and at the Sound of those Words, she turn'd her Head; and with a trembling Hand, lifting up her Vail, she espy'd Zadig himself. Upon which, she shriek'd; and as her Heart was flutter'd between the two Extreams of Transport and Surprize, she fainted away, and gently dropp'd into his Arms. 'Twas, it seems Astarte her self; 'twas the Queen of Babylon; 'twas the very Goddess whom Zadig ador'd; 'twas, in short, the very identical Lady, whose hard Fate he had so long deplor'd; and for whose sake he had felt so many agonizing Pains. For a few Minutes he stood speechless, and depriv'd, as it were, of all his senses, whilst his Eyes were fixt on his Astarte, who began to revive; and cast a wishful Glance at him, attended with some Confusion. O ye immortal Powers, cried he, who preside over the Destiny of us frail Mortals! Ye have restor'd me my Astarte; but alas! at what a Conjuncture, in what a Place, and in what a State and Condition do I view her? He threw himself prostrate on the Ground, and kiss'd the Dust of her Feet. The Queen of Babylon rais'd him up, and oblig'd him to sit by her on the flow'ry Bank whereon she was repos'd. Every now and then she wip'd her Eyes, as the Tears trickl'd down afresh her lovely Cheeks. Twenty times she endeavour'd to renew her Discourse; but was interrupted by her Sighs; she ask'd him over and over to relate to her the Hardships he had ran thro' since their parting, and by what Chance he came to traverse that solitary Meadow; but prevented him at the same Time from returning any Answer, by repeating Question upon Question. At last, she gave him a particular Detail of her own Misfortunes, and again requested to know his. Both of them, in short, having, in some Measure, appeas'd the Tumult of their Souls; Zadig, in a few Words, inform'd her of the Motives that brought him thither.

But tell me, O unfortunate, tho' ever-venerable Queen, how I came to find you out, reclining on this verdant Bank, dress'd in this servile Habit, accompanied by other Female Slaves, who, I find, have been all Day long in Quest after a Basilisk, which, as I understand, is by Order of a celebrated Physician, to be dissolv'd in Rose-water, as a specific Medicine for his dying Patient.

Whilst they busy in their fruitless Search, said the beauteous Astarte, I'll tell you the whole Series of Sorrows which I have undergone since last we parted; and since Heav'n has thus unexpectedly blest my Eyes once more with the Sight of my dear Zadig, I'll no longer exclaim against my impropitious Stars.

You are not insensible, that the jealous King my Spouse, was disgusted to find you the most amiable of all Mortals, and that for no other Reason he determin'd to strangle you, and poison me. You know very well too, that indulgent Heav'n inspir'd, as it were, my little Dwarf, with artful Means to give me timely Notice of the rash Resolutions of the King, my cruel Husband.

No sooner had the faithful Cador oblig'd you to obey my Orders, and to fly the Court, but he ventur'd to enter my Apartment in the Dead of Night thro' a private Door. He snatch'd me up, and convey'd me directly into the Temple of Orosmades, where the holy Magus, who was his Brother, lock'd me up in that august and awful Statue, that stands erect upon the Pavement of the Temple, and Colossus-like, touches the lofty Ceiling with his Head. There I lay conceal'd, or rather buried for some Time; tho' taken all imaginable Care of, and furnish'd with all the Necessaries of Life by that venerable, and loyal Priest. In the mean Time, his Apothecary enter'd at Break of Day into my Apartment, with a Potion in his Hand, compos'd of Opium, black Hellebore, Aconite, and other Ingredients still more baneful. Whilst this mercenary Officer of the King's Vengeance was thus employ'd, another as inhuman as himself, went to your Lodgings with the silken Cord. Both, however, were disappointed, as both of us were fled. Cador, very officious, flew to the King, in order the more artfully to blind him; and in a feign'd Passion, rail'd at us both, and charg'd us both as perfidious Traitors. As for that Villain Zadig, said he, he has taken his Flight towards India; and your false, ungrateful Consort, Sire, said he, is fled to Memphis. The Guards were order'd that Moment to pursue us both.

The Couriers, who flew after me, knew nothing of me. I had never expos'd my Face unveil'd to any one but your self, and that too in the Presence, and by the express Order of my Royal Master. As they had no other Marks to distinguish me from others but my Stature, as it had been describ'd, a young Lady, just of my Size, but in all Probability much more handsome, presented herself to their View, on the Frontiers of Egypt. She was found alone, and in a very disconsolate Condition. This Lady must, doubtless, said they to themselves, be the Queen of Babylon: And without listning to her Complaints, convey'd her instantly to my Husband Moabdar. Their gross Blunder at first incens'd his Majesty to the last Degree; but after he had view'd the Lady with an attentive Eye, he found she was extremely pretty, and was soon pacify'd. Her Name was Missouf. I have been since inform'd, that her Name in the Egyptian Language signifies the Fair Coquet. And in Effect, she was so: She had as much Art, however, as Caprice. For she pleas'd the King of Kings: In short, she had such an Ascendancy over him, that he didn't scruple in publick to own her as his Wife. When she had secur'd him thus far in her Toils, she never conceal'd her Power, but play'd the Part of a perfect Humourist. She indulg'd herself in every Whim that came in her Head, without Fear of being brow-beat. In the first Place, She insisted that the Chief Magus, who was old and gouty, should dance a Saraband before her; and upon his modest Refusal to comply with so preposterous a Request, she persecuted him without Mercy: Nothing would serve her Turn, in the next Place, but his Majesty's grand Master of the Horse must make her a Minc'd-pye. The Gentleman took the Liberty to let her know, that he was no profess'd Cook; a Tart, however, he must make for her, and she got him turn'd out of his Place for being so monstrously careless, as to burn one Corner of the Crust. Whereupon she gave his Post to her favourite Dwarf, and made her Fop of a Page the Keeper of his Majesty's great Seal, and Confidence. Thus she reign'd arbitrary, and was the Female Tyrant of Babylon. All the World deplor'd the Loss of me their former Queen. The King, who never acted the Part of a Tyrant, till the Moment he would have imprison'd me, and strangled you, seem'd to have drown'd all his good Qualities in his Dotage on that capricious Enchantress. He came to the Temple on the solemn Festival of the sacred Fire. I saw him prostrate on the Pavement before the Statue, wherein I was enclos'd, imploring the Gods to show'r down their choicest Blessings on his beauteous Missouf. I, with an audible and distinct, but hollow Tone, address'd my self thus, like an Oracle, to the King of Kings. The Gods reject the Vows of a Monarch, that acts the Tyrant o'er his Subjects; One, who could think of murdering an innocent Wife; and admit of a worthless Beauty to supply her Place. Moabdar was so startled at this unexpected Answer from the God he ador'd, that he was just at the Point of Distraction. The Oracle that I had deliver'd, and the tyrannical Proceedings of his new Spouse Missouf, were enough to deprive him of his Senses. In short, in a few Days he became a perfect Mad-man. Her Caprice, which seem'd a Judgement from above, portended a sudden Revolution. His Subjects accordingly revolted, and were instantly up in Arms. Babylon, that had so long indulg'd herself in Indolence and Ease, became the Seat, or Theatre of a bloody Civil War. Whereupon I was taken from my magnificent Prison, the Bowels of his God, and set up at the Head of a very powerful Party. Your Friend Cador flew to Memphis in hopes to find you there, and bring you back to Babylon. The Prince of Hyrcania, hearing of these intestine Broils, return'd with a powerful Army, in order to form a third Party, among the Babylonians. He attack'd the King, who fled with his fair, but fickle Egyptian before him. Moabdar, however, was so closely pursu'd, that he dy'd of the Wounds he receiv'd in his Retreat. Missouf became the fair Victim of the Conqueror. As for my own Part, I had the Misfortune to be over-power'd likewise, and taken Prisoner by an Hyrcanian Party, who brought me into the Presence of the young Prince, at the very Juncture when Missouf stood before him. You'll smile, doubtless, when I tell you the Prince look'd upon me as the most amiable Captive of the two; but then, I presume you will be sorry to hear, that my hard Fate doom'd me to be a Vassal in his Seraglio. He told me, in direct Terms, that as soon as he had put an happy Issue to one Military Expedition, which would not, he flatter'd himself, be long unexecuted, he would honour me with a Visit. Judge the dreadful Apprehensions I was under, upon his making such a peremptory Declaration. My Obligations to Moabdar were all cancell'd, and I was free to be the Bride of Zadig; but instead of that, I fell into the Toils of a Barbarian. I answer'd him with all the Resentment becoming one of my high Character and unspotted Virtue. I had always heard say, that Heav'n bestow'd on Persons of my Rank, such a peculiar Mark of Majesty and Grandeur, that with a bare Word, or the Glance of an angry Eye, they could bring down, and abase the Pride of those audacious Creatures that durst to thwart their Inclinations. I talk'd as big as a Queen; but I was treated like the most servile Domestic. The saucy Hyrcanian, without so much as vouchsafing me one Single Word, turn'd to his black Eunuch, and told him that I was very impertinent; but yet he could not help thinking I was very pretty. He gave him therefore particular Orders to take care of me, and put me under the same Regimen, with respect to my Diet, as one of his Favourites, in order that I might recover my Colour, which was somewhat too languid; in a Word, that I might become worthy in a little Time of his Royal Favours, and be duely qualified to receive him, when he should honour me so far as to fix the Day. I told him, I would die first: He replied, with a Sneer, that young Ladies, like me, seldom kill'd themselves, and that they were made for Enjoyment; and then turn'd upon his Heel, with as careless an Air, as a Man would part with his Paroquet, when he had shut her up close in her gilded Cage. What a shocking State was I in for the first Queen of the Universe! Nay, I'll say more, for a Heart that was wholly devoted to her Zadig!

At these endearing Words, Zadig threw himself at her Feet, and bath'd them with his Tears. Astarte immediately rais'd him in the most courteous and engaging Manner, and thus continu'd her Narration.—I too plainly perceiv'd, that I was subject to the Tyranny of a Barbarian, and the Rival of a Coquet, that was a Slave like myself. She related to me all her past Adventures in Egypt. From the Description she gave of her Gallant, the Time and Place, the Dromedary he was mounted on, and from every other minute Circumstance, I imagin'd it was your self that play'd the Hero in her Favour. As I made no Doubt but that you resided somewhere in Memphis, I determin'd to go thither my self, but in Disguise. Beauteous Missouf, said I, you are of a much sprightlier Disposition than I am; you will be able to amuse the gay young Prince of Hyrcania a thousand Times better than I shall. Find out some Way therefore for my Escape; by which you will be sole Lady Regent. You will oblige me to the last Degree, by your friendly Assistance, and at the same Time get rid of a Rival. Missouf, (cajol'd with the Hint) came into my Measures directly. She took care to send me packing forthwith, with no other Attendant than an old Egyptian Slave.

No sooner had I reach'd the Borders of Arabia, but a notorious Free-booter, (one Arbogad by Name) pick'd me up, as I was strolling along, and sold me to some Merchants, who convey'd me to yonder Castle, the magnificent Residence of the Emir Ogul. He purchas'd me at all Adventures, without enquiring what, or who I was. He is a perfect Debauchee; his sole Delight lies in good Eating, Wine, and Women; and is one, who imagines, that the Almighty sent him into the World for no other Purpose but to gratify his unruly Appetites. He is excessively fat, and puffs and blows every Moment, like one half choak'd. When he has gorg'd himself so unmercifully that he is ready to burst, his chief Physician can persuade him to take any Thing for his Relief; tho' he laughs at him, and despises his Advice when he's well and sober. He has intimated to him, that at present his Life's in Danger, and nothing will restore him but a Basilisk, boil'd in Rose-Water. Whereupon the grand Ogul has promis'd his last Favours to that Slave, whoever she be, that shall be so fortunate as to catch a Basilisk, for him, since it seems they are so seldom to be met with. You see I have others to struggle for the Honour propos'd, and I never had a less Inclination to find out this Basilisk than at present, since I have once more met with my dearest Zadig.

After this Declaration, Astarte and Zadig renew'd with Warmth the virtuous Affection which they had long conceiv'd for each other; and reciprocally utter'd all the tenderest Expressions that Love in Distress could possibly devise. And the Genii, who preside over all the soft Passions, wafted their mutual Vows of eternal Constancy and Truth to the Sphere of Venus.

The whole Train of Slaves, after a long fruitless Search, attended on Ogul, to inform him that all their strictest Search was fruitless. Zadig desired that he might have the Honour to be introduc'd into his Presence. Accordingly he was, and his Address was to this or the like Effect. May immortal Health descend from Heaven to preserve a Life, Sir, so precious as yours is. I am a Physician by Profession. I flew to your Palace, on the first News of the dangerous Situation you were in, and have brought a Basilisk with me, distill'd in Rose-Water. I can have no Hopes of the Honour of your Bed, in Case I succeed in my Application: All the Favour I request, is, the Release of one of your Babylonish Slaves, who has been in your Highness's Retinue for some Time. And I am willing to be your Bond-slave in her Stead, if I fail of restoring the most illustrious and magnificent Ogul to his pristine State of Health.

The Proposition was readily embrac'd. Astarte was instantly

discharg'd, and set out for Babylon, with a proper Attendant, according to Zadig's Direction; assuring her that she should hear every Day, by a special Courier, of his Proceedings with his new Patient. The Farewel which they took of each other, was very affectionate and tender, expressive of the strongest Obligations to each other. The Moments of Meeting, and those of Parting, are (as it is written in the sacred Book of Zend) the two most remarkable Epochas of a Lover's Life. Zadig's repeated Protestations of Affection for the Queen were perfectly sincere, and the pure Dictates of his Heart; and the Queen's Love for Zadig had made a deeper Impression on hers, than she thought proper to discover.

In the mean Time, Zadig, again addressing himself to Ogul, said; my Basilisk, Sir, as others are, is not to be drest or eaten; but all its Virtues must penetrate your whole Fabrick, thro' your Pores; I have inclos'd my never-failing Sudorific in a Bladder, full-blown and carefully cover'd with the softest Leather. You must kick this Bladder, Sir, once a Day about your Hall for a whole Hour together, with all the Vigour and Activity you possibly can. This Medicine must be repeated every Morning, and I'll attend the Operation: Upon your due Observance of the Regimen I shall put you under, I doubt not, but with the Blessing of Heav'n on my honest Endeavours, I shall give you ample Demonstration of my being an Adept in Physick. Ogul, upon making the first Experiment, was ready to expire for want of Breath, and thought he should die with the Fatigue. The second Day did not prove altogether so irksome, and he slept much better at Night than he had done before. In short, our Doctor in about eight Days Time, perform'd an absolute Cure. His Patient was as brisk, active and gay, as One in the Bloom of his Youth.

Now, Sir, said Zadig, I'll be ingenuous with you, and disclose to you the important Secret. You have play'd at Foot-ball these eight Days successively; and you have liv'd all that Time, within the Bounds of Sobriety and Moderation. Know, Sir, that there is no such Animal in Nature as a Basilisk; that Health is to be secur'd by Temperance and Exercise; and that the Art of making Health consistent with Luxury, is altogether as impracticable, and an Art, in all Respects, as idle and chimerical, as those of the Philosopher's Stone, judicial Astrology, or any other Reveries of the like airy and fantastic Nature.

Ogul's Head-Physician, apprehensive that this unexpected Cure, thus wrought by a Stranger, through such an Anti-medicinal Preparation, might possibly not only render himself the Object of Contempt in the Eye of his great Master, but cast a Kind of Slur in general on his whole Fraternity, conven'd a Set of petty Doctors and Apothecaries, who were his Vassals, and entirely devoted to his Interest, to find out some sure Ways and Means to cut off in private his dreadful Rival; but whilst their wicked Plot was hatching, Zadig receiv'd a Courier from the Queen Astarte.

16

THE TOURNAMENTS

The Queen was receiv'd at Babylon with all the Transports of Joy that could possibly be express'd for the safe Return of so illustrious and so beautiful a Personage, that had run thro' such a long Series of Misfortunes. Babylon at that Time seem'd to be perfectly serene and quiet. As for the young Prince of Hyrcania, he was slain in Battle. The Babylonians, who were the Victors, declar'd that Astarte should marry that Candidate for the Crown, who should gain it by a fair and impartial Election. They were determin'd, that the most valuable Post of Honour in the World, namely, that of being the Royal Consort of Astarte, and the Sovereign of Babylon, should be the Result of Merit only; and not be procur'd by any Party-Factions or Court-Intrigues. A solemn Oath was voluntarily taken by all Parties, that he who should distinguish himself by his superior Valour and Wisdom, should unanimously be acknowledg'd the Sovereign-Elect.

A spacious List, or Circus, was pitched upon, surrounded with commodious Seats, erected in an Amphitheatrical Manner, and richly embellish'd some few Leagues from the City. Thither the Combatants, or Champions were to repair, compleatly accoutred. Each of them had a distinct Apartment to himself behind the Lists, where no Soul could either see them, or know who they were. They were to enter the Lists four several Times. Those who were so happy as to conquer four Competitors, were afterwards to engage each other in single Combat; in order that he who should remain Master of the Field should be proclaim'd the happy Victor.

Four Days afterwards, they were to meet again, accoutred as before, and to explain all such Ænigmas, or Riddles, as the Magi should think proper to propose. If their Queries should prove too intricate and perplext for them to resolve, they were to have Recourse to the Lists again, and after that, to fresh Ænigmas, before they could be entitled to the Election: So that the Tournaments were to be continu'd till One of the Candidates should be twice a Victor, and shine as conspicuous, with respect to his internal Qualities, as to his Dexterity and Address in heroic Atchievements. The Queen, in the mean Time, was to be narrowly watch'd, and allow'd only to be a Spectator of both their Amusements, at some considerable Distance; and moreover, to be cover'd with a Vail: Nor was she indulg'd so far as to speak one single Word to any Candidate whomsoever, in order to prevent the least Jealousy or Suspicion either of Partiality or Injustice.

Astarte took care, by the Courier, to inform her Lover of all the Preliminary Articles abovemention'd, not doubting but that he would exert both his Courage and Understanding for her Sake, beyond any of the other Competitors.

Zadig accordingly set out for Babylon, and besought the Goddess Venus, not only to fortify his Courage, but to illuminate his Mind with Wisdom on this important Occasion.

The Night before these martial Atchievements were to commence, Zadig arrived upon the Banks of the Euphrates. He inscrib'd his Device amongst the List of Combatants; concealing, at the same Time, both his Person and Name, as the Laws of the

Election required; and accordingly, withdrew to the Apartment that was provided for him, according to his Lot.

Cador, who was just return'd to Babylon, having hunted all Egypt over to no Purpose, in Hopes to find his Friend Zadig, brought a compleat set of Armour into his Lodge, by express Orders from the Queen: She sent him likewise One of the finest Horses in all Persia. Zadig knew that these Presents could come from No-body but his dear Astarte, which redoubled his Vigour and his Hopes.

The next Morning the Queen being seated under a Canopy of State, enrich'd with precious Stones; and the Amphitheatres being crowded with Gentlemen and Ladies of all Ranks and Conditions from Babylon; the Competitors made their personal Appearance in the Circus: Each of them went up to the grand Magus, and laid down his particular Device at his Feet. The Devices were drawn by Lot: That of Zadig was the last. The first that advanc'd was a Grandee, one Itabod by Name, immensely rich, indeed, and very haughty; but no ways couragious; exceedingly awkward, and a Man of no acquir'd Parts. The Sycophants that hover'd round about him flatter'd him, that a Man of his Merit couldn't fail of being King: He imperiously replied, One of my Merit must be King: Whereupon he was arm'd Cap-a-pee. His Armour was made of pure Gold, enamell'd with Green. The Housings of his Saddle were green, and his Lance embellish'd with green Ribbands. Every One was sensible, at first Sight, by Itobad's Manner of managing his Horse, that he was not the Man whom Heav'n had pitch'd upon to sway the Babylonish Scepter. The first Combatant that tilted with him, threw him out of the Saddle; the second flung him quite over the Crupper, and laid him sprawling on the Ground, with his Heels quiv'ring in the Air. Itobad, 'tis true, remounted, but with so ill a Grace, that an universal Laugh went round the Amphitheatre. The third, disdaining to use his Lance, made only a Feint at him: Then catch'd hold of his Right Leg, and whirling him round, threw him flat upon the Sand. The Esquires, who were the Attendants, ran to his Assistance, and with a Sneer remounted him. The fourth Combatant catch'd hold of his Left Leg, and unhors'd him again. He was convey'd thro' the hissing Multitude to his Lodge, where, according to the Law in that Case provided, he was to pass the Night. And as he hobbled along, said he, to the Esquires, what a sad Misfortune is this to One of my Birth and Character!

The other Champions play'd their Parts much better; and all came off with Credit. Some conquer'd two of their Antagonists, and others were so far successful as to get the better of three. None of them, however, except Prince Hottam, vanquish'd four. Zadig, at last, enter'd the Lists, and dismounted all his four Opponents, one after the other, with the utmost Ease, and with such an Air and Grace, as gain'd him universal Applause. As the Case stood thus, Zadig and Hottam were to close the Day's Entertainment in a single Combat. The Armour of the latter was of a blue Colour mixt with Gold, and the Housings of his Saddle were of the same. Those of the former white as Snow. The Multitude were divided in their Wishes. The Knight in blue was the Favourite of some of the Ladies; and others again were Admirers of the Cavalier in white. The Queen, whose Heart was in a perfect Palpitation, put up her secret Prayers to Venus to assist her darling Hero.

The two Champions making their Passes and their Volta's, with the utmost Dexterity and Address, and keeping firm in their Saddles, gave each other such Rebuffs with their Lances, that all the Spectators (the Queen only excepted) wish'd for two Kings of Babylon. At last, their Horses being tired, and both their Lances broke, Zadig made use of the following Stratagem, which his Antagonist wasn't any ways appriz'd of. He got artfully behind him, and shooting with a Spring on his Horses Buttocks, grasp'd him close, threw him headlong on the Sand, then jump'd into his Seat, and wheel'd round Prince Hottam, while he lay sprawling on the Ground. All the Spectators in general, with loud Acclamations, cried out, Victory! Victory! in favour of the Champion in white. Hottam, incens'd to the last Degree, got up, and drew his Sword. Zadig sprang from his Horse with his Sabre in his Hand. Now, behold the two Chieftains upon their Legs, commencing a new Trial of Skill! where they seem'd to get the better of each other alternately; for both were strong, and both were active. The Feathers of their Helmets, the Studs of their Bracelets, their Coats of Mail, flew about in Pieces, thro' the dry Blows which they a thousand Times repeated. They struck at each other sometimes with the Edge of their Swords, at other Times they push'd, as Occasion offer'd: Now on the Right, then on the Left; now on the Head, then at the Breast; they retreated; they advanc'd; they kept at a Distance; they clos'd again; they grasp'd each other, turning and twisting like two Serpents, and engag'd each other as fiercely as two Libyan Lions fighting for their Prey: Their Swords struck Fire almost at every Blow. At last, Zadig, in order to recover his Breath, for a Moment or two stood still, and afterwards, making a Feint at the Prince, threw him on his Back, and disarm'd him. Hottam, thereupon, cried out, O thou Knight of the white Armour! 'Tis you only are destin'd to be the King of Babylon. The Queen was perfectly transported. The two Champions were reconducted to their separate Lodges, as the others had been before them, in Conformity to the Laws prescrib'd. Several Mutes were order'd to wait on the Champions, and carry them some proper Refreshment. We'll leave the Reader to judge whether the Queen's Dwarf was not appointed to wait on Zadig on this happy Occasion. After Supper the Mutes withdrew, and left the Combatants to rest their wearied Limbs till the next Morning; at which Time the Victor was to produce his Device, before the Grand Magus, in order to confer Notes, and discover the Hero whoever he might be.

Zadig slept very sound, notwithstanding his amorous Regard for the Queen, being perfectly fatigu'd. Itabod, who lay in the Lodge contiguous to his, could not once close his Eyes for Vexation. He got up therefore in the Dead of the Night, stole imperceptibly into Zadig's Apartment, took his white Armour and Device away with him, and substituted his green One in its Place.

As soon as the Day began to dawn, he repair'd, with a seemingly undaunted Courage, to the Grand Magus, to inform him, that he was the mighty Hero, the happy Victor. Without the least Hesitation, he gain'd his Point, and was proclaim'd Victor before Zadig was awake. Astarte, astonish'd at this unexpected Disappointment, return'd with a Heart overwhelm'd with Despair, to the Court of Babylon. Almost all the Spectators were mov'd off from the Amphitheatre before Zadig wak'd: He hunted for his Arms; but could find nothing but those in green. He was oblig'd, tho' sorely against his Will, to put it on, having nothing else in his Lodge to appear in: Confounded, and big with Resentment, he drest himself, and made his personal Appearance in that despicable Equipage. The Populace that were left behind in the Circus, hiss'd him every Step he took, they made a Ring about him, and treated him with all the Marks of Ignominy and Contempt. The most cowardly Wretch breathing was never sure so sweated, or hunted down as poor Zadig! He grew quite out of Patience at last, and cut his Way thro' the insulting Mob, with his Rival's Sabre; but he did not know what Measures to pursue, or how to rectify so gross a Mistake. It was not in his Power to have a Sight of the Queen; he could never recover the white Armour again which She had sent him; That was the Compromise, or the Engagement, to which the Combatants had all unanimously agreed: Thus, as he was on the one Hand, plung'd in an Abyss of Sorrow; so on the other, he was almost drove distracted with Vexation and Resentment. He withdrew therefore, in a solitary Mood, to the Banks of the Euphrates, now fully persuaded, that his impropitious Star had shed its most baleful Influence on him, and that his Misfortunes were irretrievable, revolving in his Mind, all his Disappointments from his first Adventure with the Court-Coquet, who had entertain'd an utter Aversion to a blind Eye, down to his late Loss of his white Armour. See! said he, the fatal Consequence of being a Sluggard! Had I been more vigilant, I had been King of Babylon; but what is more, I had been happy in the Embraces of my dearest Astarte. All the Knowledge of Books or Mankind; all the personal Valour that I can boast of, has only prov'd an Aggravation of my Sorrows. He carried the Point so far at last, as to murmur at the unequal

Dispensations of Divine Providence; and was tempted to believe, that all Occurrences were govern'd by a malignant Destiny, which never fail'd to oppress the Virtuous, and always crown'd the Actions of such Villains as the green Knight, with uncommon Success. In one of his frantick Fits, he put on the green Armour, that had created him such a World of Disgrace. A Merchant happening to pass by, he sold it to him for a Trifle, and took in Exchange nothing more than a Mantle, and a Cap. In this Disguise, he took a solitary Walk along the Banks of the Euphrates, every Minute reflecting in his Mind on the partial Proceedings of Providence, which never ceas'd to torment him.

17

THE HERMIT

As Zadig was travelling along, he met with a Hermit, whose grey and venerable Beard descended to his Girdle. He had in his Hand a little Book, on which his Eyes were fix'd. Zadig threw himself in his Way, and made him a profound Bow. The Hermit return'd the Compliment with such an Air of Majesty and Benevolence, that Zadig's Curiosity prompted him to converse with so agreeable a Stranger. Pray, Sir, said he, what may be the Contents of the Treatise you are reading with such Attention. 'Tis call'd, said the Hermit, the Book of Fate; will you please to look at it. He put the Book into the Hands of Zadig, who, tho' he was a perfect Master of several Languages, couldn't decypher one single Character. This rais'd his Curiosity still higher. You seem dejected, said the good Father to him. Alas! I have Cause enough, said Zadig. If you'll permit me to accompany you, said the old Hermit, perhaps I may be of some Service to you. I have sometimes instill'd Sentiments of Consolation into the Minds of the Afflicted. Zadig had a secret Regard for the Air of the old Man, for his Beard, and his Book. He found, by conversing with him, that he was the most learned Person he had ever met with. The Hermit harangu'd on Destiny, Justice, Morality, the sovereign Good, the Frailty of Nature; on Virtue and Vice, in such a lively Manner, and in such a Flow of Words, that Zadig was attach'd to him by an invincible Charm. He begg'd earnestly that he would favour him with his Company to Babylon. That Favour I was going to ask my self, said the old Man. Swear to me by Orosmades, that you won't leave me, for some Days at least, let me do what I please. Zadig took the Oath requir'd, and both pursu'd their Journey.

The two Travellers arriv'd that Evening at a superb Castle. The Hermit begg'd for an hospitable Reception of himself and his young Comrade. The Porter, whom any One might have taken for some Grandee, let them in, but with a kind of Coldness and Contempt. However, he conducted them to the Head-Steward, who went with them thro' every rich Apartment of his Master's House. They were seated at Supper afterwards at the lower End, indeed, of the Table, and where they were taken little or no Notice of by the Host; but they were serv'd with as much Delicacy and Profusion, as any of the other Guests. When they arose from Table, they wash'd their Hands in a Golden Bason set with Emeralds, and other costly Stones. When 'twas Time to go to Rest, they were conducted into a Bed-chamber richly furnish'd; and the next Morning two Pieces of Gold were presented to him for their mutual Service, by a Valet in waiting; and then they were dismiss'd.

The Proprietor of this Castle, said Zadig, as they were upon the Road, seems to me to be a very hospitable Gentleman; tho' somewhat too haughty indeed, and too imperious: The Words were no sooner out of his Mouth, but he perceiv'd that the Pocket of his Comrade's Garment, tho' very large, was swell'd, and greatly extended: He soon saw what was the Cause, and that he had clandestinely brought off the Golden Laver. He durst not immediately take Notice of the Fact; but was ready to sink at the very Thoughts on't. About Noon, the Hermit rapp'd at a petty Cottage with his Staff, the beggarly Residence of an old, rich Miser. He desir'd that he and his Companion might refresh themselves there for a few Hours. An old, shabby Domestick let them in indeed, but with visible Reluctance, and carried them into the Stable, where all their Fare was a few musty Olives, and a Draught or two of sower small Beer. The Hermit seem'd as content with his Repast, as he was the Night before. At last, rising off from his Seat, he paid his Compliments to the old Valet (who had as watchful an Eye over them all the Time, as if they had been a Brace of Thieves, and intimated every now and then that he fear'd they would be benighted) and gave him the two Pieces of Gold, he had but just receiv'd that Morning, as a Token of his Gratitude for his courteous Entertainment. He added moreover, I would willingly speak one Word with your Master before I go. The Valet, thunder-struck at his unexpected Gratuity, comply'd with his Request: Most hospitable Sir, said the Hermit, I couldn't go away without returning you my grateful Acknowledgments for the friendly Reception we have met with this Afternoon. Be pleas'd to accept this Golden Bason as a small Token of my Gratitude and Esteem. The Miser started, and was ready to fall down backwards at the Sight of so valuable a Present. The Hermit gave him no Time to recover out of his Surprise, but march'd off that Moment with his young Comrade. Father, said Zadig, What is all this that I have seen? You seem to me to act in a quite different Manner from the Generality of Mankind. You plunder One, who entertain'd you with all the Pomp and Profusion in the World, to enrich a covetous, sordid Wretch, who treated you in the most unworthy Manner. Son, said the old Man, that Grandee, who receives Visits of Strangers, with no other View than to gratify his Pride, and to raise their Astonishment at the Furniture of his Palace, will henceforward learn to be wiser; and the Miser to be more liberal for the Time to come. Don't be surpris'd, but follow me. Zadig was at a stand at present; and couldn't well determine whether his Companion was a Man of greater Wisdom than ordinary, or a Mad-man. But the Hermit assum'd such an Ascendency over him, exclusive of the Oath he had taken, that he couldn't tell how to leave him. At Night they came to a House very commodiously built, but neat and plain; where nothing was wanting, and yet nothing profuse. The Master was a Philosopher, that had retir'd from the busy World, in order to live in Peace, and form his Mind to Virtue. He was pleas'd to build this little Box for the Reception of Strangers, in a handsome Manner, but without Ostentation. He came in Person to meet them at the Door, and for a Time, advis'd them to sit down and rest themselves in a commodious Apartment. After some Respite, he invited them to a frugal, yet elegant Repast; during which, he talk'd very intelligently about the late Revolutions in Babylon. He seem'd entirely to be in the Queen's Interest, and heartily wish'd that Zadig had entred the Lists for the regal Prize: But Babylon, said he, don't deserve a King of so much Merit. A modest Blush appear'd in Zadig's Face at this unexpected Compliment, which innocently aggravated his Misfortunes. It was agreed, on all Hands, that the Affairs of this World took sometimes a quite different Turn from what the wisest Patriots would wish them. The Hermit replied, the Ways of Providence are often very intricate and obscure, and Men were much to blame for casting Reflections on the Conduct of the Whole, upon the bare Inspection of the minutest Part.

The next Topick they entred upon was the Passions. Alas! said Zadig, how fatal in their Consequences! However, said the Hermit, they are the Winds that swell the Sail of the Vessel. Sometimes, 'tis true, they overset it; but there is no such Thing as sailing without them. Phlegm, indeed, makes Men peevish and sick; but then there is no living without it. Tho' every Thing here below is dangerous, yet All are necessary.

In the next Place, their Discourse turn'd on sensual Pleasures; and the Hermit demonstrated, that they were the Gifts of Heaven; for, said he, Man cannot bestow either Sensations or Ideas on himself; he receives them all; his Pain and Pleasure, as well as his Being, proceed from a superior Cause.

Zadig stood astonish'd, to think how a Man that had committed such vile Actions, could argue so well on such Moral Topicks. At the proper Hour, after an Entertainment, not only instructive, but ev'ry way agreeable, their Host conducted them to their Bed-chamber, thanking Heaven for directing two such polite and virtuous Strangers to his House. He offer'd them at the same Time some Silver, to defray their Expences on the Road; but with such an Air of Respect and Benevolence, that 'twas impossible to give the least Disgust. The Hermit, however, refus'd it, and took his leave, as he propos'd to set forward for Babylon by Break of Day. Their Parting was very affectionate and friendly; Zadig, in particular, express'd a more than common Regard for a Man of so amiable a Behaviour. When the Hermit and he were alone, and preparing for Bed, they talk'd long in Praise of their new Host. As soon as Day-light appear'd, the old Hermit wak'd his young Comrade. 'Tis Time to be gone, said he; but as all the House are fast asleep, I'll leave a Token behind me of my Respect and Affection for the Master of it. No sooner were the Words out of his Mouth, but he struck a Light, kindled a Torch, and set the Building in a Flame: Zadig, in the utmost Confusion, shriek'd out, and would, if possible, have prevented him from being guilty of such a monstrous Act of Ingratitude. The Hermit dragg'd him away, by a superior Force. The House was soon in a Blaze: When they had got at a convenient Distance, the Hermit, with an amazing Sedateness, turn'd back and survey'd the destructive Flames. Behold, said he, our fortunate Friend! In the Ruins, he will find an immense Treasure, that will enable him, from henceforth, to exert his Beneficence, and render his Virtues more and more conspicuous. Zadig, tho' astonish'd to the last Degree, attended him to their last Stage, which was to the Cottage of a very virtuous and well-dispos'd Widow, who had a Nephew of about fourteen Years of Age. He was a hopeful Youth, and the Darling of her Heart. She entertain'd her two Guests with the best Provisions her little House afforded. In the Morning she order'd her Nephew to attend them to an adjacent Bridge, which, having been broken down some few Days before, render'd the Passage dangerous to Strangers.

The Lad, being very attentive to wait on them, went formost.

When they were got upon the Bridge; come hither, my pretty Boy, said the Hermit, I must give your Aunt some small Token of my Respect for her last Night's Favours. Upon that, he twisted his Fingers in the Hair of his Head, and threw him, very calmly, into the River. Down went the little Lad; he came up once again to the Surface of the Water; but was soon lost in the rapid Stream. O thou Monster! thou worst of Villains, cry'd Zadig! Didn't you promise, said the Hermit, to view my Conduct with Patience? Know then, that had that Boy liv'd but one Year longer, he would have murder'd his Foster-Mother. Who told you so, you barbarous Wretch, said Zadig? And when did you read that inhuman Event in your Black-Book of Fate? Who gave you Permission pray, to drown so innocent a Youth, that had never disoblig'd you?

No sooner had our young Babylonian ceas'd his severe Reflections, but he perceiv'd that the old Hermit's long Beard grew shorter and shorter; that the Furrows in his Face began to fill up, and that his Cheeks glow'd with a Rose-coloured Red, as if he had been in the Bloom of Fifteen. His Mantle was vanish'd at once; and on his Shoulders, which were before cover'd, appear'd four angelic Wings, each refulgent as the Sun. O thou Messenger of Heaven! O thou angelic Form! cry'd Zadig, and fell prostrate at his Feet; thou art descended from the Empireum, I find, to instruct such a poor frail Mortal as I am, how to submit to the Mysteries of Fate. Mankind in general, said the Angel Jesrad, judge of the Whole, by only viewing the hither Link of the Chain. Thou, of all the human Race, wast the only Man that deserv'd to have thy Mind enlighten'd. Zadig, begg'd Leave to speak. I am somewhat diffident of myself, 'tis true; but may I presume, Sir, to beg the Solution of one Scruple? Would it not have been better to have chastiz'd the Lad, and by that Means reform'd him, than to have cut him off thus unprepar'd in a Moment. Jesrad, replied, had he been virtuous, and had he liv'd, 'twas his Fate not only to be murder'd himself, but his Wife, whom he would afterwards have married, and the little Infant, that was to have been the Pledge of their mutual Affection. Is it necessary then, venerable Guide, that there should be Wickedness and Misfortunes in the World, and that those Misfortunes should fall with Weight on the Heads of the Righteous? The Wicked, replied Jesrad, are always unhappy. Misfortunes are intended only as a Touch-stone, to try a small Number of the Just, who are thinly scatter'd about this terrestrial Globe: Besides, there is no Evil under the Sun, but some Good proceeds from it: But, said Zadig, Suppose the World was all Goodness, and there was no such Thing in Nature as Evil. Then, that World of yours, said Jesrad, would be another World; the Chain of Events would be another Wisdom; and that other Order, which would be perfect, must of Necessity be the everlasting Residence of the supreme Being, whom no Evil can approach. That great and first Cause has created an infinite Number of Worlds, and no two of them alike. This vast Variety is an Attribute of his Omnipotence. There are not two Leaves on the Trees throughout the Universe, nor any two Globes of Light amongst the Myriad of Stars that deck the infinite Expanse of Heaven, which are perfectly alike. And whatever you see on that small Atom of Earth, whereof you are a Native, must exist in the Place, and at the Time appointed, according to the immutable Decrees of him who comprehends the Whole. Mankind imagine, that the Lad, whom I plung'd into the River, was drown'd by Chance; and that our generous Benefactor's House was reduc'd to Ashes by the same Chance; but know, there is no such Thing as Chance, all Misfortunes are intended, either as severe Trials, Judgments, or Rewards; and are the Result of Foreknowledge. You remember, Sir, the poor Fisherman in Despair, that thought himself the most unhappy Mortal breathing. The great Orasmades, sent you to amend his Situation. Frail Mortal! Cease to contend with what you ought to adore. But, said Zadig—whilst the Sound of the Word But dwelt upon his Tongue, the Angel took his Flight towards the tenth Sphere. Zadig sunk down upon his Knees, and acknowledg'd an over-ruling Providence with all the Marks of the profoundest Submission. The Angel, as he was soaring towards the Clouds, cried out in distinct Accents; Make thy Way towards Babylon.

18

THE ÆNIGMAS, OR RIDDLES

Zadig, as one beside himself, and perfectly thunder-struck, beat his March at random. He entred, however, into the City of Babylon, on that very Day, when those Combatants who had been before engag'd in the List or Circus, were already assembled in the spacious Outer-Court of the Palace, in order to solve the Ænigmas, and give the wisest Answers they could to such Questions, as the Grand Magus should propose. All the Parties concern'd were present, except the Knight of the Green Armour. No sooner had Zadig made his Appearance in the City, but the Populace flock'd round about him: No Eye was satisfied with gazing at him: All in general were lavish of their Praises, and in their Hearts wish'd him their Sovereign, except the envious Man, who as he pass'd by, fetch'd a deep Sigh, and turn'd his Head aside. The Populace with loud Acclamations attended him to the Palace-Gate. The Queen, who had heard of his Arrival, was in the utmost Agony, between Hope and Despair. Her Vexation had almost brought her to Death's Door; she couldn't conceive why Zadig should appear without his Accoutrements, nor imagine which Way Itobad could procure the snow-white Armour. At the Sight of Zadig a confus'd Murmur ran thro' the whole Place. Every Eye was surpriz'd, tho' charm'd at the same Time to see him again: But then none were to be admitted into the Assembly-Room except the Knights.

I have fought as successfully as any one of them all, said Zadig, tho' another appears clad in my Armour; but in the mean Time, before I can possibly prove my Assertion, I insist upon being admitted into Court, in order to give my Solutions to such Ænigmas as shall be propos'd. 'Twas put to the Vote. As the Reputation of his being a Man of the strictest Honour and Veracity was so strongly imprinted on their Minds, the Motion of his Admittance was carried in the Affirmative, without the least Opposition.

The first Question the *Grand Magus* propos'd was this: What is the longest and yet the shortest Thing in the World; the most swift and the most slow; the most divisible, and the most extended; the least valu'd, and the most regretted; And without which nothing can possibly be done: Which, in a Word, devours every Thing how minute soever, and yet gives Life and Spirit to every Object or Being, however Great?

Itobad had the Honour to answer first. His reply was, that a Man of his Merit had something else to think on, than idle Riddles; 'twas enough for him, that he was acknowledg'd the Hero of the Circus. One said, the Solution of the Ænigma propos'd was Fortune; others said the Earth; and others again the Light: But Zadig pronounced it to be Time. Nothing, said he, can be longer, since 'tis the Measure of Eternity; Nothing is shorter, since there is Time always wanting to accomplish what we aim at. Nothing passes so slowly as Time to him who is in Expectation; and nothing so swift as Time to him who is in the perfect Enjoyment of his Wishes. It's Extent is to Infinity, in the Whole; and divisible to Infinity in part. All Men neglect it in the Passage; and all regret the Loss of it when 'tis past. Nothing can possibly be done without it; it buries in Oblivion whatever is unworthy of being transmitted down to Posterity; and it renders all illustrious Actions immortal. The Assembly agreed unanimously that Zadig was in the Right.

The next Question that was started, was, What is the Thing we receive, without being ever thankful for it; which we enjoy, without knowing how we came by it; which we give away to others, without knowing where 'tis to be found; and which we lose, without being any ways conscious of our Misfortune?

Each pass'd his Verdict. Zadig was the only Person that concluded it was Life. He solv'd every Ænigma propos'd, with equal Facility. Itobad, when he heard the Explications, always said that nothing in the World was more easy, than to solve such obvious Questions; and that he could interpret a thousand of them without the least Hesitation, were he inclin'd to trouble his Head about such Trifles.

Other Questions were propos'd in regard to Justice, the sovereign Good, and the Art of Government. Zadig's Answers still carried the greatest Weight. What Pity 'tis, said some who were present, that one of so comprehensive a Genius, should make such a scurvy Cavalier?

Most illustrious Grandees, said Zadig, I was the Person that had the Honour of being Victor at your Circus; the white Armour, most puissant Lords, was mine. That awkward Warrior there, Lord Itobad, dress'd himself in it whilst I was asleep. He imagin'd, it is plain, that it would do him more Honour than his own Green one. Unaccoutred as I am, I am ready, before this august Assembly, to give them incontestable Proof of my superior Skill; to engage with the Usurper of the White Armour with my Sword only in my Mantle and Bonnet; and to testify that I only was the happy Victor of the justly admired Hottam.

Itobad accepted of the Challenge with all the Assurance of Success imaginable. He did not doubt, but being properly accoutred with his Helmet, his Cuirass, and his Bracelets, he should be able to hue down an Antagonist, in his Mantle and Cap, and nothing to skreen him from his Resentment, but a single Sabre. Zadig drew his Sword, and saluted the Queen with it, who view'd him with Transport mix'd with Fear. Itobad drew his, but paid his Compliments to Nobody. He approach'd Zadig, as one, whom he imagin'd incapable of making any considerable Resistance. He concluded, 'twas in his Power to cut Zadig into Atoms. Zadig, however, knew how to parry the Blow, by dexterously receiving it upon his Fort (as the Swordsmen call it) by which Means Itobad's Sword was snapt in two. With that Zadig in an Instant clos'd his Adversary, and by his superior Strength, as well as Skill, laid him sprawling on his Back. Then holding the Point of his Sword to the opening of his Cuirass, Submit to be stripp'd of your borrow'd Plumes, or you are a dead Man this Moment. Itobad, always surpriz'd, that any Disappointment should attend a Man of such exalted Merit as himself, very tamely permitted Zadig to disrobe him by Degrees of his pompous Helmet, his superb Cuirass, his rich Bracelets, his brilliant Cuisses, or Armour for his

Thighs, and other Martial Accoutrements. When Zadig had equipp'd himself Cap-a-pee, in his now recover'd Armour, he flew to Astarte, and threw himself prostrate at her Feet. Cador prov'd, without any great Difficulty, that the White Armour was Zadig's Property. He was thereupon acknowledg'd King of Babylon, by the unanimous Content of the Whole Court; but more particularly with the Approbation of Astarte, who after such a long Series of Misfortunes, now tasted the Sweets of seeing her darling Zadig thought worthy, in the Opinion of the whole World, to be the Partner of her royal Bed. Itobad withdrew, and contented himself with being call'd *my Lord* within the narrow Compass of his own Domesticks. Zadig, in short, was elected King, and was as happy as any Mortal could be.

Now he began to reflect on what the Angel Jesrad had said to him: Nay, he reflected so far back as the Story of the Arabian Atom of Dust metamorphosed into a Diamond. The Queen and He ador'd the Divine Providence. Zadig permitted Missouf, the Fair Coquet, to make her Conquests where she could. He sent Couriers to bring the Free-booter Arbogad to Court, and gave him an Honourable Military Post in his Army, with a farther Promise of Promotion to the highest Dignity; but upon this express Condition, that he would act for the future as a Soldier of Honour; but assur'd him at the same Time, that he'd make a publick Example of him, if he follow'd his Profession of Free-booting for the future.

Setoc was sent for from the lonely Desarts of Arabia, together with the fair Almonza, his new Bride, to preside over the commercial Affairs of Babylon. Cador was advanc'd to a Post near himself, and was his Favourite Minister at Court, as the just Reward of his past Services. He was, in short, the King's real Friend; and Zadig was the only Monarch in the Universe that could boast of such an Attendant. The Dwarf, tho' dumb, was not wholly forgotten. The Fisherman was put into the Possession of a very handsome House; and Orcan was sentenc'd, not only to pay him a very considerable Sum for the Injustice done him in detaining his Wife; but to resign her likewise to the proper Owner: The Fisherman, however, grown wise by Experience, soften'd the Rigour of the Sentence, and took the Money only in full of all Accounts.

He didn't leave so much as Semira wholly disconsolate, tho' she had such an Aversion to a blind Eye; nor Azora comfortless, notwithstanding her affectionate Intention to shorten his Nose; for he sooth'd their Sorrows by very munificent Presents. The envious Informer indeed, died with Shame and Vexation. The Empire was glorious abroad, and in the full Enjoyment of Tranquility, Peace and Plenty, at home: This, in short, was the true golden Age. The whole Country was sway'd by Love and Justice. Every one blest Zadig; and Zadig blest Heav'n for his unexpected Success.

NANINE

OR THE MAN WITHOUT PREJUDICE

DRAMATIS PERSONÆ

THE COUNT D'OLBAN, *a nobleman retired into the country*
THE BARONESS DE L'ORME, *a relation of the Count's, a haughty, imperious woman, of a bad temper, and disagreeable to live with*
THE MARCHIONESS D'OLBAN, *mother of the Count*
NANINE, *a young girl, brought up in the Count's house*
PHILIP HOMBERT, *a peasant in the neighborhood*
BLAISE, *the gardener*
GERMON; MARIN, *servants*

SCENE: *The Count d'Olban's country seat*

ACT I

SCENE I

The Count D'Olban, The Baroness De L'Orme

Baroness:	In short, my lord, it is time to come to an explanation with regard to this affair; we are no children; therefore, let us talk freely: you have been a widower for these two years past, and I, a widow about as long: the lawsuit in which we were unfortunately engaged, and which gave us both so much uneasiness, is at an end; and all our animosities, I hope, now buried with those who were the causes of them.
Count:	I am glad of it; for lawsuits were always my aversion.
Baroness:	And am not I as hateful as a lawsuit?
Count:	You, madam?
Baroness:	Yes, I, sir: for these two years past we have lived together, with freedom, as relations and friends; the ties of blood, taste, and interest, seem to unite us, and to point out a more intimate connection.
Count:	Interest, madam? make use of some better term, I beseech you.
Baroness:	That, sir, I cannot; but with grief I find, your inconstant heart no longer considers me in any other light than as your relative.
Count:	I do not wear the appearance, madam, of a trifler.

Baroness:	You wear the appearance, sir, of a perjured villain.
Count (aside):	Ha! what's this?
Baroness:	Yes, sir: you know the suit my husband began against you, to recover my estate, was, by agreement, to have been terminated by a marriage; a marriage you told me, of choice; you are engaged to me, you know you are; and he who defers the execution of his promise seldom means to perform it.
Count:	You know, I wait for my mother's consent.
Baroness:	A doting old woman: well, sir, and what then?
Count:	I love and respect her yet.
Baroness:	But I do not, sir. Come, come, these are idle, frivolous excuses for your unpardonable falsehood: you wait not for her, or for anybody; perfidious, ungrateful man!
Count:	Who told you so, madam, and whence all this violence of passion? who told you so? whence comes your information, madam?
Baroness:	Who told me? yourself, yourself. Your words, your manner, your air, your whole behavior, put on on purpose to affront me: it shocks me to see it: act in another manner, or find some better excuses for your conduct: can you think me blind to the shameful, unworthy passion that directs you, a passion for the lowest, meanest object? you have deceived me, sir, basely deceived me.
Count:	'Tis false, I cannot deceive; dissimulation is no part of my character. I own to you, there was a time when you were agreeable to me; I admired you, and flattered myself that I should have found in you a treasure to make amends for that which heaven had deprived me of; I hoped in this sweet asylum to have tasted the fruits of a peaceful and

happy union: but you have found out the means to destroy your own power. Love, as I told you long since, has two quivers: one filled with darts, tipped with the purest flame, which inspires the soul with tender feelings, refines our taste and sentiments, enlivens our affection, and enhances our pleasures; the other is full of cruel arrows, that wound our hearts with quarrels, jealousy, and suspicion, bring on coldness and indifference, and remove the warmth of passion to make room for disgust and satiety: these, madam, are the darts which you have drawn forth, against us both, and yet you expect that I should love.

Baroness: There, indeed, I own myself in the wrong: I ought not to expect it: it is not in your power: but you are false, and now would reproach me for it, and I must suffer your insults, your fine similes and illustrations: but pray, sir, what is it I have done to lose this mighty treasure? what have you to find fault with?

Count: Your temper, your humors, madam: beauty pleases the eye alone, softness and complacency charm the soul.

Baroness: And have not you your humors, too, sir?

Count: Doubtless, madam; and, for that very reason, would have an indulgent wife; one whose sweet complying goodness would bend a little to my frailties, and condescend to reconcile me to myself, to heal my wounds without burning them, to correct without assuming, to govern without being a tyrant, to insinuate herself by degrees into my heart, as the light of a fine day opens gradually on the weak and delicate eye: he who feels the yoke that is put on him will always murmur at it;

and tyrannic love is a deity that I abjure: I would be a lover, but not a slave: your pride, madam, would make me contemptible: I have faults, I own I have; but heaven made woman to correct the leaven of our souls, to soften our afflictions, sweeten our bad humors, soothe our passions, and make us better and happier beings: this was what they were designed for; and, for my part, I would prefer ugliness and affability to beauty with pride and arrogance.

Baroness: Excellently well moralized, indeed; and so when you insult, abuse, and betray me, I in return, with mean complacency, must forgive the shameful extravagance of your passion; and your assumed air of grandeur and magnanimity must be a sufficient excuse to me for all the baseness of your heart.

Count: How, madam?

Baroness: Yes, sir: I know you: it is the young Nanine who has done me this injury; a child, a servant, a field beggar, whom my foolish tenderness nourished and supported; whom your fond, easy mother, touched with false pity, took up out of the bosom of penury and sorrow. O you blush, sir, do you?

Count: I, madam? I wish her well.

Baroness: You love her, sir: I know you do.

Count: Well, madam, and if I did love her, know, I would openly avow it.

Baroness: Nay, I believe you are capable of it.

Count: I am so.

Baroness: And would you break thus through all the bounds of decency, degrade your rank, demean your birth, and, plunged as you are in shame and infamy, laugh at and defy all honor?

Count: Call it prejudice: whatever you, or the world may

think, madam, I never mistake vanity for honor and glory: you love pomp and splendor, and place grandeur and nobility in a coat of arms: I look for it in the heart. The man of worth, who has modesty with courage, and the woman who has sense and spirit, though without fortune, rank, or title, are, in my eyes, the first of human kind.

Baroness: But surely they ought to have some rank and condition in life. Would you treat a low-born scholar, or an honest man of the meanest birth, because he had a little virtue, in the same manner and with the same respect as you would a lord?

Count: The virtuous should always have the preference.

Baroness: This extravagant humility is insupportable: do we owe nothing then to our rank?

Count: Yes: to be honest.

Baroness: My noble blood would aspire to a higher character.

Count: That is a high one which defies the vulgar.

Baroness: Thus you degrade all quality.

Count: No: thus I do honor to humanity.

Baroness: Ridiculous! what then becomes of the world? what is fashion?

Count: Fashion, madam, is despised by wisdom: I will obey its ridiculous commands in my dress perhaps, but not in my sentiments: no: it becomes a man to act like a man, to preserve to himself his own taste and his own thoughts: am I ridiculously to ask of others what I am to seek, or to avoid, to praise, or condemn? must the world decide my fate? surely I have my reason, and that should be my guide: apes were made for imitation only, but man should act from his own heart.

Baroness: Why, this, to be sure, is freedom of sentiment, and talking like a philosopher. Go, then, thou

	noble and sublime soul, go, and fall in love with village damsels, be the happy rival of plowmen and hedgers: go, and support the honor of your race.
Count:	Good heaven! what must I do? How am I to act?

SCENE II

The Count, The Baroness, Blaise

Count:	Well, sir, what do you want?
Blaise:	Your poor gardener, sir, humbly beseeches your honor—
Count:	My honor! well, Blaise, and what wouldst thou have of my honor?
Blaise:	And please, your honor, I would fain—be married and—
Count:	With all my heart, Blaise, you have my consent; I like your design, and will assist you. It is well folks should marry. Well, and thy spouse elect, Blaise, what is she? handsome?
Blaise:	O yes, sir, a delicate little morsel.
Baroness:	And does she like you, Blaise?
Blaise:	O yes.
Count:	Well, and her name is?
Blaise:	Yes, 'tis—
Count:	What?
Blaise:	The pretty Nanine.
Count:	Nanine?
Baroness:	Well, very well indeed! I approve of the match extremely.
Count (aside):	O heaven! how am I sunk! it cannot, must not be.
Blaise:	I'm sure, master will like it.
Count:	What! did you say she loved you, rascal?

Blaise:	I beg pardon, sir, I—
Count:	Did she tell you that she loved you, sir?
Blaise:	Why, no, sir, not absolutely, sir; not directly; but she seemed to have a little sort of a sneaking kindness for me, too: a hundred times has she said to me in the prettiest, softest, most familiar tone, "Help me, my dear friend Blaise, to make a fine nosegay for my lord, that best of masters;" then would she make the nosegay with such a pretty air, and look so thoughtful, and so absent, and so confused, and so—O it was plain enough.
Count (aside):	Away, Blaise, get thee gone—Oh! and am I agreeable to her then?
Blaise:	Nay, master, now don't put off this little affair of mine.
Count:	Ha!
Blaise:	You shall see how this little spot of land will thrive under our hands soon: why won't you answer me, sir? You say nothing.
Count (aside):	Oh! my heart is too full: I must retire—madam, your servant.

SCENE III

The Baroness, Blaise

Baroness: (to herself)	He loves her to distraction, of that I'm positive: by what charms, by what happy address, could she thus steal his heart from me? Nanine! good heaven! what a choice! what madness! Nanine! no! I shall burst with disappointment.
Blaise:	What did you say, madam, about Nanine?
Baroness: (to herself)	Insolent creature!

Blaise:	Is not Nanine a charming girl?
Baroness:	No.
Blaise:	Well, I say no more; but do speak for me, speak for poor Blaise.
Baroness:	What a dreadful stroke is this!
Blaise:	I have a little money, madam, a few crowns: my father left me three good acres of land, and they shall be hers; money, and land, everything I have, body and soul, Blaise and all.
Baroness:	Believe me, Blaise, I wish you as well as you can wish yourself, and should be glad to serve you: I should be glad to see you married this very night: nay, what's more, I'll give her a portion.
Blaise:	O good, dear baroness! how I do love you! is it possible you can make me so happy?
Baroness:	Alas! Blaise, I am afraid I cannot; we shall never succeed.
Blaise:	O but you must, madam.
Baroness:	I wish to God she was your wife: wait for my orders.
Blaise:	And must I wait? not long I hope.
Baroness:	Be gone.
Blaise:	Servant, madam: I shall have hear, I shall have her.

SCENE IV

The Baroness (alone)

What a strange adventure! could I have received a more cruel injury? a more shameful affront? the Count d'Olban rivalled by a gardener—here, boy, [she calls out to her servant] fetch Nanine to me: since I am so unhappy, I must examine her: where could she have learned this art of flattery? who taught her to gain hearts, and to preserve them, to light up a strong and a lasting flame? where? doubtless, in her eyes, in plain and simple nature: but this shameful and unworthy passion of his is still a secret; it has not dared as yet to appear openly. D'Olban, I see, has his scruples about it: so much the worse; if he had none, I might still have hopes; but he has all the symptoms of true love: O here she comes, the sight of her hurts me; nature is most unjust, to bestow so much beauty on such a creature; 'tis an affront to nobility: come this way, madam.

SCENE V

The Baroness, Nanine

Nanine:	Madam.
Baroness:	And yet, after all, she is not so very handsome; those great black eyes of hers express nothing; but if they have said, I love; ay, there's the danger: but I must—come this way, child.
Nanine:	I come, madam, as is my duty.
Baroness:	Yes: but you make me wait a little for you; prithee, child, step on: how awkwardly she is made! what a mien there is! he was never made for such a creature as you.
Nanine:	'Tis very true, madam: I assure you; I have often blushed in secret when I looked on these fine clothes: but they were your first present to me, the effect of that goodness which I shall ever acknowledge, and of that generous care with which you were pleased to honor me: you took a pride in dressing me: O madam, remember how often you have protected me: believe me, madam, I am still the same: why should you wish to humble a submissive heart, which can never forget itself?
Baroness:	Bring that couch nearer to me—O I am distracted:

	whence come you? what have you been about?
Nanine:	Reading, madam.
Baroness:	Reading what?
Nanine:	An English book that was given me.
Baroness:	What's the subject of it?
Nanine:	'Tis extremely interesting: the author would have us believe that we are all brethren, all born equal, and on a level with each other; but 'tis an idle chimera, I can't reconcile myself to his doctrine.
Baroness (aside):	She will soon, I suppose—what vanity! [To Nanine] bring me my standish, and pen and ink.
Nanine:	Yes, madam.
Baroness:	No; stay: give me something to drink.
Nanine:	What, madam?
Baroness:	Nothing: it's no matter: take my fan. Go and get my gloves—or—stay—it does not signify, you need not: come hither: I desire you to take care never to think yourself handsome.
Nanine:	That, madam, is a lesson you have so often taught me that if I had so much vanity, and self-love had such influence over my foolish heart, you would soon have cured me of it.
Baroness (aside):	Where can she have learned all this? how I hate her! beauty and wit together! 'tis intolerable—hark'ee, child, you know the tenderness I had for you in your infancy.
Nanine:	Yes, madam, and I hope my youth will be honored with equal goodness from you.
Baroness:	Be careful then to deserve it: it is my intention now, this very day, nay, this very hour, to fix and establish your happiness; judge then whether I love you.
Nanine:	To fix my happiness?
Baroness:	Yes: I will give you a portion: the husband I design

	for you is well-made, and in every way worthy of you; a proper match for you in every particular, and the only one that at present could suit you: you ought to thank me for the choice: in a word, 'tis Blaise, the gardener.
Nanine:	Blaise, madam?
Baroness:	Yes: why that simpering? do you hesitate a moment to consent? my offers, madam, I would have you know, are commands; obey, or expect my resentment.
Nanine:	But, madam—
Baroness:	Let me have no buts; they offend me: a pretty thing indeed, for your impertinence to refuse a husband at my hands! that simple heart of yours is swelled to a fine degree of vanity: but your boldness is a little premature, and your triumph will be of short duration: you take advantage of the capricious fortune of one lucky day, but shall soon see what will be the event. You ungrateful little wretch, have you the insolence to please? you understand me, madam, but I'll bring you back to that nothingness whence you came, and you shall lament your folly and your pride: I'll shut you up for the rest of your life in a convent.
Nanine:	On my knees I thank you, madam; do shut me up, my fate will be too mild: yes, madam, of all the benefits you have ever bestowed on me, this, which you call a punishment, I shall esteem the greatest favor: shut me up forever in a cloister; there, I will thank you for your goodness, and bless my dear master: there I shall learn to calm those cruel fears, those dreadful alarms, those worst of evils, those passions that are far more dangerous to me even than your resentment, which fill me

	with terror and astonishment: O madam, by that anger, I entreat you, deliver me, save me, save me, if possible, from myself; this moment I am ready to go.
Baroness:	What do I hear? can it be? are you in earnest, Nanine, or mean you to deceive me?
Nanine:	No: indeed I do not. O do me this charming, this divine favor; my heart stands too much in need of it.
Baroness: (with transport)	Rise then, and let me embrace you. O happy hour! my dear Nanine, my friend, I'll go this instant and prepare your sweet retreat; O 'tis a charming thing to live in a convent!
Nanine:	'Tis at least a shelter from the world, and all its cares.
Baroness:	O my dear, 'tis a delightful situation.
Nanine:	Do you think so, madam?
Baroness:	This world is a hateful place—jealous—
Nanine: (sighing)	'Tis so indeed.
Baroness:	Foolish, wicked, vain, deceitful, inconstant, and ungrateful: O 'tis a horrid place.
Nanine:	Yes, I see it would be fatal to me, I ought to flee from it.
Baroness:	You ought indeed: a good convent is the best haven of security. Now, my good lord, I think I shall be beforehand with you.
Nanine:	Did you say anything about my master, madam?
Baroness:	O Nanine, I love you even to madness: this moment I would, if possible, lock you up never to come out again: but to-night it is too late, we must wait till morning. Hark'ee, child, come to me at midnight to my apartment, and we will set off secretly for the convent: be ready by five at the latest.

SCENE VI

Nanine (alone)

How distressful is my condition! what trouble and uneasiness do I feel! and what various passions rise in my soul! to leave so good, so amiable a master, perhaps to offend him by it: and yet, if I had stayed, this excess of his goodness might have brought on worse calamities, and put his whole family in confusion. The baroness seems apprehensive that he has a particular regard for me: but his heart could never stoop so low; I must not, dare not think of it: and my lady seems desperately angry about it: am I hated then, and should I be afraid of being beloved? O but myself, myself I have most reason to fear, and my foolish heart, that beats so at the thought of him. What will become of me? taken out of my humble state, my notions now are too refined and too exalted: it is a misfortune, nay, and it is a fault, too, to have a mind above one's condition. I must go: I know it will kill me: but no matter.

SCENE VII

The Count, Nanine, a Servant

Count:	Stay at that door there somebody, d'ye hear? bring chairs here, quick, make haste. [He bows to Nanine, who makes him a low courtesy.] Come, sit down.
Nanine:	Who, I, sir?
Count:	Yes: I will have it so: I mean to pay you, Nanine, that respect which your conduct, your beauty, and merit deserve: shines the diamond with less lustre, or is it less valuable, because found in a desert? What's the matter? your eyes seem bathed in tears:

	O I see it but too plainly; our angry baroness, jealous of your charms, has been venting her ill-humors on you, and left my poor girl weeping.
Nanine:	No, sir, no: her goodness, I assure you, to me was never greater than at present; but everything here softens and affects me.
Count:	I'm glad to hear it; I was afraid it was some of her malice.
Nanine:	Why so, sir?
Count:	O my dear girl, jealousy reigns in every breast: every man is jealous when he is in love, and every woman even before she is so. A young and beautiful girl, who at the same time is good-natured and sincere, is sure to displease her whole sex: men are more just, and we endeavor as well as we can to revenge ourselves on you for your jealousy: but, with regard to Nanine, I only do her justice, I love that heart which is void of artifice; I admire the display of those extraordinary talents which you have so finely cultivated; and I am both surprised and charmed at the ingenuous simplicity of your manners.
Nanine:	O sir, my merit is small indeed; but I have seen you, have heard and been instructed by you: you have raised me too high above my humble birth: I owe you but too much: from you only I have learned to think.
Count:	O Nanine, wit and good sense are not to be taught.
Nanine:	I think too much, I fear, for one in my station: my fortune designed me for the lowest rank in life.
Count:	Your virtues have placed you in the highest: but tell me ingenuously, what effect had that English book I lent you?
Nanine:	Not convinced me at all, sir: I am more than ever

	of opinion, that there are hearts so noble and so generous, that all others must appear mean and vile when put in comparison with them.
Count:	True, Nanine, and you are yourself a proof of it: but permit me to raise you for the future to a rank and station here less unworthy of you.
Nanine:	My condition, sir, is already too high, and too desirable for me.
Count:	No, Nanine, that cannot be: henceforward I shall consider you as one of the family; my mother is coming, she will look on you as her daughter, my esteem, and her tender friendship, will put you on a different footing, and place you in a better rank than you have hitherto held under a proud and imperious woman.
Nanine (aside):	She only taught me my duty, sir—and a hard one it is to fulfil.
Count:	What duty? yours, Nanine, is only to please, and that you always perform; would I could do so, too! but you should be more at your ease, and appear with more splendor; you are not yet in your proper sphere.
Nanine:	I am indeed quite out of it, and it is that which makes me unhappy; 'tis my misfortune, perhaps an irreparable one. [Rising.] O my lord, my master, remove, I beseech you, from me all these vanities: I am confused, overwhelmed with your excess of goodness; let me live unknown and unenvied; heaven formed me for obscurity, and humility has nothing in it that to me is grating or disagreeable: leave me to my retreat; what should I do in the world, what should I wish to see there, after the admiration of your virtues?
Count:	It is too much, I can resist no longer. (to Nanine)

(to himself)	You remain in obscurity? you?
Nanine:	Whatever I may do, permit me to ask one favor of you.
Count:	What is it? speak.
Nanine:	For some time past you have loaded me with presents.
Count:	Pardon me, Nanine, I acted but as a tender father who loved his child: I have not the art to set off my presents by flattery, I aim not at gallantry, and only desire to be just: fortune had done you wrong, and I meant to avenge the injury: but nature, in recompense for it, lavished all her bounties on you, and her I strove to imitate.
Nanine:	You have done a great deal too much; but I flatter myself I may be permitted, without being thought ungrateful, to dispose of those noble presents, which I shall ever hold dear because they came from you.
Count:	You mean to affront me, sure.

SCENE VIII

The Count, Nanine, Germon

Germon:	My lady wants you; she waits.
Count:	Let her wait then: what! can't I speak a moment to you without being interrupted?
Nanine:	It gives me pain to leave you; but you know, sir, she was my mistress.
Count:	No: I know it not, nor ever will.
Nanine:	She has still a power over me.
Count:	No such thing: she shall have none—you sigh, Nanine, there's something at the bottom of that

	heart; what's the matter?
Nanine:	I am sorry to leave you, sir—but I must—O heaven, now all is over.

[She goes out]

SCENE IX

The Count, Germon

Count: (to himself)	She wept as she left me; for a long time she has groaned beneath the tyrannical caprice of this peevish baroness, who insults her: and by what right, or what authority? but 'tis an abuse which I will never suffer: this world is nothing but a lottery of wealth, titles, dignities, rights, and privileges, bartered for without legal claim, and scattered without distinction—here, you—
Germon:	My lord.
Count:	To-morrow morning lay this purse of a hundred louis d'ors on her toilette; be sure you don't fail; you must then go and see after her servants below, they'll wait there.
Germon:	The baroness shall certainly have them on her toilette according to your orders.
Count:	Blockhead, they're not for her: for Nanine, I tell you.
Germon:	O very well, sir, I beg pardon.
Count:	Begone, leave me. [Germon goes out.] This tenderness of mine can never be a weakness in me: true, I idolize her; but my heart was not touched by her beauty only, her character is to the last degree amiable: I admire her soul; but then her low condition—it is too high; were she lower, I should

love her yet more: but can I marry her? doubtless I may; can one pay too dear for being happy? shall I fear the censure of an idle world, and let pride deprive me of all I wish for? but then custom—a cruel tyrant: nature has a prior right, and should be obeyed: and so I am Blaise's rival, too; and why not? Blaise is a man; he loves her, and he is in the right of it: she can be but in the possession of one, though the desire of all: gardeners may sigh for her, and so may kings: my happiness will justify my choice.

ACT II

SCENE I

The Count, Marin

Count:
(to himself)
: Well; this night is a whole year to me: not once have I closed my eyelids: everybody is asleep but me; Nanine sleeps in peace, a sweet repose refreshes her charms, while I wander from place to place, and can find no rest: I sit down to write, but can't: then strive to read, but all in vain; I don't know the words before me while I am looking on them, nor can my mind retain a single idea: methinks, in every page, I see the name of Nanine imprinted by some hand divine—hullo! who's there? all asleep? German, Marin.

Marin:
(behind the scenes)
: Coming, sir.

Count: You idle rascals, make haste, it's broad daylight; come, come.

Marin: Lord, sir, what spirit has raised you up so early this morning?

Count: Love.

Marin: O ho! my lady will let none of us sleep long in this house; what did you want, sir?

Count: Why, Marin, I must have, let me see, by to-morrow at the latest, six new horses, a new equipage, a clever chambermaid, notable and careful, a valet de chambre, and two footmen, young and well-made, and no libertines; some diamonds, some very fine buckles, some gold trinkets, and some new stuffs; therefore, be gone, ride post to Paris this instant,

	never mind killing a few horses.
Marin:	O ho, I see how it is; you are caught; my lady baroness is to be our mistress to-day, I suppose; you are going to be married to her at last?
Count:	Whatever my intention is, go you about your business; fly, and make haste back.
Marin:	I'm gone, sir.

SCENE II

The Count, Germon

Count: (to himself)	And shall I then enjoy the sweet pleasure of honoring, of making happy the dear object of my love? The baroness, I know, will be in a rage: with all my heart, let her rave as long as she will; I despise her, and the world, and its opinion; and am afraid of nobody: I will never be the slave of prejudice; it is an enemy whom we ought to subdue, those who make a rational mind more virtuous, and those only are respectable: but hark! what noise is that in the court? a chariot sure: it must be so; yet who could come at this time in the morning? my mother perhaps. Germon—
Germon:	Sir.
Count:	What is that?
Germon:	A chariot, sir.
Count:	Whose is it? anybody coming here?
Germon:	No, sir, they're going.
Count:	Going? who? where?
Germon:	The baroness, sir, going out immediately.
Count:	O with all my heart, let her go forever if she pleases!

Germon:	Nanine and she are this minute setting out.
Count:	O heaven! what sayest thou? Nanine?
Germon:	So the maid says, sir.
Count:	How is this?
Germon:	My lady, sir, is going with her this morning, to put her into a neighboring convent.
Count:	Away: fly: let us begone: but what am I about? I am too warm to talk to them: no matter, I'll go; I ought—but stop, that must not be, I should at once discover all my passion: no—go, Germon, stop them, let everything be fast; bring Nanine to me, or answer it with your life. [Germon goes out.] So they would have carried her off! what a dreadful stroke! ungrateful, cruel, unjust woman! how have I deserved this! what have I done! I only loved and adored her; but never declared my passion; never endeavored to force her inclinations, or to alarm her timid innocence: why should she fly from me? the more I think of it, the more I am astonished.

SCENE III

The Count, Nanine

Count:	My sweet girl, is it you? what, run away from me? answer me, explain this mystery to me: terrified, I suppose, with the baroness's threats, you were willing to escape; and that tender regard which I have long had for your virtues, I know, has quickened her resentment; surely you could not yourself have thought of leaving me, of depriving this place of its fairest ornament: last night, when I saw you in tears, tell me, Nanine, had you any

	intention of this? answer me, tell me, why would you have wished to leave me?
Nanine:	Behold me on my knees, and trembling before you.
Count: (raising her up)	Rise, Nanine, and tell me—I tremble more myself.
Nanine:	My lady, sir—
Count:	Well—what of her?
Nanine:	That lady, sir, whom I honor and esteem, did not, I assure you, force me to the convent.
Count:	And could it then be your own choice? O misery!
Nanine:	It was, I own it was: I entreated her to restrain my wandering thoughts—she wanted to marry me.
Count:	Indeed? to whom?
Nanine:	To your gardener.
Count:	O the worthy choice!
Nanine:	I, sir, was ashamed, and to the last degree unhappy: I who in vain endeavor to stifle sentiments far above my condition, I whom your bounty had raised too high, must now be punished by the loss of that goodness which I never deserved.
Count:	You punish yourself, Nanine, and for what?
Nanine:	For having dared to raise the resentment of your relation, sir, who was once my mistress; I know, sir, I am disagreeable to her; the very sight of me disgusts her: she has reason indeed, for when I was near her, I was guilty of a weakness which I shall ever feel; it grows on me every hour: but I would have torn it from my breast; I would have humbled, by the austerities of a convent, this proud heart, exalted by your goodness, and revenged on it the involuntary crime: but the bitterest grief I felt, was my fear of offending you.

Count: (turning from her, and walking about)	What sentiments! what a noble and ingenuous mind! Can she be prejudiced in my favor? was she afraid of loving me? O exalted virtue!
Nanine:	If I have offended you, I beg a thousand pardons; but permit me, sir, in some deep retreat to hide my sorrows, and to reflect in secret on my own duty, and your goodness to me.
Count:	No more of that: now, observe me, the baroness is your friend, and out of her generosity has provided you with a servant, a rustic, a boor, for your husband. I know of one who will at least be less unworthy of you: in birth and fortune far superior to Blaise; young, honest, and well provided for: a man, I assure you, of sense and reflection: his character very different from those of the present age: if I am not much mistaken, he'll make you an excellent husband: is not this better than a convent?
Nanine:	No: sir, I own to you, this new favor which you would bestow on me has nothing in it that can give me any real satisfaction: you know my grateful heart, read there my real sentiments, and see why I wish to retreat from the world: a gardener, or the monarch of the whole world, who should offer marriage to me, would be equally displeasing.
Count:	You have determined me: and now, Nanine, know the man for whom I have designed you: you already esteem him: he is yours; he adores you: that husband is—myself. I see, you are troubled and surprised: but speak to me; my life depends on you: O recollect yourself, you are strangely agitated.
Nanine:	What do I hear? can it be?

Count:	It is no more than you deserve.
Nanine:	In love with me? O do not think, do not imagine I will ever dare to claim my conquest: no, sir, never will I suffer you to descend thus low for me: such marriages, believe me, sir, are always unhappy: fancy vanishes, and repentance alone remains. No, I will call your ancestors to witness—alas! sir, think not on me: you took pity on my youth: this heart, which you have formed, which is your own work, would be unworthy of your care, if it could accept from you this noblest present. No, sir, I owe you at least this refusal: my heart shall sacrifice itself for your sake.
Count:	No more: for I am resolved, and you shall be my wife. Did you not this moment assure me you would refuse every other man, though he were a prince?
Nanine:	I did, and repent not of the resolution.
Count:	Do you hate me then?
Nanine:	Should I have fled, should I have avoided, should I have feared, if I had hated you?
Count:	It is enough, and I am fixed.
Nanine:	What then have you determined on?
Count:	Our marriage.
Nanine:	Think, sir.
Count:	I have thought of everything.
Nanine:	And foreseen too?
Count:	I have.
Nanine:	If you love me, believe me, sir—
Count:	I do believe—that I have resolved on the only means to make myself happy.
Nanine:	But you forget—
Count:	I have forgotten nothing: everything is ordered, and everything shall be ready.
Nanine:	What! in spite of all I say, will your obstinate

	passion—
Count:	Yes, in spite of you, my impatient love must urge the happy moment. I will quit you for a minute, that henceforth we may never part: adieu, my dear Nanine.

SCENE IV

Nanine (alone)

Good heaven! do I dream? or am I indeed arrived at the summit of earthly happiness? 'tis not the honor, great as it is; 'tis not the splendor that dazzles me: no: I despise it all: but to wed the most generous of men, the dear object of all my timid wishes, him whom I was so much afraid of loving, him whom I adore, yet I love him too much to wish he should demean himself for my sake: but it is impossible to avoid it; I cannot now escape him: what can I do? heaven, I trust, will direct me, and support my weakness, perhaps even—but I'll write to him—and yet how to begin, and what to say—what a surprise! I will write immediately before I enter into this solemn engagement.

SCENE V

Nanine, Blaise

Blaise:	O there she is: well, my little maid, my lady has spoken to you in my favor, has she not? ha! she writes on, and takes no notice of me.
Nanine: (writing on)	O Blaise, good morrow to you.
Blaise:	Good morrow is but a cold compliment.

Nanine: (writing)	Every word I write doubles my distress, and my whole letter is full of doubts and uneasiness.
Blaise:	How she writes offhand! O she's a great genius; and a monstrous wit: I wish I was a wit too, then I'd tell her—
Nanine:	Well, sir.
Blaise:	Lackaday, she's so clever, I'm afraid to speak: I shall never be able to break my mind to her—yet I was hot upon't, and came here o' purpose; that I did.
Nanine:	Dear Blaise, you must do me a piece of service.
Blaise:	Marry, two an' you will.
Nanine:	I shall trust to your discretion, to your good heart, Blaise; nay, I do you but justice.
Blaise:	O no ceremony; for look you, ma'am, Blaise is ready to serve you, and there's an end of it. Come, come, make no secret.
Nanine:	You often go to the neighboring village, to Remival, the right hand side of the road.
Blaise:	Yes, yes.
Nanine:	Could you find one Philip Hombert for me there?
Blaise:	Philip Hombert? I know nothing of him: what sort of a man is he?
Nanine:	He came there, I believe, but yesterday evening; do you look him up, and give him immediately this money, and this letter.
Blaise:	Oh, money is it?
Nanine:	And at the same time deliver him this packet: go on horse-back that you may return the sooner: away, make haste, and be assured I'll remember you for it.
Blaise:	I would go for you to the world's end—this Philip Hombert is a happy rogue: the purse is full: all ready rhino. What, is it a debt?
Nanine:	Yes: and well proved; nothing can be more sacred,

	therefore take care of it: hark'ee, Blaise, Hombert may not be known in the village, perhaps he is not yet returned: if you can't give the letter into his own hands, bring it me back again: my dear friend, remember that.
Blaise:	My dear friend!
Nanine:	I shall depend on you.
Blaise:	Her dear friend! O lud!
Nanine:	I rely entirely upon you, and expect everything from your fidelity.

SCENE VI

The Baroness, Blaise

Blaise:	What a message! and where the deuce could this money come from? it would have been of service to me in housekeeping: but she has a friendship for me, and that's better than money, so away we go.

[As he is putting the money and letter into his pocket, he meets the baroness, and runs full against her]

Baroness:	How now, booby? a little more and you'd have broken my head.
Blaise:	I beg your pardon, madam.
Baroness:	Where are you going? have you heard anything of Nanine? what is she about? is the count in a violent passion? what have you got there, a letter?
Blaise:	O that's a secret: poise on her!
Baroness:	Let me look at it.
Blaise:	Nanine will be angry.
Baroness:	Nanine! could she write, and send it by you? give it me this minute, or I'll break off your match

	immediately; give it me, I say.
Blaise: (laughing)	He! he!
Baroness:	What do you laugh at?
Blaise : (still laughing)	Ah! ah!
Baroness:	I must know the contents of this;—[Breaks open the letter] if I am not mistaken, they concern me nearly.
Blaise (laughing):	Ah! ah! ah! how she is nicked now! she has got nothing there but a scrap of paper: but I shall keep the money, and carry it to Philip Hombert: yes, yes, must obey my mistress. Servant, ma'am.

SCENE VII

The Baroness (alone)

Now let's see what we have got. [Reads.] "Both my joy and tenderness are unspeakable, as is my happiness also: what a moment was this for you to come in! when I cannot see or hear you, cannot throw myself into your arms: but, I conjure you, take these packets, and accept the contents of them. Know, I have been offered a most noble and truly enviable condition in life, such as I might well be dazzled with the prospect of: but there is nothing which I would not sacrifice to the only one on earth whom my heart ought to love." Very fine indeed! upon my word, Nanine, an excellent style: how prettily she writes! the innocent orphan: her passion speaks most eloquently: a rare billet this! O thou sly jade: thus you deceived poor Blaise, and thus deprived me of my lover: this going into a convent, I find, was all a feint, a pretence; and the count's money, it seems, is for Philip Hombert: thou little coquette! but I am glad of it: the count's perfidiousness to me deserved this return: I thought indeed Nanine's heart was as mean as her birth, and now I am satisfied of it.

SCENE VIII

The Count, Baroness

Baroness:	But here comes the philosopher, the sentimental Count d'Olban, the wise lover, the man above prejudice: your servant, noble count, approach and laugh, my dear lover, at the most ridiculous circumstance: do you know Philip Hombert, of Remival? but, to be sure, you can't be a stranger to your—rival.
Count:	What is all this, pray?
Baroness:	This billet perhaps will inform you: this Hombert must be a handsome lad.
Count:	You are too late, madam, now with your schemes; my resolution once made, I am not to be shaken: be satisfied, madam, with the shameful trick you wanted to play me this morning.
Baroness:	You'll find this new one worse, I believe: there, read: [Gives him the letter] you'll like it vastly: you know the hand, and you know the virtue of the dear nymph that has subdued you: [While he is reading it he seems confounded, grows pale and angry] well, sir, what think you of the style?—he sees nothing, says nothing, hears nothing: poor man! but he deserves it.
Count:	Did I read aright? it cannot be. I am astonished, thunder-struck; ungrateful sex! perfidious creature!
Baroness (aside):	I know his temper well; naturally violent, quick and resolute: he'll do something immediately.

SCENE IX

The Count, Baroness, Germon

Germon:	Yonder comes Madam d'Olban: she's in the avenue already.
Baroness:	Is the old woman returned?
Germon:	Sir, sir, my lady, your mother, is coming.
Baroness:	His anger has taken away his hearing: the letter operates finely.
Germon: (bawling out to him)	Sir.
Count:	Does she think—
Germon (aloud):	My lady, sir, your mother.
Count:	What is Nanine doing at this instant?
Germon:	Writing in her own apartment—but, sir—
Count: (with an air of coolness)	Go, seize her papers; bring me what she writes, and then let her be sent away.
Germon:	Who, sir?
Count:	Nanine.
Germon:	I can never have the heart to do it, sir: O sir, if you knew how she charms us all, so noble, so good!
Count:	Do it, sir, or see my face no more.
Germon:	I obey, sir.

[He goes out]

SCENE X

The Count, Baroness

Baroness:	Now, the day is ours: I give you joy, sir, of your return to reason: now, sir, is it not true as I told

	you, the low-bred always retain something of their former condition, and persons of family alone have hearts truly noble? Blood, sir, let me tell you, does everything, and meanness of birth will inspire Nanine with sentiments you never suspected her of.
Count:	That I don't believe: but come, we'll talk no more about it, but endeavor to make amends for past errors: every man has his follies, at some part of his life; we all go wrong; and he is least to blame who repents the soonest.
Baroness:	'Tis well observed.
Count:	Never mention her to me again: be silent on that head, I entreat you.
Baroness:	Most willingly.
Count:	I beg this subject of our dispute may be entirely forgotten.
Baroness:	But will you remember then your former vows?
Count:	Well, well, I understand you, I will.
Baroness:	And quickly, too, or you will not repair the injury: our marriage so shamefully deferred is an affront—
Count:	That shall be made amends for; but, madam, we must have—
Baroness:	Have what? we must have a lawyer.
Count:	You know, madam, that—I waited for my mother.
Baroness:	And here she comes.

SCENE XI

The Marchioness D'olban, The Count, Baroness

Count: (to his mother)	Madam, I should have—[Aside] O Philip Hombert! [To his mother] but you have prevented me: my respect and tenderness—[Aside] with that air of innocence too! perfidious wretch!

Marchioness:	Why, you rave, child; I heard indeed, as I passed through Paris, that your head was a little touched, and I find there was some truth in it; how long has this misfortune—
Count:	Good heaven! how confused I am!
Marchioness:	Does it seize you often?
Count:	It never will again, madam.
Marchioness:	I should be glad to speak with you alone. [Turns to the baroness and makes her a formal courtesy.] Good morrow, madam.
Baroness (aside):	The old fool! [Turning to the Marchioness] Madam, I leave you the pleasure of entertaining the count at your leisure, and retire.

[She goes out]

SCENE XII

The Marchioness, The Count

Marchioness: (talking very fast, and in the manner of a little prattling old woman)	Well, sir, and so you intend to make the baroness my daughter-in-law: 'twas this, to tell you the truth, that brought me here so soon: she's a peevish, impertinent, proud, opinionated creature, and one who never had the least regard for me: last year, when I supped with the Marchioness Agard, she said before all the company, I was a babbler. Lord forbid I should ever sup there again: a babbler! besides, I know, between you and me, she is not so rich; and that, let me tell you, son, is a great point, and we ought to be well-informed about it: they tell me that the Château d'Orme did but half of it belong to her husband, and that the other half was disputed by a long lawsuit, that is not finished to

	this day: that I had from your grandpapa, and he always told the truth: ay, he was a man; there are few such nowadays: there is nothing now at Paris but a set of half-men, vain, foolish, impertinent coxcombs, talking on every subject, and laughing at times past. Oh, their eternal clack distracts me, prating about new kitchens, and new fashions: we hear of nothing now but bankrupts, and distress, and ruin: the wives, in short, are licentious, and the husbands simpletons: everything grows worse and worse.
Count: (reading the letter over again)	Who could have thought it? this is a desperate stroke indeed. Well, Germon?

SCENE XIII

The Marchioness, The Count, Germon

Germon:	Here's your lawyer, sir.
Count:	O let him wait.
Germon:	And here's the paper, sir, she sent you.
Count (reading):	Give it me—well, let me see: she loves me, she says here, and refuses me out of—respect. Faithless woman! thou hast not told me the true reason of that refusal.
Marchioness:	My son's head is certainly turned: 'tis the baroness's doing: love has taken away his senses.
Count: (to Germon)	Is Nanine gone! shall I be rid of her?
Germon:	Alas! sir, she has already put on her old rustic garb with the greatest modesty, and never murmured or complained.

Count:	Very likely so.
Germon:	She bore her misfortune with the utmost tranquillity, while everybody about her was in tears.
Count:	With tranquillity, sayest thou?
Marchioness:	Whom are you talking about?
Germon:	O madam, poor Nanine, she is going to be driven away, and everybody laments the loss of her.
Marchioness:	To be driven away? how is this? I don't understand it: what! my little Nanine go! call her back again: my charming orphan! what has she done, pray? why, Nanine was my present to you. O I remember, at ten years of age she delighted everybody that saw her: our baroness took her, and I said then she would be ill-used; I knew it would be so: but you never mind what I say; you will do everything of your own head: but let me tell you, turning Nanine out of doors thus is a very bad action.
Count:	Alone, on foot, without money, without assistance!
Germon:	O sir, I forgot to tell you: an old man asked after you below, and says he wants to speak to you on an affair of importance, which he can communicate to none but yourself: he wants to throw himself at your feet.
Count:	In my present unhappy situation of mind, am I fit to converse with anybody?
Marchioness:	You are uneasy enough, I believe, child, and so am I, too, to drive away poor Nanine, and make up a marriage which you knew would be disagreeable to me: come, it was not a wise thing: in three months' time you will be weary of one another: I'll tell you what happened exactly like this to my cousin the Marquis of Marmure: his wife was as sour as verjuice, though, by the by, yours is worse; when

they married, they thought they loved one another, and in two months after they were parted. My lady went to live with her gallant, a foolish, sharking, extravagant fop; and my lord took a vile, tricking, ridiculous coquette! fine suppers, country houses, horses, clothes, a rascally steward, new trinkets bought on trust, lawyers, contracts, interest-money, all together soon ruined them, and in two years both went together to the hospital. O, and now I think of it, I remember another story, more tragical, and more extraordinary than the other, it was of a—

Count: My dear mother, we must go in to dinner: come—could I ever have suspected such infidelity!

Marchioness: 'Tis really dreadful: but I'll tell it you all at table: in proper time and place, son, it may be of great use to you. Away.

ACT III

SCENE I

Nanine, clothed as a country girl; Germon

Germon:	We are all in tears at the thought of losing you.
Nanine:	It is time to go: I've staid too long already.
Germon:	But you won't leave us forever, I hope, and in this dress, too?
Nanine:	Obscurity was my first condition.
Germon:	What a change! and only from this morning: to suffer is nothing, but to be degraded is terrible.
Nanine:	No, no, there are a thousand times worse misfortunes.
Germon:	I admire your patience and humility; surely my master must have been ill-advised: our baroness has certainly abused her power: she must have done you this injury, the count could never have the heart.
Nanine:	I am indebted to him for everything; and, if he thinks fit to banish me, I must submit; his favors are his own, and he has a right to recall them.
Germon:	Who would ever have expected such a change? what do you intend to do with yourself?
Nanine:	To retire, and repent.
Germon:	How we shall all detest the baroness!
Nanine:	They have made me miserable, but I forgive them.
Germon:	But what shall I tell my master from you when you are gone?
Nanine:	Tell him, I thank him for restoring me to my former condition: tell him that, forever sensible of his goodness, I shall forget nothing but his—cruelty.

Germon:	You melt my very soul; I could leave this house immediately to go along with you wherever you went: but Blaise is beforehand with us all: he will go and live with you, and we are all ready to follow him.
Nanine:	No, Germon, that I'm sure you are not. O Germon, to be driven out in this manner—and by whom?
Germon:	The devil is certainly at the bottom of this business: you are leaving us, and my master is going to be married.
Nanine:	Married, sayest thou? indeed? nay, then let us be gone: O he was too dangerous for me—farewell.
Germon:	Well! after all, my master must have a cruel heart, to banish so sweet a creature: she seems a most amiable girl, but in this world one should swear to nothing.

SCENE II

The Count, Germon

Count:	Well, is she gone at last?
Germon:	Yes, sir, 'tis done.
Count:	I'm glad of it.
Germon:	Then, sir, you have a heart of iron.
Count:	Did Philip Hombert meet and give her his hand?
Germon:	What Philip Hombert, sir? alas! sir, poor Nanine went off without a creature to give her his hand; she would not even accept of mine.
Count:	And where is she gone?
Germon:	That I know not; most probably to her friends.
Count:	Ay, at Remival, I suppose.
Germon:	Yes, I believe she went that road.

Count:	Go, Germon, immediately, and conduct her to that convent where the baroness was going this morning, I'll lodge her in that safe retreat: these hundred louis d'ors will secure her reception; carry them to her, but take care she does not know they come from me: tell her 'tis a present from my mother: on no account mention my name to her.
Germon:	Very well, sir, I shall obey your orders.

[He goes towards the door]

Count:	Germon, you saw her as she went off?
Germon:	I did, sir.
Count:	Did she seem dejected? did she weep?
Germon:	She behaved still better, sir; a few tears dropped from her, but she strove as much as she could to repress them.
Count:	Did she let fall anything that betrayed her sentiments? did you remark—
Germon:	What, sir?
Count:	Did she say anything of me?
Germon:	Yes, sir; a great deal.
Count:	Tell me, then, rascal, what did she say?
Germon:	That you were her master, her best and kindest benefactor; that she shall forget everything—but your cruelty.
Count:	Away—be sure you take care she never returns; [Germon going out] and hark'ee, Germon.
Germon:	Sir.
Count:	One word more: remember, if, by chance, as you are conducting her, one Philip Hombert should follow you, that you treat him in a proper manner.
Germon:	O, sir, I'll use him most politely, and treat him with a good drubbing, that you may depend on: I'll do the business honestly, I warrant you: young

	Hombert, you say?
Count:	The same.
Germon:	Very well: I have not the honor to know him, but the first man I see will I trim most heartily, and afterwards make him tell me his name. [He goes towards the door and comes back.] This young Hombert, I'll lay my life, is some lover of hers, a beau, a prig, I suppose, the cock of the village. Let me alone to deal with him.
Count:	Do as I bid you, and immediately.
Germon:	I thought there was some lover in the case—and Blaise, too, puts in his claim, I suppose. Ay: they always love their equals better than their masters.
Count:	Begone, I tell you.

SCENE III

The Count (alone)

He's in the right, and has hit on the true cause of my unhappiness, but I shall myself be the punisher of my own folly. I must now marry the baroness; it is determined, and I can't avoid it: 'tis dreadful; but I have deserved it; 'twill at least be a convenient match: she's not very tractable indeed, but every man may rule, if he has a mind to it; and he who has resolution may, at any time, be master in his own house.

SCENE IV

The Count, Baroness, Marchioness

Marchioness:	Well, son, you are going to marry this lady here?
Count:	Yes, madam.
Marchioness:	This night she is to be your wife and my daughter-in-law?
Baroness:	If you approve of it, madam; I suppose I shall have your consent.
Marchioness:	Why, I must give it, I think: but to-morrow I shall take my leave of you.
Count:	Your leave, madam, why so?
Marchioness:	I shall take my Nanine with me: since you have thought fit to turn her out of doors, I shall take her under my protection: I have a match in my eye for ner: I propose marrying her to the young chief justice, nephew to the attorney-general, Jean Roc Souci; he whose father met with that comical adventure at Corbeil; you must have heard of him: yes, I will take care of this poor child, I'm determined: she is a jewel, and deserves to be well set. I'll marry her off immediately. Your servant.
Count:	My dear mother, don't be in a passion: leave me to manage my own affairs, and let Nanine go into a convent.
Baroness:	Indeed, madam, you may believe us, such a girl as Nanine is not fit to go into a family.
Marchioness:	Ha! why, what's the matter?
Baroness:	O a little affair only.
Marchioness:	But pray—
Baroness:	O nothing at all.
Marchioness:	Nothing! a great deal, I'm afraid: I understand you mighty well: some little indiscretion I suppose: nothing more likely, for to be sure, she's very handsome. Ay, ay, we are all frail; we tempt, and are tempted; the heart has its weakness: young girls are always a little coquettish: but come, it is not so

	bad as you make it; tell me fairly, what my poor child has done?
Count:	I tell you, madam?
Marchioness:	You seem, after all, at the bottom to have some regard for the girl, and perhaps you may—

SCENE V

The Count, Marchioness, Baroness, Marin (booted)

Marin:	I've done it, sir; it's all agreed for.
Marchioness:	What's agreed for?
Baroness:	Ay, what, sir, what?
Marin:	Why, sir, I've done as you ordered me, spoke to the tradesmen, and you'll have your equipage tomorrow.
Baroness:	What equipage?
Marin:	Everything, madam, that your future spouse had ordered; six fine horses, and a charming berlin; I'm sure your ladyship will like it; it's very fine; the panels all varnished by Martin: the diamonds, too, are brilliant, and well-chosen; and the new stuffs quite in taste.—O nothing comes up to them.
Baroness: (to the count)	And had you ordered all this?
Count:	I had—[Aside] but for whom!
Marin:	Everything will come to-morrow morning in the coach, and will be ready for your wedding in the evening: O there's nothing like Paris for getting everything at a minute's warning, if you have but money. As I came back, I called on the lawyer; he's just by, finishing your affair.
Baroness:	It has hung a long time in suspense.

Marchioness: (aside)	I wish it would hang these forty years.
Marin:	In the hall I met a poor old man, sighing and in tears; he has waited a long time, he says, and begs to speak to you.
Baroness:	An impertinent fellow! let him go about his business: he has chosen the wrong time to trouble us now.
Marchioness:	Why, so, madam? have a little consideration: son, let me tell you, it's very wrong to repulse poor people in this manner; I have told you over and over, when you were a child, you ought to treat them with indulgence; hear what they have to say; be courteous, and affable to them: are not they men as well as yourself? we don't know perhaps whom we affront, and may repent our hardness of heart: the proud never prosper. [To Marin.] Go, see to that old man.
Marin:	I will, ma'am. [He goes out.]
Count:	Forgive me, madam, my respects are always due to you, and I am ready to see this man, in spite of my present embarrassment.

SCENE VI

The Count, Marchioness, Baroness, a Peasant

Marchioness: (to the Peasant)	Come, come, speak, don't be afraid.
Peasant:	O my lord, for heaven's sake, hear me; permit me to fall at your feet, and to give you back—
Count:	Rise, friend; I'll not be knelt to; do not imagine me capable of such pride: you seem to be an honest

	man, do you want employment in my family? who are you?
Marchioness:	Cheer up, man.
Peasant:	Alas! sir, I am the father of—Nanine.
Count:	You?
Baroness:	Your daughter's a slut.
Peasant:	This, sir, is what I feared: this is the cruel stroke that has wounded my poor heart: I thought indeed so much money could not fairly belong to one in her condition: we little folks soon lose our integrity when we come among the great.
Baroness:	There he's right enough: but still he's a deceiver, for Nanine is not his daughter, she was an orphan.
Peasant:	It is too true, she was so: I left her with her poor relatives in her infant years, having lost her mother, with all my fortune; obliged by necessity, I went to serve abroad; and as I would not have her pass for the daughter of a soldier, forbade her ever to mention my name.
Marchioness:	Why so? for my part, I respect a soldier: we stand in need of them sometimes.
Count:	What is there shameful in the profession?
Peasant:	It meets indeed with less honor than it deserves.
Count:	The prejudice against them is inexcusable. I own, I esteem an honest soldier, who hazards his life in the defence of his king and country, much more than an important, self-sufficient scoundrel, whose knavish industry sucks up the blood of his fellow subjects.
Marchioness:	You must have been in a great many battles: let me have an account of them all; I long to hear it.
Peasant:	In my present unhappy condition you must excuse me: let it suffice to inform you, that I received a thousand promises of advancement; but, without friends, how was it possible to rise? thrown

	amongst the common crowd, all I could do was to distinguish myself, and honor my only reward.
Marchioness:	You were then well-born?
Baroness:	Fie: how can you think so! well-born indeed!
Peasant:	No, madam: but I was born of honest parents, and merited—a better daughter.
Marchioness:	Could you have had a better?
Count:	Well! go on.
Marchioness:	A better than Nanine?
Count:	Prithee, go on.
Peasant:	My daughter, I understood, was brought up here, and treated in the kindest manner; I thought myself happy, and blessed heaven for your goodness, and paternal care of her; I came to the neighboring village, full of hopes and fears; I own I trembled for her dangerous youth; and, by this lady's intimation, find I had but too much reason; it has shocked me to the soul; but I thought a hundred louis d'ors, besides diamonds, was a treasure too great to be fairly come by: she could never be mistress of them, but at the expense of her innocence: the bare suspicion makes me shudder; if it be so, I shall die with grief and shame: but I came as soon as possible, to give them you back again: they are yours, therefore, I beseech you, take them: if my daughter is to blame, punish me, but don't ruin her.
Marchioness:	O my dear son, I cannot bear this; it overpowers me.
Baroness:	What is all this? a dream? a trick?
Count:	O what have I done?
Peasant: (taking out the purse and the letter)	Here, sir, take them.

Count:	I take them! no: they were given to her, and she has made a noble use of them: was it to you, then, the message was delivered? who brought it?
Peasant:	Your gardener, sir, in whom Nanine ventured to confide.
Count:	Was it directed to you?
Peasant:	It was, I own it, sir.
Count:	O grief! O tenderness! what excess of virtue in them both! but now your name?—O I am lost, distracted.
Marchioness:	Ay, your name. What mystery is this?
Peasant:	Philip Hombert de Gatine.
Count:	O my father!
Baroness:	What does he say?
Count:	How day breaks in upon me! I have done wrong, and I must make amends for it: O if you knew how culpable I have been! I have injured the sublimest virtue. [He steps aside, and speaks to one of his servants.] away: fly.
Baroness:	What is all this emotion for?
Count:	My coach immediately.
Marchioness:	Now, madam, you must be her protectress: when we have done such an injury, we should blush at nothing so much as an imperfect repentance; my son often has his whims, which people are too apt to mistake for unpardonable follies; but at bottom he has a generous soul, and is naturally good; I can do what I please with him: you, my daughter-in-law, are not so well-disposed.
Baroness:	I shall grow out of all patience: how confused and thoughtful he looks! what strange scheme now is he meditating upon? well, sir, what do you intend to do?
Marchioness:	Ay, for Nanine?

Baroness:	Make her a handsome present, and satisfy her.
Marchioness:	That will be the least we can do.
Baroness:	But as to seeing her that I never will: she shall not come nigh the castle: do you hear me?
Count:	Yes, I hear you.
Marchioness: (aside)	What a heart of stone!
Baroness:	Don't give my suspicions cause to break out, sir. Ha! you hesitate.
Count: (after a pause of some time)	No, madam, I am resolved.
Baroness:	That respect at least is owing to me; nay, to both of us.
Marchioness:	And can you be so cruel, son?
Baroness:	What step do you propose to take?
Count:	'Tis taken already: you know my heart, madam, and the frankness of it: I must be plain with you: I had promised you my hand; but the design of our marriage was only to put an end to a tedious lawsuit between us, which I will now do immediately, by willingly resigning to you all those rights and pretensions which were the foundation of it: even the interest shall be yours; I give up everything, take, and enjoy it: if we cannot be man and wife, let us at least live as friends and relatives: let everything that gave mutual uneasiness be forgotten; there is no reason why, because we can't love, we should hate each other.
Baroness:	Your falsehood is what I expected: but I renounce your presents, and yourself: yes, traitor, I see now who you mean to live with, and how low your passion sinks you: go, and be a slave to her, I leave you to your unworthy choice.

[She goes out]

SCENE VII

The Count, Marchioness, Philip Hombert

Count: No, madam, 'tis not unworthy, my soul is not blinded by an idle passion: that virtue which it is my duty to reward ought to melt, but cannot debase me: what they call meanness in this old man constitutes his merit, and makes him truly noble: if I would be so, I must pay the price of it: where souls are thus ennobled by themselves, and distinguished by superior characters, we should pass over common rules: their birth, low as it is, when attended with such virtues, will make my family but more illustrious.

Marchioness: What are you talking about?

SCENE VIII

The Count, Marchioness, Nanine, Philip Hombert

Count: Look at her, and guess.
(to his mother)

Marchioness: My dearest child, come to my arms: but she is strangely clothed, and yet how handsome she looks, and modest too!
(to Nanine)

Nanine: O nature demands my first acknowledgments, my dear father!
(pays her respects to the Marchioness, and then runs to her father)

Philip Hombert:	O heaven! my daughter! O sir, you have made me amends for forty years' afflictions.
Count:	Ay, but how must I repair the injury I have done to such exalted virtue! to come back in this dress, how mean it is, but she adorns it; Nanine does honor to everything: speak, my Nanine, can your goodness pardon the affront?
Nanine:	Can you, sir, doubt my forgiveness of it? I never thought, after all your bounty to me, you could injure me.
Count:	If you have indeed forgotten the wrong I did you, give me a proof of it: once more, and only once, I take upon me to command you; but this once you must swear—to obey me.
Philip Hombert:	I am sure she owes it to you, and her gratitude—
Nanine: (to her father)	He need not doubt, sir, of my obedience.
Count:	I shall depend on it: let me tell you then, that all your duty is not yet paid: I have seen you on your knees to my mother, and to your own father; one thing still remains for you, and that is, now, before them, to embrace—your husband.
Nanine:	Who? I?
Marchioness:	Are you in earnest? can it be?
Philip Hombert:	O my child!
Count: (to his mother)	By your permission, madam.
Marchioness:	My dear child, the family will be in a strange uproar about it.
Count:	O when they see Nanine, they must approve.
Philip Hombert:	What a stroke of fortune! O sir, I never thought you could descend thus low.

Count:	You promised to obey, and I must have it so.
Marchioness:	My son.
Count:	My happiness, madam, depends on this important moment: interest alone, we know, has made a thousand marriages; we have seen the wisest men consult fortune and character only: her character is irreproachable; and as to fortune, she wants it not: justice and inclination shall do what avarice has so often done before: let me, then, madam, have your consent, and finish all.
Nanine:	No, madam, you must not consent; indeed you must not; oppose his passion, oppose mine: let me entreat you, do: love has blinded him, do you, madam, remove the veil: let me live far from him, and at a distance only adore his virtues: you know my condition; you see my father: can I, ought I, ever to wish to call you mother?
Marchioness:	Yes; you can, you ought: it is enough: I can hold out no longer: this last generosity has entirely subdued me: it tells me how much I ought to love: it is as singular, as extraordinary, as Nanine herself.
Nanine:	Then, madam, I obey; my heart can no longer resist the power of love.
Marchioness:	Let this happy day be the worthy recompense of virtue, but let it not be made a precedent.

ANDRÉ DES TOUCHES IN SIAM

André Des Touches was a very agreeable musician in the brilliant reign of Louis XIV., before the science of music was perfected by Rameau, and before it was corrupted by those who prefer the art of surmounting difficulties to nature and the real graces of composition.

Before he had recourse to these talents he had been a musketeer, and before that, in 1688, he went into Siam with the Jesuit Tachard, who gave him many marks of his affection, for the amusement he afforded on board the ship; and Des Touches spoke with admiration of Father Tachard for the rest of his life.

In Siam he became acquainted with the first commissary of Barcalon, whose name was Croutef, and he committed to writing most of those questions which he asked of Croutef, and the answers of that Siamese. They are as follows:

DES TOUCHES	How many soldiers have you?
CROUTEF	Fourscore thousand, very indifferently paid.
DES TOUCHES	And how many talapoins?
CROUTEF	A hundred and twenty thousand, very idle and very rich. It is true that in the last war we were beaten, but our talapoins have lived sumptuously and built fine houses.
DES TOUCHES	Nothing could have discovered more judgment. And your finances, in what state are they?
CROUTEF	In a very bad state. We have, however, about ninety thousand men employed to render them prosperous, and if they have not succeeded, it has not been their fault, for there is not one of them who does not honorably

	seize all that he can get possession of, and strip and plunder those who cultivate the ground for the good of the state.
DES TOUCHES	Bravo! And is not your jurisprudence as perfect as the rest of your administration?
CROUTEF	It is much superior. We have no laws, but we have five or six thousand volumes on the laws. We are governed in general by customs; for it is known that a custom, having been established by chance, is the wisest principle that can be imagined. Besides, all customs being necessarily different in different provinces, the judges may choose at their pleasure a custom which prevailed four hundred years ago or one which prevailed last year. It occasions a variety in our legislation which our neighbors are forever admiring. This yields a certain fortune to practitioners. It is a resource for all pleaders who are destitute of honor, and a pastime of infinite amusement for the judges, who can, with safe consciences, decide causes without understanding them.
DES TOUCHES	But in criminal cases—you have laws which may be depended upon?
CROUTEF	God forbid! We can condemn men to exile, to the galleys, to be hanged; or we can discharge them, according to our own fancy. We sometimes complain of the arbitrary power of the Barcalon, but we choose that all our decisions should be arbitrary.
DES TOUCHES	That is very just. And the torture—do you put people to the torture?
CROUTEF	It is our greatest pleasure. We have found it an infallible secret to save a guilty person, who has vigorous muscles, strong and supple

hamstrings, nervous arms, and firm loins, and we gayly break on the wheel all those innocent persons to whom nature has given feeble organs. It is thus we conduct ourselves with wonderful wisdom and prudence. As there are half proofs, I mean half truths, it is certain there are persons who are half innocent and half guilty. We commence, therefore, by rendering them half dead; we then go to breakfast; afterwards ensues entire death, which gives us great consideration in the world, which is one of the most valuable advantages of our offices.

DES TOUCHES It must be allowed that nothing can be more prudent and humane. Pray tell me what becomes of the property of the condemned?

CROUTEF The children are deprived of it. For you know that nothing can be more equitable than to punish the single fault of a parent on all his descendants.

DES TOUCHES Yes. It is a great while since I have heard of this jurisprudence.

CROUTEF The people of Laos, our neighbors, admit neither the torture, nor arbitrary punishments, nor the different customs, nor the horrible deaths which are in use among us; but we regard them as barbarians who have no idea of good government. All Asia is agreed that we dance the best of all its inhabitants, and that, consequently, it is impossible they should come near us in jurisprudence, in commerce, in finance, and, above all, in the military art.

DES TOUCHES Tell me, I beseech you, by what steps men arrive at the magistracy in Siam.

CROUTEF	By ready money. You perceive that it may be impossible to be a good judge if a man has not by him thirty or forty thousand pieces of silver. It is in vain a man may be perfectly acquainted with all our customs; it is to no purpose that he has pleaded five hundred causes with success—that he has a mind which is the seat of judgment, and a heart replete with justice; no man can become a magistrate without money. This, I say, is the circumstance which distinguishes us from all Asia, and particularly from the barbarous inhabitants of Laos, who have the madness to recompense all kinds of talents, and not to sell any employment.

André Des Touches, who was a little off his guard, said to the Siamese that most of the airs which he had just sung sounded discordant to him, and wished to receive information concerning real Siamese music. But Croutef, full of his subject, and enthusiastic for his country, continued in these words:

"What does it signify that our neighbors, who live beyond our mountains, have better music than we have, or better pictures, provided we have always wise and humane laws? It is in that circumstance we excel. For example:

"If a man has adroitly stolen three or four hundred thousand pieces of gold we respect him, and we go and dine with him. But if a poor servant gets awkwardly into his possession three or four pieces of copper out of his mistress' box we never fail of putting that servant to a public death; first, lest he should not correct himself; secondly, that he may not have it in his power to produce a great number of children for the state, one or two of whom might possibly steal a few little pieces of copper, or become great men; thirdly, because it is just to proportion the punishment to the crime, and that it would be ridiculous to give any useful employment in a prison to a person guilty of so enormous a crime.

"But we are still more just, more merciful, more reasonable in the chastisements which we inflict on those who have the audacity to make use of their legs to go wherever they choose. We treat those warriors so well who sell us their lives, we give them so prodigious a salary, they have so considerable a part in our conquests, that they must be the most criminal of all men to wish to return to their parents on the recovery of their reason, because they had been enlisted in a state of intoxication. To oblige them to remain in one place, we lodge about a dozen leaden balls in their heads, after which they become infinitely useful to their country.

"I will not speak of a great number of excellent institutions which do not go so far as to shed the blood of men, but which render life so pleasant and agreeable that it is impossible the guilty should avoid becoming virtuous. If a farmer has not been able to pay promptly a tax which exceeds his ability, we sell the pot in which he dresses his food; we sell his bed in order that, being relieved of all his superfluities, he may be in a better condition to cultivate the earth."

DES TOUCHES	That is extremely harmonious!
CROUTEF	To comprehend our profound wisdom you must know that our fundamental principle is to acknowledge in many places as our sovereign a shaven-headed foreigner who lives at the distance of nine hundred miles from us. When we assign some of our best territories to any of our talapoins, which it is very prudent in us to do, that Siamese talapoin must pay the revenue of his first year to that shaven-headed Tartar, without which it is clear our lands would be unfruitful. But the time, the happy time, is no more when that tonsured priest induced one-half of the nation to cut the throats of the other half in order to decide whether Sammonocodom had played at leap-frog or at some other game; whether he had been disguised in an elephant or in a cow; if he had slept three hundred and ninety days on the right side or on the left. Those grand questions, which so essentially affect morality, agitated all minds; they shook the world; blood flowed plentifully for it; women were massacred on the bodies of their husbands; they dashed out the brains of their little infants on the stones with a devotion, with a grace, with a contrition truly angelic. Woe to us! degenerate offspring of pious ancestors, who never offer such holy sacrifices! But, heaven be praised, there are yet among us at least a few good souls who would imitate them if they were permitted.
DES TOUCHES	Tell me, I beseech you, sir, if in Siam you divide the tone major into two commas, or

	into two semi-commas, and if the progress of the fundamental sounds are made by one, three, and nine?
CROUTEF	By Sammonocodom, you are laughing at me. You observe no bounds. You have interrogated me on the form of our government, and you speak to me of music!
DES TOUCHES	Music is everything. It was at the foundation of all the politics of the Greeks. But I beg your pardon; you have not a good ear, and we will return to our subject. You said that in order to produce a perfect harmony—
CROUTEF	I was telling you that formerly the tonsured Tartar pretended to dispose of all the kingdoms of Asia, which occasioned something very different from perfect harmony. But a very considerable benefit resulted from it; for people were then more devout toward Sammonocodom and his elephant than they are now, for, at the present time, all the world pretends to common sense, with an indiscretion truly pitiable. However, all things go on; people divert themselves, they dance, they play, they dine, they sup, they make love; this makes every man shudder who entertains good intentions.
DES TOUCHES	And what would you have more? You only want good music. If you had good music you might call your nation the happiest in the world.

PLATO'S DREAM

Plato was a great dreamer, as many others have been since his time. He dreamed that mankind were formerly double, and that, as a punishment for their crimes, they were divided into male and female.

He undertook to prove that there can be no more than five perfect worlds, because there are but five regular mathematical bodies. His republic was one of his principal dreams. He dreamed, moreover, that watching arises from sleep, and sleep from watching, and that a person who should attempt to look at an eclipse otherwise than in a pail of water would surely lose his sight. Dreams were at that time in great repute.

Here follows one of his dreams, which is not one of the least interesting. He thought that the great Demiurgos, the eternal geometer, having peopled the immensity of space with innumerable globes, was willing to make a trial of the knowledge of the genii who had been witnesses of his works. He gave to each of them a small portion of matter to arrange, nearly in the same manner as Phidias and Zeuxis would have given their scholars a statue to carve or a picture to paint, if we may be allowed to compare small things to great.

Demogorgon had for his lot the lump of mould which we call the earth, and, having formed it such as it now appears, he thought he had executed a masterpiece. He imagined he had silenced Envy herself, and expected to receive the highest panegyrics, even from his brethren; but how great was his surprise, when, at his next appearing among them, they received him with a general hiss.

One among them, more satirical than the rest, accosted him thus:

"Truly you have performed mighty feats! you have divided your world into two parts; and, to prevent the one from communication with the other, you have carefully placed a vast collection of waters between the two hemispheres. The inhabitants must perish with cold under both your poles and be scorched to death under the equator. You have, in your great prudence, formed immense deserts of sand, so that all who travel over them may die with hunger and thirst. I have no fault to find with your cows, your sheep, your cocks, and your hens, but can never be reconciled to your serpents and your spiders. Your onions and your artichokes are very good things, but I cannot conceive what induced you to scatter such a heap of poisonous plants over the face of the earth, unless it was to poison its inhabitants. Moreover, if I am not mistaken, you have created about thirty different kinds of monkeys, a still greater number of dogs, and only four or five species of the human race. It is true, indeed, you have bestowed on the latter of these animals a faculty by you called reason, but, in truth, this same reason is a very ridiculous thing, and borders very near upon folly. Besides, you do not seem to have shown any very great regard to this two-legged creature, seeing you have left him with so few means of defence, subjected him to so many disorders and provided him with so few remedies, and formed him with such a multitude of passions and so small a portion of wisdom or prudence to resist them. You certainly were not willing that there should remain any great number of these animals on the earth at once, for, without reckoning the dangers to which you have exposed them, you have so ordered matters that, taking every day throughout the year, smallpox will regularly carry off the tenth part of the species, and sister maladies will taint the springs of life in the nine remaining parts; and then, as if this were not sufficient, you have so disposed things that one-half of those who survive will be occupied in going to law with each other or cutting one another's throats.

"Now, they must doubtless be under infinite obligations to you, and it must be owned you have executed a masterpiece."

Demogorgon blushed. He was sensible there was much moral

and physical evil in this affair, but still he insisted there was more good than ill in it.

"It is an easy matter to find fault, good folks," said the genius, "but do you imagine it is so easy to form an animal, who, having the gift of reason and free-will, shall not sometimes abuse his liberty? Do you think that, in rearing between nine and ten thousand different plants, it is so easy to prevent some few from having noxious qualities? Do you suppose that with a certain quantity of water, sand, and mud you could make a globe that should have neither seas nor deserts?

"As for you, my sneering friend, I think you have just finished the planet Jupiter. Let us see now what figure you make with your great belts and your long nights with four moons to enlighten them. Let us examine your worlds and see whether the inhabitants you have made are exempt from follies or diseases."

Accordingly the genius fell to examining the planet Jupiter, when the laugh went strongly against the laugher. The serious genius who had made the planet Saturn did not escape without his share of the censure, and his brother operators, the makers of Mars, Mercury, and Venus, had each in his turn some reproaches to undergo.

Several large volumes and a great number of pamphlets were written on this occasion; smart sayings and witty repartees flew about on all sides; they railed against and ridiculed each other, and, in short, the disputes were carried on with all the warmth of party heat, when the eternal Demiurgos thus imposed silence on them all:

"In your several performances there is both good and bad, because you have a great share of understanding, but at the same time fall short of perfection. Your works will not endure above a hundred millions of years, after which you will acquire more knowledge and perform much better. It belongs to me alone to create things perfect and immortal."

This was the doctrine Plato taught his disciples. One of them, when he had finished his harangue, cried out: "And so you then awoke?"

AN ADVENTURE IN INDIA

All the world knows that Pythagoras, while he resided in India, attended the school of the Gymnosophists and learned the language of beasts and plants. One day while he was walking in a meadow near the sea-shore he heard these words:

"How unfortunate that I was born an herb! I scarcely attain two inches in height, when a voracious monster, a horrid animal, tramples me under his large feet; his jaws are armed with rows of sharp scythes, by which he cuts, then grinds, and then swallows me. Men call this monster a sheep. I do not suppose there is in the whole creation a more detestable creature."

Pythagoras proceeded a little way and found an oyster yawning on a small rock. He had not yet adopted that admirable law by which we are enjoined not to eat those animals which have a resemblance to us. He had scarcely taken up the oyster to swallow it, when it spoke these affecting words:

"O Nature, how happy is the herb, which is, as I am, thy work! Though it be cut down, it is regenerated and immortal, and we, poor oysters, in vain are defended by a double cuirass; villains eat us by dozens at their breakfast, and all is over with us forever. What a horrible fate is that of an oyster, and how barbarous are men!"

Pythagoras shuddered; he felt the enormity of the crime he had nearly committed; he begged pardon of the oyster, with tears in his eyes, and replaced it very carefully on the rock.

As he was returning to the city, profoundly meditating on this adventure, he saw spiders devouring flies; swallows eating spiders, and sparrow-hawks eating swallows. "None of these," said he, "are philosophers."

On his entrance, Pythagoras was stunned, bruised, and thrown down by a lot of tatterdemalions, who were running and crying: "Well done, he fully deserved it." "Who? What?" said Pythagoras, as he was getting up. The people continued running and crying: "Oh, how delightful it will be to see them boiled!"

Pythagoras supposed they meant lentils or some other vegetables, but he was in error; they meant two poor Indians. "Oh!" said Pythagoras, "these Indians, without doubt, are two great philosophers weary of their lives; they are desirous of regenerating under other forms; it affords pleasure to a man to change his place of residence, though he may be but indifferently lodged; there is no disputing on taste."

He proceeded with the mob to the public square, where he perceived a lighted pile of wood and a bench opposite to it, which was called a tribunal. On this bench judges were seated, each of whom had a cow's tail in his hand and a cap on his head, with ears resembling those of the animal which bore Silenus when he came into that country with Bacchus, after having crossed the Erytrean sea without wetting a foot, and stopping the sun and moon, as it is recorded with great fidelity by the Orphics.

Among these judges there was an honest man with whom Pythagoras was acquainted. The Indian sage explained to the sage of Samos the nature of that festival to be given to the people of India.

"These two Indians," said he, "have not the least desire to be committed to the flames. My grave brethren have adjudged them to be burnt; one for saying that the substance of Xaca is not that of Brahma, and the other for supposing that the approbation of the Supreme Being was to be obtained at the point of death without holding a cow by the tail. 'Because,' said he, 'we may be virtuous at all times, and we cannot always have a cow to lay hold of just when we may have occasion.' The good women of the city were greatly terrified at two such heretical opinions; they would not allow the judges a moment's peace until they had ordered the execution of those unfortunate men."

Pythagoras was convinced that from the herb up to man there

were many causes of chagrin. However, he obliged the judges and even the devotees to listen to reason, which happened only at that time.

He went afterwards and preached toleration at Crotona; but a bigot set fire to his house, and he was burned—the man who had delivered the two Hindoos from the flames! Let those save themselves who can!

BABABEC

When I was in the city of Benares, on the borders of the Ganges, the country of the ancient Brahmins, I endeavored to instruct myself in their religion and manners. I understood the Indian language tolerably well. I heard a great deal and remarked everything. I lodged at the house of my correspondent, Omri, who was the most worthy man I ever knew. He was of the religion of the Brahmins; I have the honor to be a Mussulman. We never exchanged one word higher than another about Mahomet or Brahma. We performed our ablutions each on his own side; we drank of the same sherbet, and we ate of the same rice, as if we had been two brothers.

One day we went together to the pagoda of Gavani. There we saw several bands of fakirs, some of whom were janguis, that is to say, contemplative fakirs, and others were disciples of the ancient Gymnosophists, who led an active life. They all have a learned language peculiar to themselves; it is that of the most ancient Brahmins; and they have a book written in this language, which they call the "*Shasta*." It is, beyond all contradiction, the most ancient book in all Asia, not excepting the "*Zend*."

I happened by chance to cross in front of a fakir who was reading in this book.

"Ah! wretched infidel!" cried he, "thou hast made me lose a number of vowels that I was counting, which will cause my soul to pass into the body of a hare instead of that of a parrot, with which I had before the greatest reason to flatter myself."

I gave him a rupee to comfort him for the accident. In going a few paces farther I had the misfortune to sneeze. The noise I made roused a fakir, who was in a trance.

"Heavens!" cried he, "what a dreadful noise. Where am I? I can no longer see the tip of my nose—the heavenly light has disappeared."

"If I am the cause," said I, "of your not seeing farther than the length of your nose, here is a rupee to repair the great injury I have done you. Squint again, my friend, and resume the heavenly light."

Having thus brought myself off discreetly enough, I passed over to the side of the Gymnosophists, several of whom brought me a parcel of mighty pretty nails to drive into my arms and thighs, in honor of Brahma. I bought their nails and made use of them to fasten down my boxes. Others were dancing upon their hands, others cut capers on the slack rope, and others went always upon one foot. There were some who dragged a heavy chain about with them, and others carried a packsaddle; some had their heads always in a bushel—the best people in the world to live with. My friend Omri took me to the cell of one of the most famous of these. His name was Bababec; he was as naked as he was born, and had a great chain about his neck that weighed upwards of sixty pounds. He sat on a wooden chair, very neatly decorated with little points of nails that penetrated into his flesh, and you would have thought he had been sitting on a velvet cushion. Numbers of women flocked to him to consult him. He was the oracle of all the families in the neighborhood, and was, truly speaking, in great reputation. I was witness to a long conversation that Omri had with him.

"Do you think, father," said my friend, "that after having gone through seven metempsychoses, I may at length arrive at the habitation of Brahma?"

"That is as it may happen," said the fakir. "What sort of life do you lead?"

"I endeavor," answered Omri, "to be a good subject, a good husband, a good father, and a good friend. I lend money without interest to the rich who want it, and I give it to the poor; I always strive to preserve peace among my neighbors."

"But have you ever run nails into your flesh?" demanded the Brahmin.

"Never, reverend father."

"I am sorry for it," replied the father, "very sorry for it, indeed. It is a thousand pities, but you will certainly not reach above the nineteenth heaven."

"No higher!" said Omri. "In truth, I am very well contented with my lot. What is it to me whether I go into the nineteenth or the twentieth, provided I do my duty in my pilgrimage, and am well received at the end of my journey? Is it not as much as one can desire to live with a fair character in this world and be happy with Brahma in the next? And pray what heaven do you think of going to, good master Bababec, with your chain?"

"Into the thirty-fifth," said Bababec.

"I admire your modesty," replied Omri, "to pretend to be better lodged than me. This is surely the result of an excessive ambition. How can you, who condemn others that covet honors in this world, arrogate such distinguished ones to yourself in the next? What right have you to be better treated than me? Know that I bestow more alms to the poor in ten days than the nails you run into your flesh cost for ten years. What is it to Brahma that you pass the whole day stark naked with a chain about your neck? This is doing a notable service to your country, doubtless! I have a thousand times more esteem for the man who sows pulse or plants trees than for all your tribe, who look at the tips of their noses or carry packsaddles to show their magnanimity."

Having finished this speech, Omri softened his voice, embraced the Brahmin, and, with an endearing sweetness, besought him to throw aside his nails and his chain, to go home with him and live with decency and comfort.

The fakir was persuaded: he was washed clean, rubbed with essences and perfumes and clad in a decent habit; he lived a fortnight in this manner, behaved with prudence and wisdom and acknowledged that he was a thousand times happier than before; but he lost his credit among the people; the women no longer crowded to consult him; he therefore quitted the house of the friendly Omri and returned to his nails and his chain—to regain his reputation.

14u